# Science in Arcady by Grant Allen

Charles Grant Blairfindie Allen was born on February 24th, 1848 at Alwington, near Kingston, Canada West (now part of Ontario).

Home schooled until 13 when his family moved to England, Grant was to become a highly regarded science writer who branched out to a fiction career and became enormously popular.

His work helped propel several genres of fiction and whilst his career was short it was enormously productive.

Grant's scientific background enabled him to root much of his work in a plausibility that was denied to others. He had little fear in challenging a society that treated women as second class citizens and creating best sellers from such works.

On October 25th 1899 Grant Allen died at his home in Hindhead, Haslemere, Surrey, England. He died just before finishing Hilda Wade. The novel's final episode, which he dictated to his friend, doctor and neighbour Sir Arthur Conan Doyle from his bed appeared under the appropriate title, The Episode of the Dead Man Who Spoke in 1900.

## Index of Contents

I0553514

These essays deal for the most part with Science in Arcady. 'Tis my native country: for I am not of those who 'praise the busy town.' On the contrary, in the words of the great poet who has just departed to join Milton and Shelley in a place of high collateral glory, I 'love to rail against it still,' with a naturalist's bitterness. For the town is always dead and lifeless. There are who admire it, they say, poor purblind creatures, because, forsooth, 'there is so much life there.' So much life, indeed! No grass in the streets; no flowers in the lanes; no beetles or butterflies on the dull stone pavements! Brick and mortar have killed out all life over square miles of Middlesex. For myself, I love better the densely-peopled fields than this human desert, this beflagged and macadamised man-made solitude. The country teems with life on every hand; a thousand different plants and flowers in the spangled meadows; a thousand varied denizens of pond, and air, and heath, and copses. Their ways are endless. They attract me far more with their infinite diversity than the grey and gloomy haunts of the cab-horse and the stock-broker.

But my Arcady, as you will see, is none the less tolerably broad and eclectic in its limits. These various essays have been suggested to my pen by rambles far and wide between its elastic confines. The little tractate on Mud, for example, recalls to mind some pleasant weeks among the Italian lakes and on the plain of Lombardy. A Desert Fruit owes its origin to a morning at Luxor. High Life had its key-note struck by a fortnight in the Tyrol. Tropical Education is a dim reminiscence of old Jamaican experiences. Our Eight-Legged Friends were observed at leisure on the window-panes of our own little nook at Dorking. A Hill-Top Stronghold was sketched in situ at Florence by a window that looked across the valley to Fiesole. Excursions into books or into the remoter past have given occasion for the archæological essays relegated here to the end of the volume.

G.A.

Hind Head, Surrey, Oct., 1892.

## MY ISLANDS

About the middle of the Miocene period, as well as I can now remember (for I made no note of the precise date at the moment), my islands first appeared above the stormy sheet of the North-West Atlantic as a little rising group of mountain tops, capping a broad boss of submarine volcanoes. My attention was originally called to the new archipelago by a brother investigator of my own aerial race, who pointed out to me on the wing that at a spot some 900 miles to the west of the Portuguese coast, just opposite the place where your mushroom city of Lisbon now stands, the water of the ocean, as seen in a bird's-eye view from some three thousand feet above, formed a distinct greenish patch such as always betokens shoals or rising ground at the bottom. Flying out at once to the point he indicated, and poising myself above it on my broad pinions at a giddy altitude, I saw at a glance that my friend was quite right. Land making was in progress. A volcanic upheaval was taking place on the bed of the sea. A new island group was being forced right up by lateral pressure or internal energies from a depth of at least two thousand fathoms.

I had always had a great liking for the study of material plants and animals, and I was so much interested in the occurrence of this novel phenomenon, the growth and development of an oceanic island before my very eyes, that I determined to devote the next few thousand centuries or so of my æonian existence to watching the course of its gradual evolution.

If I trusted to unaided memory, however, for my dates and facts, I might perhaps at this distance of time be uncertain whether the moment was really what I have roughly given, within a geological age or two, the period of the Mid-Miocene. But existing remains on one of the islands constituting my group (now called in your new-fangled terminology Santa Maria) help me to fix with comparative certainty the precise epoch of their original upheaval. For these remains, still in evidence on the spot, consist of a few small marine deposits of Upper Miocene age; and I recollect distinctly that after the main group had been for some time raised above the surface of the ocean, and after sand and streams had formed a small sedimentary deposit containing Upper Miocene fossils beneath the shoal water surrounding the main group, a slight change of level occurred, during which this minor island was pushed up with the Miocene deposits on its shoulders, as a sort of natural memorandum to assist my random scientific recollections. With that solitary exception, however, the entire group remains essentially volcanic in its composition, exactly as it was when I first saw its youthful craters and its red-hot ash-cones pushed gradually up, century after century, from the deep blue waters of the Mid-Miocene ocean.

All round my islands the Atlantic then, as now, had a depth, as I said before, of two thousand fathoms; indeed, in some parts between the group and Portugal the plummet of your human navigators finds no bottom, I have often heard them say, till it reaches 2,500; and out of this profound sea-bed the volcanic energies pushed up my islands as a small submarine mountain range, whose topmost summits alone stood out bit by bit above the level of the surrounding sea. One of them, the most abrupt and cone-like, by name now Pico, rises to this day, a magnificent sight, sheer seven thousand feet into the sky from the placid sheet that girds it round on every side. You creatures of to-day, approaching it in one of your clumsy new-fashioned fire-driven canoes that you call steamers, must admire immensely its conical peak, as it stands out silhouetted against the glowing horizon in the deep red glare of a sub-tropical Atlantic sunset.

But when I, from my solitary aerial perch, saw my islands rise bare and massive first from the water's edge, the earliest idea that occurred to me as an investigator of nature was simply this: how will they ever get clad with soil and herbage and living creatures? So naked and barren were their black crags and rocks of volcanic slag, that I could hardly conceive how they could ever come to resemble the other smiling oceanic islands which I looked down upon in my flight from day to day over so many wide and scattered oceans. I set myself to watch, accordingly, whence they would derive the first seeds of life, and what changes would take place under dint of time upon their desolate surface.

For a long epoch, while the mountains were still rising in their active volcanic state, I saw but little evidence of a marked sort of the growth of living creatures upon their loose piles of pumice. Gradually, however, I observed that spores of lichens, blown towards them by the wind, were beginning to sprout upon the more settled rocks, and to discolour the surface in places with grey and yellow patches. Bit by bit, as rain fell upon the new-born hills, it brought down from their weathered summits sand and mud, which the torrents ground small and deposited in little hollows in the valleys; and at last something like earth was found at certain spots, on which seeds, if there had been any, might doubtless have rooted and flourished exceedingly.

My primitive idea, as I watched my islands in this their almost lifeless condition, was that the Gulf Stream and the trade winds from America would bring the earliest higher plants and animals to our shores. But in this I soon found I was quite mistaken. The distance to be traversed was so great, and the current so slow, that the few seeds or germs of American species cast up upon the shore from time to time were mostly far too old and water-logged to show signs of life in such ungenial conditions. It was from the nearer coasts of Europe, on the contrary, that our earliest colonists seemed to come. Though the prevalent winds set from the west, more violent storms reached us occasionally from the eastward direction; and these, blowing from Europe, which lay so much closer to our group, were far more likely to bring with them by waves or wind some waifs and strays of the European fauna and flora.

I well remember the first of these great storms that produced any distinct impression on my islands. The plants that followed in its wake were a few small ferns, whose light spores were more readily carried on the breeze than any regular seeds of flowering plants. For a month or two nothing very marked occurred in the way of change, but slowly the spores rooted, and soon produced a small crop of ferns, which, finding the ground unoccupied, spread when once fairly started with extraordinary rapidity, till they covered all the suitable positions throughout the islands.

For the most part, however, additions to the flora, and still more to the fauna, were very gradually made; so much so that most of the species now found in the group did not arrive there till after the end of the Glacial epoch, and belong essentially to the modern European assemblage of plants and animals. This was partly because the islands themselves were surrounded by pack-ice during that chilly period, which interrupted for a time the course of my experiment. It was interesting, too, after the ice cleared away, to note what kinds could manage by stray accidents to cross the ocean with a fair chance of sprouting or hatching out on the new soil, and which were totally unable by original constitution to survive the ordeal of immersion in the sea. For instance, I looked anxiously at first for the arrival of some casual acorn or some floating filbert, which might stock my islands with waving greenery of oaks and hazel bushes. But I gradually discovered, in the course of a few centuries, that these heavy nuts never floated securely so far as the outskirts of my little archipelago; and that consequently no chestnuts, apple trees, beeches, alders, larches, or pines ever came to diversify my island valleys. The seeds that did really reach us from time to time belonged rather to one or other of four special classes. Either they were very small and light, like the spores of ferns, fungi, and club-mosses; or they were winged and feathery, like dandelion and thistle-down; or they were the stones of fruits that are eaten by birds, like rose-hips and hawthorn; or they were chaffy grains, enclosed in papery scales, like grasses and sedges, of a kind well adapted to be readily borne on the surface of the water. In all these ways new plants did really get wafted by slow degrees to the islands; and if they were of kinds adapted to the climate they grew and flourished, living down the first growth of ferns and flowerless herbs in the rich valleys.

The time which it took to people my archipelago with these various plants was, of course, when judged by your human standards, immensely long, as often the group received only a single new addition in the lapse of two or three centuries. But I noticed one very curious result of this haphazard and lengthy mode of stocking the country: some of the plants which arrived the earliest, having the coast all clear to themselves, free from the fierce competition to which they had always been exposed on the mainland of Europe, began to sport a great deal in various directions, and being acted upon here by new conditions, soon assumed under stress of natural selection totally distinct specific forms. (You see, I have quite mastered your best modern scientific vocabulary.) For instance, there were at first no insects of any sort on the islands; and so those plants which in Europe depended for their fertilisation upon bees or butterflies had here either to adapt themselves somehow to the wind as a carrier of their pollen or else to die out for want of crossing. Again, the number of enemies being reduced to a minimum, these early plants tended to lose various defences or protections they had acquired on the mainland against slugs or ants, and so to become different in a corresponding degree from their European ancestors. The consequence was that by the time you men first discovered the archipelago no fewer than forty kinds of plants had so far diverged from the parent forms in Europe or elsewhere that your savants considered them at once as distinct species, and set them down at first as indigenous creations. It amused me immensely.

For out of these forty plants thirty-four were to my certain knowledge of European origin. I had seen their seeds brought over by the wind or waves, and I had watched them gradually altering under stress of the new conditions into fresh varieties, which in process of time became distinct species. Two of the oldest were flowers of the dandelion and daisy group, provided with feathery seeds which enable them to fly far before the carrying breeze; and these two underwent such profound modifications in their insular home that the systematic botanists who at last examined them insisted upon putting each into a new genus, all by itself, invented for the special purpose of their reception. One almost equally ancient inhabitant, a sort of harebell, also became in process of time extremely unlike any other harebell I had ever seen in any part of my airy wanderings. But the remaining thirty new species or so evolved in the islands by the special circumstances of the group had varied so comparatively little from their primitive European ancestors, that they hardly deserved to be called anything more than very distinct and divergent varieties.

Some five or six plants, however, I noted arrive in my archipelago, not from Europe, but from the Canaries or Madeira, whose distant blue peaks lay dim on the horizon far to the south-west of us, as I poised in mid-air high above the topmost pinnacle of my wild craggy Pico. These kinds, belonging to a much warmer region, soon, as I noticed, underwent considerable modification in our cooler climate, and were all of them adjudged distinct species by the learned gentlemen who finally reported upon my island realm to British science.

As far as I can recollect, then, the total number of flowering plants I noted in the islands before the arrival of man was about 200; and of these, as I said before, only forty had so far altered in type as to be considered at present peculiar to the archipelago. The remainder were either comparatively recent arrivals or else had found the conditions of their new home so like those of the old one from which they migrated, that comparatively little change took place in their forms or habits. Of course, just in proportion as the islands got stocked I noticed that the changes were less and less marked; for each new plant, insect, or bird that established itself successfully tended to make the balance of nature more similar to the one that obtained in the mainland opposite, and so decreased the chances of novelty of variation.

Hence, it struck me that the oldest arrivals were the ones which altered most in adaptation to the circumstances, while the newest, finding themselves in comparatively familiar surroundings, had less occasion to be selected for strange and curious freaks or sports of form or colour.

The peopling of the islands with birds and animals, however, was to me even a more interesting and engrossing study in natural evolution than its peopling by plants, shrubs, and trees. I may as well begin, therefore, by telling you at once that no furry or hairy quadruped of any sort, no mammal, as I understand your men of science call them, was ever stranded alive upon the shores of my islands. For twenty or thirty centuries indeed, I waited patiently, examining every piece of driftwood cast up upon our beaches, in the faint hope that perhaps some tiny mouse or shrew or water-vole might lurk half drowned in some cranny or crevice of the bark or trunk. But it was all in vain. I ought to have known beforehand that terrestrial animals of the higher types never by any chance reach an oceanic island in any part of this planet. The only three specimens of mammals I ever saw tossed up on the beach were two drowned mice and an unhappy squirrel, all as dead as doornails, and horribly mauled by the sea and the breakers. Nor did we ever get a snake, a lizard, a frog, or a fresh-water fish, whose eggs I at first fondly supposed might occasionally be transported to us on bits of floating trees or matted turf, torn by floods from those prehistoric Lusitanian or African forests. No such luck was ours. Not a single terrestrial vertebrate of any sort appeared upon our shores before the advent of man with his domestic animals, who played havoc at once with my interesting experiment.

It was quite otherwise with the unobtrusive small deer of life, the snails, and beetles, and flies, and earthworms, and especially with the winged things: birds, bats, and butterflies. In the very earliest days of my islands' existence, indeed, a few stray feathered fowls of the air were driven ashore here by violent storms, at a time when vegetation had not yet begun to clothe the naked pumice and volcanic rock; but these, of course, perished for want of food, as did also a few later arrivals, who came under stress of weather at the period when only ferns, lichens, and mosses had as yet obtained a foothold on the young archipelago. Sea-birds, of course, soon found out our rocks; but as they live off fish only, they contributed little more than rich beds of guano to the permanent colonising of the islands. As well as I can remember, the land-snails were the earliest truly terrestrial casuals that managed to pick up a stray livelihood in these first colonial days of the archipelago. They came oftenest in the egg, sometimes clinging to water-logged leaves cast up by storms, sometimes hidden in the bark of floating driftwood, and sometimes swimming free on the open ocean. In one case, as I recall to myself well, a swallow, driven off from the Portuguese coast, a little before the Glacial period had begun to whiten the distant mountains of central and northern Europe, fell exhausted at last upon the shore of Terceira. There were no insects then for the poor bird to feed upon, so it died of starvation and weariness before the day was out; but a little earth that clung in a pellet to one of its feet contained the egg of a land-shell, while the prickly seed of a common Spanish plant was entangled among the winged feathers by its hooked awns. The egg hatched out, and became the parent of a large brood of minute snails, which, outliving the cold spell of the Ice Age, had developed into a very distinct type in the long period that intervened before the advent of man in the islands; while the seed sprang up on the natural manure heap afforded by the swallow's decaying body, and clinging to the valleys during the Glacial Age on the hill-tops, gave birth in due season to one of the most markedly indigenous of our Terceira plants.

Occasionally, too, very minute land-snails would arrive alive on the island after their long sea-voyage on bits of broken forest-trees, a circumstance which I would perhaps hesitate to mention in mere human society were it not that I have been credibly informed your own great naturalist, Darwin, tried the experiment himself with one of the biggest European land-molluscs, the great edible Roman snail, and found that it still lived on in vigorous style after immersion in sea-water for twenty days. Now, I myself observed that several of these bits of broken trees, torn down by floods in heavy storm time from the banks of Spanish or Portuguese rivers, reached my island in eight or ten days after leaving the mainland, and sometimes contained eggs of small land-snails. But as very long periods often passed without a single new species being introduced into the group, any kind that once managed to establish itself on any of the islands usually remained for ages undisturbed by new arrivals, and so had plenty of opportunity to adapt itself perfectly by natural selection to the new conditions. The consequence was, that out of some seventy land-snails now known in the islands, thirty-two had assumed distinct specific features before the advent of man, while thirty-seven (many of which, I think, I never noticed till the introduction of cultivated plants) are common to my group with Europe or with the other Atlantic islands. Most of these, I believe, came in with man and his disconcerting agriculture.

As to the pond and river snails, so far as I could observe, they mostly reached us later, being conveyed in the egg on the feet of stray waders or water-birds, which gradually peopled the island after the Glacial epoch.

Birds and all other flying creatures are now very abundant in all the islands; but I could tell you some curious and interesting facts, too, as to the mode of their arrival and the vicissitudes of their settlement. For example, during the age of the Forest Beds in Europe, a stray bullfinch was driven out to sea by a violent storm, and perched at last on a bush at Fayal. I wondered at first whether he would effect a settlement. But at that time no seeds or fruits fit for bullfinches to eat existed on the islands. Still, as it turned out, this particular bullfinch happened to have in his crop several undigested seeds of European plants exactly suited to the bullfinch taste; so when he died on the spot, these seeds, germinating abundantly, gave rise to a whole valleyful of appropriate plants for bullfinches to feed upon. Now, however, there was no bullfinch to eat them. For a long time, indeed, no other bullfinches arrived at my archipelago. Once, to be sure, a few hundred years later, a single cock bird did reach the island alone, much exhausted with his journey, and managed to pick up a living for himself off the seeds introduced by his unhappy predecessor. But as he had no mate, he died at last, as your lawyers would say, without issue.

It was a couple of hundred years or so more before I saw a third bullfinch, which didn't surprise me, for bullfinches are very woodland birds, and non-migratory into the bargain, so that they didn't often get blown seaward over the broad Atlantic. At the end of that time, however, I observed one morning a pair of finches, after a heavy storm, drying their poor battered wings upon a shrub in one of the islands. From this solitary pair a new race sprang up, which developed after a time, as I imagined they must, into a distinct species. These local bullfinches now form the only birds peculiar to the islands; and the reason is one well divined by one of your own great naturalists (to whom I mean before I end to make the amende honorable). In almost all other cases the birds kept getting reinforced from time to time by others of their kind blown out to sea accidentally, for only such species were likely to arrive there, and this kept up the purity of the original race, by ensuring a cross every now and again with the European community. But the bullfinches, being the merest casuals, never again to my knowledge were reinforced from the mainland, and so they have produced at last a special island type, exactly adapted to the peculiarities of their new habitat.

You see, there was hardly ever a big storm on land that didn't bring at least one or two new birds of some sort or other to the islands. Naturally, too, the newcomers landed always on the first shore they could sight; and so at the present day the greatest number of species is found on the two easternmost islands nearest the mainland, which have forty kinds of land-birds, while the central islands have but thirty-six, and the western only twenty-nine. It would have been quite different, of course, if the birds came mainly from America with the trade winds and the Gulf Stream, as I at first anticipated. In that case, there would have been most kinds in the westernmost islands, and fewest stragglers in the far eastern. But your own naturalists have rightly seen that the existing distribution necessarily implies the opposite explanation.

Birds, I early noticed, are always great carriers of fruit-seeds, because they eat the berries, but don't digest the hard little stones within. It was in that way, I fancy, that the Portugal laurel first came to my islands, because it has an edible fruit with a very hard seed; and the same reason must account for the presence of the myrtle, with its small blue berry; the laurustinus with its currant-like fruit; the elder-tree, the canary laurel, the local sweet-gale, and the peculiar juniper. Before these shrubs were introduced thus unconsciously by our feathered guests, there were no fruits on which berry-eating birds could live; but now they are the only native trees or large bushes on the islands, I mean the only ones not directly planted by you mischief-making men, who have entirely spoilt my nice little experiment.

It was much the same with the history of some among the birds themselves. Not a few birds of prey, for example, were driven to my little archipelago by stress of weather in its very early days; but they all perished for want of sufficient small quarry to make a living out of. As soon, however, as the islands had got well stocked with robins, black-caps, wrens, and wagtails, of European types, as soon as the chaffinches had established themselves on the seaward plains, and the canary had learnt to nest without fear among the Portugal laurels, then buzzards, long-eared owls, and common barn-owls, driven westward by tempests, began to pick up a decent living on all the islands, and have ever since been permanent residents, to the immense terror and discomfort of our smaller song-birds. Thus the older the archipelago got the less chance was there of local variation taking place to any large degree, because the balance of life each day grew more closely to resemble that which each species had left behind it in its native European or African mainland.

I said a little while ago we had no mammal in the islands. In that I was not quite strictly correct. I ought to have said, no terrestrial mammal. A little Spanish bat got blown to us once by a rough nor'easter, and took up its abode at once among the caves of our archipelago, where it hawks to this day after our flies and beetles. This seemed to me to show very conspicuously the advantage which winged animals have in the matter of cosmopolitan dispersion; for while it was quite impossible for rats, mice, or squirrels to cross the intervening belt of three hundred leagues of sea, their little winged relation, the flitter-mouse, made the journey across quite safely on his own leathery vans, and with no greater difficulty than a swallow or a wood-pigeon.

The insects of my archipelago tell very much the same story as the birds and the plants. Here, too, winged species have stood at a great advantage. To be sure, the earliest butterflies and bees that arrived in the fern-clad period were starved for want of honey; but as soon as the valleys began to be thickly tangled with composites, harebells, and sweet-scented myrtle bushes, these nectar-eating insects established themselves successfully, and kept their breed true by occasional crosses with fresh arrivals blown to sea afterwards. The development of the beetles I watched with far greater interest, as they assumed fresh forms much more rapidly under their new conditions of restricted food and limited enemies. Many kinds I observed which came originally from Europe, sometimes in the larval state, sometimes in the egg, and sometimes flying as full-grown insects before the blast of the angry tempest. Several of these changed their features rapidly after their arrival in the islands, producing at first divergent varieties, and finally, by dint of selection, acting in various ways, through climate, food, or enemies, on these nascent forms, evolving into stable and well-adapted species. But I noticed three cases where bits of driftwood thrown up from South America on the western coasts contained the eggs or larvae of American beetles, while several others were driven ashore from the Canaries or Madeira; and in one instance even a small insect, belonging to a type now confined to Madagascar, found its way safely by sea to this remote spot, where, being a female with eggs, it succeeded in establishing a flourishing colony. I believe, however, that at the time of its arrival it still existed on the African continent, but becoming extinct there under stress of competition with higher forms, it now survives only in these two widely separated insular areas.

It was an endless amusement to me during those long centuries, while I devoted myself entirely to the task of watching my fauna and flora develop itself, to look out from day to day for any chance arrival by wind or waves, and to follow the course of its subsequent vicissitudes and evolution. In a great many cases, especially at first, the new-comer found no niche ready for it in the established order of things on the islands, and was fain at last, after a hard struggle, to retire for ever from the unequal contest. But often enough, too, he made a gallant fight for it, and, adapting himself rapidly to his new environment, changed his form and habits with surprising facility. For natural selection, I found, is a hard schoolmaster. If you happen to fit your place in the world, you live and thrive, but if you don't happen to fit it, to the wall with you without quarter. Thus sometimes I would see a small canary beetle quickly take to new food and new modes of life on my islands under my very eyes, so that in a century or so I judged him myself worthy of the distinction of a separate species; while in another case, I remember, a south European weevil evolved before long into something so wholly different from his former self that a systematic entomologist would have been forced to enrol him in a distinct genus. I often wish now that I had kept a regular collection of all the intermediate forms, to present as an illustrative series to one of your human museums; but in those days, of course, we none of us imagined anybody but ourselves would ever take an interest in these problems of the development of life, and we let the chance slide till it was too late to recover it.

Naturally, during all these ages changes of other sorts were going on in my islands, elevations and subsidences, separations and reunions, which helped to modify the life of the group considerably. Indeed, volcanic action was constantly at work altering the shapes and sizes of the different rocky mountain-tops, and bringing now one, now another, into closer relations than before with its neighbours. Why, as recently as 1811 (a date which is so fresh in my memory that I could hardly forget it) a new island was suddenly formed by submarine eruption off the coast of St. Michael's, to which the name of Sabrina was momentarily given by your human geographers. It was about a mile around and 300 feet high; but, consisting as it did of loose cinders only, it was soon washed away by the force of the waves in that stormy region. I merely mention it here to show how recently volcanic changes have taken place in my islands, and how continuously the internal energy has been at work modifying and re-arranging them.

Up to the moment of the arrival of man in the archipelago the whole population, animal and vegetable, consisted entirely of these waifs and strays, blown out to sea from Europe or Africa, and modified more or less on the spot in accordance with the varying needs of their new home. But the advent of the obtrusive human species spoilt the game at once for an independent observer. Man immediately introduced oranges, bananas, sweet potatoes, grapes, plums, almonds, and many other trees or shrubs, in which, for selfish reasons, he was personally interested. At the same time he quite unconsciously and unintentionally stocked the islands with a fine vigorous crop of European weeds, so that the number of kinds of flowering plants included in the modern flora of my little archipelago exceeds, I think, by fully one-half that which I remember before the date of the Portuguese occupation. In the same way, besides his domestic animals, this spoil-sport colonist man brought in his train accidentally rabbits, weasels, mice, and rats, which now abound in many parts of the group, so that the islands have now in effect a wild mammalian fauna. What is more odd, a small lizard has also got about in the walls, not as you would imagine, a native-born Portuguese subject, but of a kind found only in Madeira and Teneriffe, and, as far as I could make out at the time, it seemed to me to come over with cuttings of Madeira vines for planting at St. Michael's. It was about the same time, I imagine, that eels and gold-fish first got loose from glass globes into the ponds and water-courses.

I have forgotten to mention, what you will no doubt yourself long since have inferred, that my archipelago is known among human beings in modern times as the Azores; and also that traces of all these curious facts of introduction and modification, which I have detailed here in their historical order, may still be detected by an acute observer and reasoner in the existing condition of the fauna and flora. Indeed, one of your own countrymen, Mr. Goodman, has collected all the most salient of these facts in his 'Natural History of the Azores,' and another of your distinguished men of science, Mr. Alfred Russel Wallace, has given essentially the same explanations beforehand as those which I have here ventured to lay, from another point of view, before a critical human audience. But while Mr. Wallace has arrived at them by a process of arguing backward from existing facts to prior causes and probable antecedents, it occurred to me, who had enjoyed such exceptional opportunities of watching the whole process unfold itself from the very beginning, that a strictly historical account of how I had seen it come about, step after step, might possess for some of you a greater direct interest than Mr. Wallace's inferential solution of the self-same problem. If, through lapse of memory or inattention to detail at so remote a period, I have set down aught amiss, I sincerely trust you will be kind enough to forgive me. But this little epic of the peopling of a single oceanic archipelago by casual strays, which I alone have had the good fortune to follow through all its episodes, seemed to me too unique and valuable a chapter in the annals of life to be withheld entirely from the scientific world of your eager, ephemeral, nineteenth century humanity.

## TROPICAL EDUCATION

If any one were to ask me (which is highly unlikely) 'In what university would an intelligent young man do best to study?' I think I should be very much inclined indeed to answer offhand, 'In the Tropics.'

No doubt this advice sounds on first hearing just a trifle paradoxical; and no doubt, too, the proposed university has certain serious drawbacks (like many others) on the various grounds of health, expense, faith, and morals. Senior Proctors are unknown at Honolulu; Select Preachers don't range as far as the West Coast. But it has always seemed to me, nevertheless, that certain elements of a liberal education are to be acquired tropically which can never be acquired in a temperate, still less in an arctic or antarctic academy. This is more especially true, I allow, in the particular cases of the biologist and the sociologist; but it is also true in a somewhat less degree of the mere common arts course, and the mere average seeker after liberal culture. Vast aspects of nature and human life exist which can never adequately be understood aright except in tropical countries; vivid side-lights are cast upon our own history and the history of our globe which can never adequately be appreciated except beneath the searching and all too garish rays of a tropical sun.

Whenever I meet a cultivated man who knows his Tropics, and more particularly one who has known his Tropics during the formative period of mental development, say from eighteen to thirty, I feel instinctively that he possesses certain keys of man and nature, certain clues to the problems of the world we live in, not possessed in anything like the same degree by the mere average annual output of Oxford or of Heidelberg. I feel that we talk like Freemasons together, we of the Higher Brotherhood who have worshipped the sun, præsentiorem deum, in his own nearer temples.

Let me begin by positing an extreme parallel. How obviously inadequate is the conception of life enjoyed by the ordinary Laplander or the most intelligent Fuegian! Suppose even he has attended the mission school of his native village, and become learned there in all the learning of the Egyptians, up to the extreme level of the sixth standard, yet how feeble must be his idea of the planet on which he moves! How much must his horizon be cabined, cribbed, confined by the frost and snow, the gloom and poverty, of the bare land around him! He lives in a dark cold world of scrubby vegetation and scant animal life: a world where human existence is necessarily preserved only by ceaseless labour and at severe odds; a world out of which all the noblest and most beautiful living creatures have been ruthlessly pressed; a world where nothing great has been or can be; a world doomed by its mere physical conditions to eternal poverty, discomfort, and squalor. For green fields he has snow and reindeer moss: for singing birds and flowers, the ptarmigan and the tundra. How can he ever form any fitting conception of the glory of life, of the means by which animal and vegetable organisms first grew and flourished? How can he frame to himself any reasonable picture of civilised society, or of the origin and development of human faculty and human organisation?

Somewhat the same, though of course in a highly mitigated degree, are the disadvantages under which the pure temperate education labours, when compared with the education unconsciously drunk in at every pore by an intelligent mind in tropical climates. And fully to understand this pregnant educational importance of the Tropics we must consider with ourselves how large a part tropical conditions have borne in the development of life in general, and of human life and society in particular.

The Tropics, we must carefully remember, are the norma of nature: the way things mostly are and always have been. They represent to us the common condition of the whole world during by far the greater part of its entire existence. Not only are they still in the strictest sense the biological head-quarters: they are also the standard or central type by which we must explain all the rest of nature, both in man and beast, in plant and animal.

The temperate and arctic worlds, on the other hand, are a mere passing accident in the history of our planet: a hole-and-corner development; a special result of the great Glacial epoch, and of that vast slow secular cooling which preceded and led up to it, from the beginning of the Miocene or Mid-Tertiary period. Our European ideas, poor, harsh, and narrow, are mainly formed among a chilled and stunted fauna and flora, under inclement skies, and in gloomy days, all of which can give us but a very cramped and faint conception of the joyous exuberance, the teeming vitality, the fierce hand-to-hand conflict, and the victorious exultation of tropical life in its full free development.

All through the Primary and Secondary epochs of geology, it is now pretty certain, hothouse conditions practically prevailed almost without a break over the whole world from pole to pole. It may be true, indeed, as Dr. Croli believes (and his reasoning on the point I confess is fairly convincing), that from time to time glacial periods in one or other hemisphere broke in for a while upon the genial warmth that characterised the greater part of those vast and immeasurable primæval æons. But even if that were so, if at long intervals the world for some hours in its cosmical year was chilled and frozen in an insignificant cap at either extremity, these casual episodes in a long story do not interfere with the general truth of the principle that life as a whole during the greater portion of its antique existence has been carried on under essentially tropical conditions. No matter what geological formation we examine, we find everywhere the same tale unfolded in plain inscriptions before our eyes. Take, for example, the giant club-mosses and luxuriant tree-ferns nature-printed on shales of the coal age in Britain: and we see in the wild undergrowth of those palæozoic forests ample evidence of a warm and almost West Indian climate among the low basking islets of our northern carboniferous seas. Or take once more the oolitic epoch in England, lithographed on its own mud, with its puzzle-monkeys and its sago-palms, its crocodiles and its deinosaurs, its winged pterodactyls and its whale-like lizards. All these huge creatures and these broad-leaved trees plainly indicate the existence of a temperature over the whole of Northern Europe almost as warm as that of the Malay Archipelago in our own day. The weather report for all the earlier ages stands almost uninterruptedly at Set Fair.

Roughly speaking, indeed, one may say that through the long series of Primary and Secondary formations hardly a trace can be found of ice or snow, autumn or winter, leafless boughs or pinched and starved deciduous vegetation. Everything is powerful, luxuriant, vivid. Life, as Comus feared, was strangled with its waste fertility. Once, indeed, in the Permian Age, all over the temperate regions, north and south, we get passing indications of what seems very like a glacial epoch, partially comparable to that great glaciation on whose last fringe we still abide to-day. But the Ice Age of the Permian, if such there were, passed away entirely, leaving the world once more warm and fruitful up to the very poles under conditions which we would now describe as essentially tropical.

It was with the Tertiary period, perhaps, indeed, only with the middle subdivision of that period, that the gradual cooling of the polar and intermediate regions began. We know from the deposits of the chalk epoch in Greenland that late in Secondary times ferns, magnolias, myrtles, and sago-palms, an Indian or Mexican flora, flourished exceedingly in what is now the dreariest and most ice-clad region of the northern hemisphere. Later still, in the Eocene days, though the plants of Greenland had grown slightly more temperate in type, we still find among the fossils, not only oaks, planes, vines, and walnuts, but also wellingtonias like the big trees of California, Spanish chestnuts, quaint southern salisburias, broad-leaved liquidambars, and American sassafras. Nay, even in glacier-clad Spitzbergen itself, where the character of the flora already begins to show signs of incipient chilling, we nevertheless see among the Eocene types such plants as the swamp-cyprus of the Carolinas and the wellingtonias of the Far West, together with a rich forest vegetation of poplars, birches, oaks, planes, hazels, walnuts, water-lilies, and irises. As a whole, this vegetation still bespeaks a climate considerably more genial, mild, and equable than that of modern England.

It was in this basking world of the chalk and the Eocene that the great mammalian fauna first took its rise; it was in this easy world of fruits and sunshine that the primitive ancestors of man first began to work upwards toward the distinctively human level of the palæolithic period.

But then, in the mid-career of that third day of the geological drama, came a frost, a nipping-frost; and slowly but surely the whole arctic and antarctic worlds were chilled and cramped, degree after degree, by the gradual on-coming of the Great Ice Age. I am not going to deal here with either the causes or the extent of that colossal cataclysm; I shall take all those for granted at present: what we are concerned with now are the results it left behind, the changes which it wrought on fauna and flora and on human society. Especially is it of importance in this connection to point out that the Glacial epoch is not yet entirely finished, if, indeed, it is ever destined to be finished. We are living still on the fringe of the Ice Age, in a cold and cheerless era, the legacy of the accumulated glaciers of the northern and southern snow-fields.

If once that ice were melted off, ah, well, there is much virtue in an if. Still, Mr. Alfred Russel Wallace seems to suggest somewhere that the sun is gradually making inroads even now on those great glacier-sheets of the northern cap, just as we know he is doing on the smaller glacier-sheets of Switzerland (most of which are receding), and that in time perhaps (say in a hundred thousand years or so) warm ocean currents may once more penetrate to the very poles themselves. That, however, is neither here nor there. The fact remains that we of Northern Europe live to-day in a cramped, chilled, contracted world; a world from which all the larger, fiercer, and grander types have either been killed off or driven south; a world which stands to the full and vigorous world of the Eocene and Miocene periods in somewhat the same relation as Lapland stands to-day to Italy or the Riviera.

This being so, it naturally results that if we want really to understand the history of life, its origin and its episodes, we must turn nowadays to that part of our planet which still most nearly preserves the original conditions, that is to say, the Tropics. And it has always seemed to me, both à priori and à posteriori, that the Tropics on this account do really possess for every one of us a vast and for the most part unrecognised educational importance.

I say 'for every one of us,' of deliberate design. I don't mean merely for the biologist, though to him, no doubt, their value in this respect is greatest of all. Indeed, I doubt whether the very ideas of the struggle for life, natural selection, the survival of the fittest, would ever have occurred at all to the stay-at-home naturalists of the Linnæan epoch. It was in the depths of Brazilian forests, or under the broad shade of East Indian palms, that those fertile conceptions first flashed independently upon two southern explorers. It is very noteworthy indeed that all the biologists who have done most to revolutionise the science of life in our own day, Darwin, Huxley, Wallace, Bates, Fritz Müller, and Belt, have without exception formed their notions of the plant and animal world during tropical travels in early life. No one can read the 'Voyage of the Beagle,' the 'Naturalist on the Amazons,' or the 'Malay Archipelago' without feeling at every page how profoundly the facts of tropical nature had penetrated and modified their authors' minds. On the other hand, it is well worth while to notice that the formal opposition to the new and more expansive evolutionary views came mainly from the museum and laboratory type of naturalists in London and Paris, the official exponents of dry bones, who knew nature only through books and preserved specimens, or through her impoverished and far less plastic developments in northern lands. The battle of organic evolution has been waged by the Darwins, the Huxleys, and the Müllers on the one hand, against the Cuviers, the Owens, and the Virchows on the other.

Still, it is not only in biology, as I said just now, that a taste of the Tropics in early life exerts a marked widening and philosophic influence upon a man's whole mental horizon. In ten thousand ways, in that great tropical university, men feel themselves in closer touch than elsewhere with the ultimate facts and truths of nature. I don't know whether it is all fancy and preconceived opinion, but I often imagine when I talk with new-met men that I can detect a certain difference in tone and feeling at first sight between those who have and those who have not passed the Tropical Tripos. In the Tropics, in short, we seem to get down to the very roots of things. Thousands of questions, social, political, economical, ethical, present themselves at once in new and more engagingly simple aspects. Difficulties vanish, distinctions disappear, conventions fade, clothes are reduced to their least common measure, man stands forth in his native nakedness. Things that in the North we had come to regard as inevitable, garments, firing, income tax, morality, evaporate or simplify themselves with instructive ease and phantasmagoric readiness. Malthus and the food question assume fresh forms, as in dissolving views, before our very eyes. How are slums conceivable or East Ends possible where every man can plant his own yam and cocoa-nut, and reap their fruit four-hundred-fold? How can Mrs. Grundy thrive where every woman may rear her own ten children on her ten-rood plot without aid or assistance from their indeterminate fathers? What need of carpentry where a few bamboos, cut down at random, can be fastened together with thongs into a comfortable chair? What use of pottery where calabashes hang on every tree, and cocoa-nuts, with the water fresh and pure within, supply at once the cup, and the filter, and the Apollinaris within?

Of course I don't mean to assert, either, that this tropical university will in itself suffice for all the needs of educated or rather of educable men. It must be taken, bien entendu, as a supplementary course to the Literæ Humaniores. There are things which can only be learnt in the crowded haunts and cities of men, in London, Paris, New York, Vienna. There are things which can only be learnt in the centres of culture or of artistic handicraft, in Oxford, Munich, Florence, Venice, Rome. There is only one Grand Canal and only one Pitti Palace. We must have Shakespeare, Homer, Catullus, Dante; we must have Phidias, Fra Angelico, Rafael, Mendelssohn; we must have Aristotle, Newton, Laplace, Spencer. But after all these, and before all these, there is something more left to learn. Having first read them, we must read ourselves out of them. We must forget all this formal modern life; we must break away from this cramped, cold, northern world; we must find ourselves face to face at last, in Pacific isles or African forests, with the underlying truths of simple naked nature. For that, in its perfection, we must go to the Tropics; and there, we shall learn and unlearn much, coming back, no doubt, with shattered faiths and broken gods, and strangely disconcerted European prejudices, but looking out upon life with a new outlook, an outlook undimmed by ten thousand preconceptions which hem in the vision and obstruct the view of the mere temperately educated.

Nor is it only on the élite of the world that this tropical training has in its own way a widening influence. It is good, of course, for our Galtons to have seen South Africa; good for our Tylors to have studied Mexico; good for our Hookers to have numbered the rhododendrons and deodars of the Himalayas. I sometimes fancy, even, that in the works of our very greatest stay-at-home thinkers on anthropological or sociological subjects, I detect here and there a certain formalist and schematic note which betrays the want of first-hand acquaintance with the plastic and expansive nature of tropical society. The beliefs and relations of the actual savage have not quite that definiteness of form and expression which our University Professors would fain assign to them. But apart from the widening influence of the Tropics on these picked minds, there is a widening influence exerted insensibly on the very planters or merchants, the rank and file of European settlers, which can hardly fail to impress all those who have lived amongst them. The cramping effect of the winter cold and the artificial life is all removed. Men live in a freer, wider, warmer air; their doors and windows stand open day and night; the scent of flowers and the hum of insects blow in upon them with every breeze; their brother man and sister woman are more patent in every action to their eyes; the world shows itself more frankly; it has fewer secrets, and readier sympathies. I don't mean to say the result is all gain. Far from it. There are evils inherent in tropical life which, as a noble lord remarks of nature generally, "no preacher can heal." But viewed as education, like Saint-Simon's thieving, it is all valuable. I should think most men who have once passed through a tropical experience would no more wish that full chapter blotted out of their lives than they would consent to lose their university culture, their Continental travel, or their literary, scientific, or artistic education.

And what are the elements of this tropical curriculum which give it such immense educational value? I think they are manifold. A few only may be selected as of typical importance.

In the first place, because first in order of realisation, there is its value as a mental bouleversement, a revolution in ideas, a sort of moral and intellectual cold shower-bath, a nervous shock to the system generally. The patient or pupil gets so thoroughly upset in all his preconceived ideas; he finds all round him a life so different from the life to which he has been accustomed in colder regions, that he wakes up suddenly, rubs his eyes hard, and begins to look about him for some general explanation of the world he lives in. It is good for the ordinary man to get thus unceremoniously upset. Take the average young intelligence of the London streets, with its glib ideas already formed from supply and demand in a civilised country, where soil is appropriated, and classes distinct, and commodities drop as it were from the clouds upon the middle-class breakfast-table, take such an intelligence, self-satisfied and empty, and place its possessor all at once in a new environment, where everything material, mental, and moral seems topsy-turvy, where life is real and morals are rudimentary, and unless he is a very particular fool indeed, what a lot you must really give that blithe new-comer to turn over and think about! The sun that shifts now north, now south of him; the seasons that go by fours instead of twos; the trees that blossom and bear fruit from January to December, with no apparent regard for the calendar months as by law established; the black, brown, or yellow people, who know not his creed or his social code; the castes and cross-divisions that puzzle and surprise him; the pride and the scruples, deeper than those of civilised life, but that nevertheless run counter to his own; the economic conditions that defy his preconceptions; the virtues and the vices that equally rub him up the wrong way, all these things are highly conducive to the production of that first substratum of philosophic thinking, a Socratic attitude of supreme ignorance, a pure Cartesian frame of universal doubt.

Then again there is the marvellous exuberance and novelty of the fauna and flora. And this once more has something better for us all than mere specialist interest. Sugar and ginger grow for all alike. For we must remember that not only do the Tropics represent the vastly greater portion of the world's past: they also represent the vastly greater portion of the world's present. By far the larger part of the land surface of the earth is tropical or subtropical; the temperate and arctic regions make up but a minor and unimportant fraction of the soil of our planet. And if we include the sea as well, this truth becomes even more strikingly evident: the Tropics are even now the rule of life; the colder regions are but an abnormal and outlying eccentricity of nature. Yet it is from this starved and dwarfed and impoverished northern area that most of us have formed our views of life, to the total exclusion of the wider, richer, more varied world that calls for our admiration in tropical latitudes.

Insensibly this richness and vividness of nature all around one, on a first visit to the Tropics, sinks into one's mind, and produces profound, though at first unconscious, modifications in one's whole mode of regarding man and his universe. Especially is this the case in early life, when the character is still plastic and the eye still keen: pictures are formed in that brilliant sunshine and under those dim arches of hot grey sky that photograph themselves for ever on the lasting tablets of the human memory. John Stuart Mill in his Autobiography dwells lovingly, I remember, on the profound effect produced on himself by his childish visits to Jeremy Bentham at Ford Abbey in Dorsetshire, on the delightful sense of space and freedom and generous expansion given to his mind by the mere act of living and moving in those stately halls and wide airy gardens. Every university man must look back with pleasure of somewhat the same sort to the free breezy memories of the quadrangles and common rooms of Christ Church or of Trinity. But in the tropical university everybody passes his time in arcades of Greek or Pompeian airiness: the palm-trees wave and whisper around his head as he sits for coolness on his wide verandah; the humming-birds dart from flower to flower on the delicate bouquets that crowd his drawing-room. I knew a lady who made a capital collection of butterflies and moths at her own dinner-table by simply impounding in paper boxes the insects that flitted about the lamp at dessert. Why, if it comes to that, the very bread itself comprises generally a whole entomological cabinet, and contains in fragments the disjecta membra of specimens enough to stock entire glass cases at severe South Kensington. How's that for an inducement to study life where it is richest and most abundant in its native starting-place?

But above all in educational importance I rank the advantage of seeing human nature in its primitive surroundings, far from the squalid and chilly influences of the tail-end of the Glacial epoch. I admit at once that cold has done much, exceeding much, for human development, has been the mother of civilisation in somewhat the same sense that necessity has been the mother of invention. To it, no doubt, we owe to a great extent, in varying stages, clothing, the house, fire, the steam-engine. Yet none the less is it true that the first levels of society must needs have been passed under essentially tropical conditions, and that nascent civilisation spread but slowly northward, from Egypt and Asia, through Greece and Italy, to the cloudy regions where its chief centres are at present domiciled under canopies of coal smoke. And even to-day the sight of the tropics, green and luxuriant, brings us into touch at once with earlier ideas and habits of the race, makes us more able not only to understand, but also to sympathise with, our ancient ancestors of the naked-and-not-ashamed era of culture. Views formed exclusively in the North tend too much to imitate the reduced gentlewoman's outlook upon life; views formed in the Tropics correct this refractive influence by a certain genial and tolerant virile expansion, not to be learned at the Common, Clapham.

To one whose economic pendulum has hitherto oscillated between selfish luxury in Mayfair and squalid poverty in Seven Dials, there is indeed a world of novelty in the first view of the tropical poverty that is not squalid but contentedly luxurious, of the dusky father with his wife or wives (the mere number is a detail) sprawling at full length, half clad, in the eye of the sun, before the palm-thatched hut, while the fat black babies and the fat black little pigs wallow together almost indistinguishably in the dust at his side, just out of reach of the muscular foot that might otherwise of pure wantonness molest them. What a flood of light it all casts upon the future possibilities of society, that leisured, cultureless household, on whose garden-plot yam or bread-fruit or bananas or sweet potatoes can be grown in sufficient quantity to support the family without more labour than in England would pay for its kitchen coals; where the hut is but a shelter from rain, or a bed-curtain for night, and where the untaxed sun supplies the place of a drawing-room fire all the year round, and warms the water for the baby's bath at nothing the gallon! If there is any man who doesn't sympathise with his dusky brother when he sees him thus at home in his airy palace, any man who doesn't fraternise closely with his kind when thus brought face to face with our primitive existence, I don't envy him his stern and wild Caledonian ethics. The beach-comber instinct should be strong in all sane minds. Or if that blunt way of putting it perchance offend the weaker brethren, let us say rather, the spirit of the Lotus-eaters. For the man who doesn't want to eat of the Lotus just once in his life has become too civilised: the iron of the Gradgrind era of universal competition and payment by results has entered to deeply into his sordid soul. He wants a course of Egypt and Tahiti.

Oh, yes; I know what you are going to object, and I grant it at once: the influence of the Tropics is by no means an ascetic one. They, tend rather to encourage a certain genial and friendly tolerance of all possible human forms of society, even the lowest. They are essentially democratic, not to say socialistic and revolutionary in tone. By bringing us all down to the underlying verities of life, apart from its conventions, they beget perhaps a somewhat hasty impatience of Court dress and the Lord Chamberlain's regulations. But, per contra, they teach us to feel that every man, whether black, brown, or white, is very human, and every woman and child, if possible, even a trifle more so. Wicked as it all is, there is yet in tropical political economy more of the Gospel according to St. John, and less of Adam Smith, Ricardo, and Malthus, than in any orthodox political economy prescribed by examiners for the University of London. It is something to see a world where ceaseless toil is not the necessary and inevitable lot of all who don't pay income tax on a thousand a year, even if Board schools are unknown and quadratic equations a vanishing quantity. It is something to see a stick of sugar-cane protruding from the mouth of every child, and oranges retailed at twelve for a ha'penny. It is something to know how the vast majority of the human race still live and move and have their being, and to feel that after all their mode of life, though lacking in Greek iambics, wallpapers, and the Saturday Review, yet appeals in its own beach-comberish way to some of one's inmost and deepest yearnings. The hibiscus that flames before the wattled hut, the parrot that chatters from the green and golden mango-tree, the lithe, healthy figures of the children in the stream, are some compensation for the lack of London mud, London fog, and London illustrations of practical Christianity in the Isle of Dogs and the Bermondsey purlieus. I don't know whether I am knocking the last nail into the completed coffin of my own contention, but I believe every right-minded man returns from the Tropics a good deal more of a Communist than when he went there.

One word of explanation to prevent mistake. I am not myself, like Kingsley or Wallace, an enthusiastic tropicist. On the contrary, viewed as a place of permanent residence, I don't at all like the Tropics to live in. I am pleading here only for their educational value, in small doses. Spending two or three years there in the heyday of life is very much like reading Herodotus, a thing one is glad one had once to do, but one would never willingly do again for any money. We northern creatures are remote products of the Great Ice Age, and by this time, like Polar bears, we have grown adapted to our glacial environment. All the more, therefore, is it a useful shaking-up for us to get transported bodily from our cramped and poverty-stricken northern slums, just once in our life, to the palms and temples of the South, the lands where the human body is a hardy plant, not a frail exotic. We come back to our chilly home among the fogs and bogs with wider projects for the thawing down of the social ice-heap, and the introduction of the bread-fruit-tree and the currant-bun-bush into the remotest wilds of the borough of Hackney. I am not even quite sure that tropical experience doesn't predispose us somewhat in favour of planting the sweet potato instead of grazing battering-rams in the uplands of Connemara. But hush; I hear an editorial frown. No more of this heresy.


## ON THE WINGS OF THE WIND

Of course, you know my friend the squirting cucumber. If you don't, that can be only because you've never looked in the right place to find him. On all waste ground outside most southern cities, Nice, Cannes, Florence: Rome, Algiers, Granada: Athens, Palermo, Tunis, where you will, the soil is thickly covered by dark trailing vines which bear on their branches a queer hairy green fruit, much like a common cucumber at that early stage of its existence when we know it best in the commercial form of pickled gherkins. As long as you don't interfere with them, these hairy green fruits do nothing out of the common in the way of personal aggressiveness. Like the model young lady of the books on etiquette, they don't speak unless they're spoken to. But if peradventure you chance to brush up against the plant accidentally, or you irritate it of set purpose with your foot or your cane, then, as Mr. Rider Haggard would say, 'a strange thing happens': off jumps the little green fruit with a startling bounce, and scatters its juice and pulp and seeds explosively through a hole in the end where the stem joined on to it. The entire central part of the cucumber, in short (answering to the seeds and pulp of a ripe melon), squirts out elastically through the breach in the outer wall, leaving the hollow shell behind as a mere empty windbag.

Naturally, the squirting cucumber knows its own business best, and is not without sufficient reasons of its own for this strange and, to some extent, unmannerly behaviour. By its queer trick of squirting, it manages to kill at least two birds with one stone. For, in the first place, the sudden elastic jump of the fruit frightens away browsing animals, such as goats and cattle. Those meditative ruminants are little accustomed to finding shrubs or plants take the aggressive against them; and when they see a fruit that quite literally flies in their faces of its own accord, they hesitate to attack the uncanny vine which bristles with such magical and almost miraculous defences. Moreover, the juice of the squirting cucumber is bitter and nauseous, and if it gets into the eyes or nostrils of man or beast, it impresses itself on the memory by stinging like red pepper. So the trick of squirting serves in a double way as a protection to the plant against the attacks of herbivorous animals and other enemies.

But that's not all. Even when no enemy is near, the ripe fruits at last drop off of themselves, and scatter their seeds elastically in every direction. This they do simply in order to disseminate their kind in new and unoccupied spots, where the seedlings will root and find an opening in life for themselves. Observe, indeed, that the very word 'disseminate' implies a general vague recognition of this principle of plant-life on the part of humanity. It means, etymologically, to scatter seed; and it points to the fact that everywhere in nature seeds are scattered broadcast, infinite pains being taken by the mother-plant for their general diffusion over wide areas of woodland, plain, or prairie.

Let us take as examples a single little set of instances, familiar to everybody, but far commoner in the world at large than the inhabitants of towns are at all aware of: I mean, the winged seeds, that fly about freely in the air by means of feathery hairs or gossamer, like thistle-down and dandelion. Of these winged types we have many hundred varieties in England alone. All the willow-herbs, for example, have such feathery seeds (or rather fruits) to help them on their way through life; and one kind, the beautiful pink rose-bay, flies about so readily, and over such wide spaces of open country, that the plant is known to farmers in America as fireweed, because it always springs up at once over whole square miles of charred and smoking soil after every devastating forest fire. It travels fast, for it travels like Ariel. In much the same way, the coltsfoot grows on all new English railway banks, because its winged seeds are wafted everywhere in myriads on the winds of March. All the willows and poplars have also winged seeds: so have the whole vast tribe of hawkweeds, groundsels, ragworts, thistles, fleabanes, cat's-ears, dandelions, and lettuces. Indeed, one may say roughly, there are very few plants of any size or importance in the economy of nature which don't deliberately provide, in one way or another, for the dispersal and dissemination of their fruits or seedlings.

Why is this? Why isn't the plant content just to let its grains or berries drop quietly on to the soil beneath, and there shift for themselves as best they may on their own resources?

The answer is a more profound one than you would at first imagine. Plants discovered the grand principle of the rotation of crops long before man did. The farmer now knows that if he sows wheat or turnips too many years running on the same plot, he 'exhausts the soil,' as we say, deprives it of certain special mineral or animal constituents needful for that particular crop, and makes the growth of the plant, therefore, feeble or even impossible. To avoid this misfortune, he lets the land lie fallow, or varies his crops from year to year according to a regular and deliberate cycle. Well, natural selection forced the same discovery upon the plants themselves long before the farmer had dreamed of its existence. For plants, being, in the strictest sense, 'rooted to the spot,' absolutely require that all their needs should be supplied quite locally. Hence, from the very beginning, those plants which scattered their seeds widest throve the best; while those which merely dropped them on the ground under their own shadow, and on soil exhausted by their own previous demands upon it, fared ill in the struggle for life against their more discursive competitors. The result has been that in the long run few species have survived, except those which in one way or another arranged beforehand for the dispersal of their seeds and fruits over fresh and unoccupied areas of plain or hillside.

I don't, of course, by any means intend to assert that seeds always do it by the simple device of wings or feathery projections. Every variety of plan or dodge or expedient has been adopted in turn to secure the self-same end; and provided only it succeeds in securing it, any variety of them all is equally satisfactory. One might parallel it with the case of hatching birds' eggs. Most birds sit upon their eggs themselves, and supply the necessary warmth from their own bodies. But any alternative plan that attains the same end does just as well. The felonious cuckoo drops her foundlings unawares in another bird's nest: the ostrich trusts her unhatched offspring to the heat of the burning desert sand: and the Australian brush-turkeys, with vicarious maternal instinct, collect great mounds of decaying and fermenting leaves and rubbish, in which they deposit their eggs to be artificially incubated, as it were, by the slow heat generated in the process of putrefaction. Just in the same way, we shall see in the case of seeds that any method of dispersion will serve the plant's purpose equally well, provided only it succeeds in carrying a few of the young seedlings to a proper place in which they may start fair at last in the struggle for existence.

As in the case of the fertilization of flowers, so in that of the dispersal of seeds, there are two main ways in which the work is effected, by animals and by wind-power. I will not insult the intelligence of the reader at the present time of day by telling him that pollen is usually transferred from blossom to blossom in one or other of these two chief ways, it is carried on the heads or bodies of bees and other honey-seeking insects, or else it is wafted on the wings of the wind to the sensitive surface of a sister-flower. So, too, seeds are for the most part either dispersed by animals or blown about by the breezes of heaven to new situations. These are the two most obvious means of locomotion provided by nature; and it is curious to see that they have both been utilized almost equally by plants, alike for their pollen and their seeds, just as they have been utilized by man for his own purposes on sea or land, in ship, or windmill, or pack-horse, or carriage.

There are two ways in which animals may be employed to disperse seeds, voluntarily and involuntarily. They may be compelled to carry them against their wills: or they may be bribed and cajoled and flattered into doing the plant's work for it in return for some substantial advantage or benefit the plant confers upon them. The first plan is the one adopted by burrs and cleavers. These adhesive fruits are like the man who buttonholes you and won't be shaken off: they are provided with little curved hooks or bent and barbed hairs which catch upon the wool of sheep, the coat of cattle, or the nether integuments of wayfaring humanity, and can't be got rid of without some little difficulty. Most of them, you will find on examination, belonged to confirmed hedgerow or woodside plants: they grow among bushes or low scrub, and thickets of gorse or bramble. Now, to such plants as these, it is obviously useful to have adhesive fruits and seeds: for when sheep or other animals get them caught in their coats, they carry them away to other bushy spots, and there, to get rid of the annoyance caused by the foreign body, scratch them off at once against some holly-bush or blackthorn. You may often find seeds of this type sticking on thorns as the nucleus of a little matted mass of wool, so left by the sheep in the very spots best adapted for the free growth of their vigorous seedlings.

Even among plants which trust to the involuntary services of animals in dispersing their seeds, a great many varieties of detail may be observed on close inspection. For example, in hound's-tongue and goose-grass, two of the best-known instances among our common English weeds, each little nut is covered with many small hooks, which make it catch on firmly by several points of attachment to passing animals. These are the kinds we human beings of either sex oftenest find clinging to our skirts or trousers after a walk in a rabbit-warren. But in herb-bennet and avens each nut has a single long awn, crooked near the middle with a very peculiar S-shaped joint, which effectually catches on to the wool or hair, but drops at the elbow after a short period of withering. Sometimes, too, the whole fruit is provided with prehensile hooks, while sometimes it is rather the individual seeds themselves that are so accommodated. Oddest of all is the plan followed by the common burdock. Here, an involucre or common cup-shaped receptacle of hooked bracts surrounds an entire head of purple tubular flowers, and each of these flowers produces in time a distinct fruit; but the hooked involucre contains the whole compound mass, and, being pulled off bodily by a stray sheep or dog, effects the transference of the composite lot at once to some fitting place for their germination.

Those plants, on the other hand, which depend rather, like London hospitals, upon the voluntary system, produce that very familiar form of edible capsule which we commonly call in the restricted sense a fruit or berry. In such cases, the seed-vessel is usually swollen and pulpy: it is stored with sweet juices to attract the birds or other animal allies, and it is brightly coloured so as to advertise to their eyes the presence of the alluring sugary foodstuff. These instances, however, are now so familiar to everybody that I won't dwell upon them at any length. Even the degenerate schoolboy of the present day, much as he has declined from the high standard set forth by Macaulay, knows all about the way the actual seed itself is covered (as in the plum or the cherry) by a hard stony coat which 'resists the action of the gastric juice' (so physiologists put it, with their usual frankness), and thus passes undigested through the body of its swallower. All I will do here, therefore, is to note very briefly that some edible fruits, like the two just mentioned, as well as the apricot, the peach, the nectarine, and the mango, consist of a single seed with its outer covering; in others, as in the raspberry, the blackberry, the cloudberry, and the dew-berry, many seeds are massed together, each with a separate edible pulp; in yet others, as in the gooseberry, the currant, the grape, and the whortleberry, several seeds are embedded within the fruit in a common pulpy mass; and in others again, as in the apple, pear, quince, and medlar, they are surrounded by a quantity of spongy edible flesh. Indeed, the variety that prevails among fruits in this respect almost defies classification: for sometimes, as in the mulberry, the separate little fruits of several distinct flowers grow together at last into a common berry: sometimes, as in a fig, the general flower-stalk of several tiny one-seeded blossoms forms the edible part: and sometimes, as in the strawberry, the true little nuts or fruits appear as mere specks or dots on the bloated surface of the swollen and overgrown stem, which forms the luscious morsel dear to the human palate.

Yet in every case it is interesting to observe that, while the seeds which depend for dispersion upon the breeze are easily detached from the parent plant and blown about by every wind of doctrine, the seeds or fruits which depend for their dispersion upon birds or animals always, on the contrary, hang on to their native boughs to the very last, till some unconscious friend pecks them off and devours them. Haws, rose-hips, and holly-berries will wither and wilt on the tree in mild winters, because they can't drop off of themselves without the aid of birds, while the birds are too well supplied with other food to care for them. One of the strangest cases of all, however, is that of the mistletoe, which, living parasitically upon the forest-boughs and apple-trees, would of course be utterly lost if its berries dropped their seeds on to the ground beneath it. To avoid such a misfortune, the mistletoe berries are filled with an exceedingly viscid and sticky pulp, surrounding the hard little nut-like seeds: and this pulp makes the seeds cling to the bills and feet of various birds which feed upon the fruit, but most particularly of the missel thrush, who derives his common English name from his devotion to the mistletoe. The birds then carry them away unwittingly to some neighbouring tree, and rub them off, when they get uncomfortable, against a forked branch, the exact spots that best suits the young mistletoe for sprouting in. Man, in turn, makes use of the sticky pulp for the manufacture of bird-lime, and so employs against the birds the very qualities which the plant intended as a bribe for their kindly services.

Among seeds that trust for their disposal to the wind, the commonest, simplest, and least evolved type is that of the ordinary capsule, as in the poppies and campions. At first sight, to be sure, a casual observer might suppose there existed in these cases no recognisable device at all for the dissemination of the seedlings. But you and I, most excellent and discreet reader, are emphatically not, of course, mere casual observers. We look close, and go to the very root of things. And when we do so, we see for ourselves at once that almost all capsules open—where? why, at the top, so that the seeds can only be shaken out when there is a high enough wind blowing to sway the stems to and fro with some violence, and scatter the small black grains inside to a considerable distance. Furthermore, in many instances, of which the common poppy-head is an excellent example, the capsule opens by lateral pores at the top of a flat head, a further precaution which allows the seeds to get out only by a few at a time, after a distinct jerk, and so scatters them pretty evenly, with different winds, over a wide circular space around the mother plant. Experiment will show how this simple dodge works. Try to shake out the poppy-seed from a ripe poppy-head on the plant as it grows, without breaking the stem or bending it unnaturally, and you will easily see how much force of wind is required in order to put this unobtrusive but very effective mechanism into working order.

The devices of this character employed by various plants for the dispersal of seeds even in ordinary dry capsules are far too numerous for me to describe in full detail, though they form a delightful subject for individual study in any small suburban garden. I will only give one more illustrative case, just to show the sort of point an amateur should always be on the look-out for. There is an extremely common, though inconspicuous, English weed, the mouse-ear chickweed, found everywhere in flower-beds or grass-plots, however small, and noticeable for its quaint little horn-shaped capsules. These have a very odd sort of twist or cock-up in the middle, just above the part where the seeds lie; and they open at the top by ten small teeth, pointed obliquely outward for no apparent reason. Yet every point has a meaning of its own for all that. The plant is one that lies rather close upon the ground; and the effect of this twist in the capsule is that the seeds, which are relatively heavy, and well stored with nutriment, can never get out at all, unless a very strong wind is blowing, which sweeps over the herbage in long quick waves, and carries everything it shakes out for great distances before it. So much design have even the smallest weeds put into the mechanism for the dispersion of their precious seeds, the hope of their race and the earnest of their future!

Artillery marks a higher stage than the sling and the stone. Just so, in many plants, a step higher in the evolutionary scale as regards the method of dispersion, the capsule itself bursts open explosively, and scatters its contents to the four winds of heaven. Such plants may be said to discharge their grains on the principle of the bow and arrow. The balsam is a familiar example of this startling mode of moving to fresh fields and pastures new: its capsule consists of five long straight valves, which break asunder elastically the moment they are touched, when fully ripe, and shed their seeds on all sides, like so many small bombshells. Our friend the squirting cucumber, which served as the prime text for this present discourse, falls into somewhat the same category, though in other ways it rather resembles the true succulent fruits, and belongs, indeed, to the same family as the melon, the gourd, the pumpkin, and the vegetable-marrow, almost all of which are edible and in every way fruit-like. Among English weeds, the little bittercress that grows on dry walls and hedge-banks forms an excellent example of the same device. Village children love to touch the long, ripe, brown capsules on the top with one timid finger, and then jump away, half laughing, half terrified, when the mild-looking little plant goes off suddenly with a small bang and shoots its grains like a catapult point-blank in their faces.

It is in the tropics, however, that these elastic fruits reach their highest development. There they have to fight, not merely against such small fry as robins, squirrels, and harvest-mice, but against the aggressive parrot, the hard-billed toucan, the persistent lemur, and the inquisitive monkey. Moreover, the elastic fruits of the tropics grow often on spreading forest trees, and must therefore shed their seeds to immense distances if they are to reach comparatively virgin soil, unexhausted by the deep-set roots of the mother trunk. Under such exceptional circumstances, the tropical examples of these elastic capsules are by no means mere toys to be lightly played with by babes and sucklings. The sand-box tree of the West Indies has large round fruits, containing seeds about as big as an English horsebean; and the capsule explodes, when ripe, with a detonation like a pistol, scattering its contents with as much violence as a shot from an air-gun. It is dangerous to go too near these natural batteries during the shooting season. A blow in the eye from one would blind a man instantly. I well remember the very first night I spent in my own house in Jamaica, where I went to live shortly after the repression of 'Governor Eyre's rebellion,' as everybody calls it locally. All night long I heard somebody, as I thought, practising with a revolver in my own back garden: a sound which somewhat alarmed me under those very unstable social conditions. An earthquake about midnight, it is true, diverted my attention temporarily from the recurring shots, but didn't produce the slightest effect upon the supposed rebel's devotion to the improvement of his marksmanship. When morning dawned, however, I found it was only a sand-box tree, and that the shots were nothing more than the explosions of the capsules. As to the wonderful tales told about the Brazilian cannon-ball tree, I cannot personally endorse them from original observation, and will not stain this veracious page with any second-hand quotations from the strange stories of modern scientific Munchausens.

Still higher in the evolutionary scale than the elastic fruits are those airy species which have taken to themselves wings like the eagle, and soar forth upon the free breeze in search of what the Americans describe as 'fresh locations.' Of this class the simplest type may be seen in those forest-trees, like the maple and the sycamore, whose fruits are flattened out into long expansions or parachutes, technically known as 'keys,' by whose aid they flutter down obliquely to the ground at a considerable distance. The keys of the sycamore, to take a single instance, when detached from the tree in autumn, fall spirally through the air owing to the twist of the winged arm, and are carried so far that, as every gardener knows, young sycamore trees rank among the commonest weeds among our plots and flower-beds. A curious variant upon this type is presented by the lime, or linden, whose fruits are in themselves small wingless nuts; but they are born in clusters upon a common stalk, which is winged on either side by a large membranous bract. When the nuts are ripe, the whole cluster detaches itself in a body from the branch, and flutters away before the breeze by means of the common parachute, to some spot a hundred yards or more, where the wind chances to land it.

The topmost place of all in the hierarchy of seed life, it seems to me, is taken by the feathery fruits and seeds which float freely hither and thither wherever the wind may bear them. An immense number of the very highest plants, the aristocrats of the vegetable kingdom, such as the lordly composites, those ultimate products of plant evolution, possess such floating feathery seeds; though here, again, the varieties of detail are too infinite for rapid or popular classification. Indeed, among the composites alone, the thistle and dandelion tribe with downy fruits, I can reckon up more than a hundred and fifty distinct variations of plan among the winged seeds known to me in various parts of Europe. But if I am strong, I am merciful: I will let the public off with a hundred and forty-eight of them. My two exceptions shall be John-go-to-bed-at-noon and the hairy hawkweed, both of them common English meadow-plants. The first, and more quaintly named, of the two has little ribbed fruits that end in a long and narrow beak, supporting a radial rib-work of spokes like the frame of an umbrella; and from rib to rib of this framework stretch feathery cross-pieces, continuous all round, so as to make of the whole mechanism a perfect circular parachute, resembling somewhat the web of a geometrical spider. But the hairy hawkweed is still more cunning in its generation; for that clever and cautious weed produces its seeds or fruits in clustered heads, of which the central ones are winged, while the outer are heavy, squat, and wingless. Thus does the plant make the best of all chances that may happen to open before it: if one lot goes far and fares but ill, the other is pretty sure to score a bull's-eye.

These are only a few selected examples of the infinite dodges employed by enlightened herbs and shrubs to propagate their scions in foreign parts. Many more, equally interesting, must be left undescribed. Only for a single case more can I still find room, that of the subterranean clover, which has been driven by its numerous enemies to take refuge at last in a very remarkable and almost unique mode, of protecting its offspring. This particular kind of clover affects smooth and close-cropped hillsides, where the sheep nibble down the grass and other herbage almost as fast as it springs up again. Now, clover seeds resemble their allies of the pea and bean tribe in being exceedingly rich in starch and other valuable foodstuffs. Hence, they are much sought after by the inquiring sheep, which eat them off wherever found, as exceptionally nutritious and dainty morsels. Under these circumstances, the subterranean clover has learnt to produce small heads of bloom, pressed close to the ground, in which only the outer flowers are perfect and fertile, while the inner ones are transformed into tiny wriggling corkscrews. As soon as the fertile flowers have begun to set their seed, by the kind aid of the bees, the whole stem bends downward, automatically, of its own accord; the little corkscrews then worm their way into the turf beneath; and the pods ripen and mature in the actual soil itself, where no prying ewe can poke an inquisitive nose to grub them up and devour them. Cases like this point in certain ways to the absolute high-water-mark of vegetable ingenuity: they go nearest of all in the plant-world to the similitude of conscious animal intelligence.


## A DESERT FRUIT

Who knows the Mediterranean, knows the prickly pear. Not that that quaint and uncanny-looking cactus, with its yellow blossoms and bristling fruits that seem to grow paradoxically out of the edge of thick fleshy leaves, is really a native of Italy, Spain, and North Africa, where it now abounds on every sun-smitten hillside. Like Mr. Henry James and Mr. Marion Crawford, the Barbary fig, as the French call it, is, in point of fact, an American citizen, domiciled and half naturalised on this side of the Atlantic, but redolent still at heart of its Columbian origin. Nothing is more common, indeed, than to see classical pictures of the Alma-Tadema school, not, of course, from the brush of the master himself, who is impeccable in such details, but fair works of decent imitators, in which Caia or Marcia leans gracefully in her white stole on one pensive elbow against a marble lintel, beside a courtyard decorated with a Pompeian basin, and overgrown with prickly pear or "American aloes." I need hardly say that, as a matter of plain historical fact, neither cactuses nor agaves were known in Europe till long after Christopher Columbus had steered his wandering bark to the sandy shores of Cat's Island in the Bahamas. (I have seen Cat's Island with these very eyes, and can honestly assure you that its shores are sandy.) But this is only one among the many pardonable little inaccuracies of painters, who thrust scarlet geraniums from the Cape of Good Hope into the fingers of Aspasia, or supply King Solomon in all his glory with Japanese lilies of the most recent introduction.

At the present day, it is true, both the prickly-pear cactus and the American agave (which the world at large insists upon confounding with the aloe, a member of a totally distinct family) have spread themselves in an apparently wild condition over all the rocky coasts both of Southern Europe and of Northern Africa. The alien desert weeds have fixed their roots firmly in the sunbaked clefts of Ligurian Apennines; the tall candelabrum of the western agave has reared its great spike of branching blossoms (which flower, not once in a century, as legend avers, but once in some fifteen years or so) on all the basking hillsides of the Mauritanian Atlas. But for the origin, and therefore for the evolutionary history, of either plant, we must look away from the shore of the inland sea to the arid expanse of the Mexican desert. It was there, among the sweltering rocks of the Tierras Calientes, that these ungainly cactuses first learned to clothe themselves in prickly mail, to store in their loose tissues an abundant supply of sticky moisture, and to set at defiance the persistent attacks of all external enemies. The prickly pear, in fact, is a typical instance of a desert plant, as the camel is a typical instance of a desert animal. Each lays itself out to endure the long droughts of its almost rainless habitat by drinking as much as it can when opportunity offers, hoarding up the superfluous water for future use, and economising evaporation by every means in its power.

If you ask that convenient fiction, the Man in the Street, what sort of plant a cactus is, he will probably tell you it is all leaf and no stem, and each of the leaves grows out of the last one. Whenever we set up the Man in the Street, however, you must have noticed we do it in order to knock him down again like a nine-pin next moment: and this particular instance is no exception to the rule; for the truth is that a cactus is practically all stem and no leaves, what looks like a leaf being really a branch sticking out at an angle. The true leaves, if there are any, are reduced to mere spines or prickles on the surface, while the branches, in the prickly-pear and many of the ornamental hot-house cactuses, are flattened out like a leaf to perform foliar functions. In most plants, to put it simply, the leaves are the mouths and stomachs of the organism; their thin and flattened blades are spread out horizontally in a wide expanse, covered with tiny throats and lips which suck in carbonic acid from the surrounding air, and disintegrate it in their own cells under the influence of sunlight. In the prickly pears, on the contrary, it is the flattened stem and branches which undertake this essential operation in the life of the plant, the sucking-in of carbon and giving-out of oxygen, which is to the vegetable exactly what the eating and digesting of food is to the animal organism. In their old age, however, the stems of the prickly pear display their true character by becoming woody in texture and losing their articulated leaf-like appearance.

Everything on this earth can best be understood by investigating the history of its origin and development, and in order to understand this curious reversal of the ordinary rule in the cactus tribe we must look at the circumstances under which the race was evolved in the howling waste of American deserts. (All deserts have a prescriptive right to howl, and I wouldn't for worlds deprive them of the privilege.) Some familiar analogies will help us to see the utility of this arrangement. Everybody knows our common English stone-crops, or if he doesn't he ought to, for they are pretty and ubiquitous. Now stone-crops grow for the most part in chinks of the rock or thirsty sandy soil; they are essentially plants of very dry positions. Hence they have thick and succulent little stems and leaves, which merge into one another by imperceptible gradations. All parts of the plant alike are stumpy, green, and cylindrical. If you squash them with your finger and thumb you find that though the outer skin or epidermis is thick and firm, the inside is sticky, moist, and jelly-like. The reason for all this is plain; the stone-crops drink greedily by their roots whenever they get a chance, and store up the water so obtained to keep them from withering under the hot and pitiless sun that beats down upon them for hours In the baked clefts of their granite matrix. It's the camel trick over again. So leaves and stem grow thick and round and juicy within; but outside they are enclosed in a stout layer of epidermis, which consists of empty glassy cells, and which can be peeled off or flayed with a knife like the skin of an animal. This outer layer prevents evaporation, and is a marked feature of all succulent plants which grow exposed to the sun on arid rocks or in sandy deserts.

The tendency to produce rounded stems and leaves, little distinguishable from one another, is equally noticeable in many seaside plants which frequent the strip of thirsty sand beyond the reach of the tides. That belt of dry beach that stretches between high-water mark and the zone of vegetable mould, is to all intents and purpose a miniature desert. True, it is watered by rain from time to time; but the drops sink in so fast that in half an hour, as we know, the entire strip is as dry as Sahara again. Now there are many shore weeds of this intermediate sand-belt which mimic to a surprising degree the chief external features of the cactuses. One such weed, the common salicornia, which grows in sandy bottoms or hollows of the beach, has a jointed stem, branched and succulent, after the true cactus pattern, and entirely without leaves or their equivalents in any way. Still more cactus-like in general effect is another familiar English seaside weed, the kali or glasswort, so called because it was formerly burnt to extract the soda. The glasswort has leaves, it is true, but they are thick and fleshy, continuous with the stem, and each one terminating in a sharp, needle-like spine, which effectually protects the weed against all browsing aggressors.

Now, wherever you get very dry and sandy conditions of soil, you get this same type of cactus-like vegetation, plantes grasses, as the French well call them. The species which exhibit it are not necessary related to one another in any way; often they belong to most widely distinct families; it is an adaptive resemblance alone, due to similarity of external circumstances only. The plants have to fight against the same difficulties, and they adopt for the most part the same tactics to fight them with. In other words, any plant of whatever family, which wishes to thrive in desert conditions, must almost, as a matter of course, become thick and succulent, so as to store up water, and must be protected by a stout epidermis to prevent its evaporation under the fierce heat of the sunlight. They do not necessarily lose their leaves in the process; but the jointed stem usually answers the purpose of leaves under such conditions far better than any thin and exposed blade could do in the arid air of a baking desert. And therefore, as a rule, desert plants are leafless.

In India, for example, there are no cactuses. But I wouldn't advise you to dispute the point with a peppery, fire-eating Anglo-Indian colonel. I did so once, myself, at the risk of my life, at a table d'hôte on the Continent; and the wonder is that I'm still alive to tell the story. I had nothing but facts on my side, while the colonel had fists, and probably pistols. And when I say no cactuses, I mean, of course, no indigenous species; for prickly pears and epiphyllums may naturally be planted by the hand of man anywhere. But what people take for thickets of cactus in the Indian jungle are really thickets of cactus-like spurges. In the dry soil of India, many spurges grow thick and succulent, learn to suppress their leaves, and assume the bizarre forms and quaint jointed appearance of the true cactuses. In flower and fruit, however, they are euphorbias to the end; it is only in the thick and fleshy stem that they resemble their nobler and more beautiful Western rivals. No true cactus grows truly wild anywhere on earth except in America. The family was developed there, and, till man transplanted it, never succeeded in gaining a foothold elsewhere. Essentially tropical in type, it was provided with no means of dispersing its seeds across the enormous expanse of intervening ocean which separated its habitat from the sister continents.

But why are cactuses so almost universally prickly? From the grotesque little melon-cactuses of our English hothouses to the huge and ungainly monsters which form miles of hedgerows on Jamaican hillsides, the members of this desert family are mostly distinguished by their abundant spines and thorns, or by the irritating hairs which break off in your skin if you happen to brush incautiously against them. Cactuses are the hedgehogs of the vegetable world; their motto is Nemo me impune lacessit. Many a time in the West Indies I have pushed my hand for a second into a bit of tangled 'bush,' as the negroes call it, to seize some rare flower or some beautiful insect, and been punished for twenty-four hours afterwards by the stings of the almost invisible and glass-like little cactus-needles. When you rub them they only break in pieces, and every piece inflicts a fresh wound on the flesh where it rankles. Some of the species have large, stout prickles; some have clusters of irritating hairs at measured distances; and some rejoice in both means of defence at once, scattered impartially over their entire surface. In the prickly pear, the bundles of prickles are arranged geometrically with great regularity in a perfect quincunx. But that is a small consolation indeed to the reflective mind when you've stung yourself badly with them.

The reason for this bellicose disposition on the part of the cactuses is a tolerably easy one to guess. Fodder is rare in the desert. The starving herbivores that find themselves from time to time belated on the confines of such thirsty regions would seize with avidity upon any succulent plant which offered them food and drink at once in their last extremity. Fancy the joy with which a lost caravan, dying of hunger and thirst in the byways of Sahara, would hail a great bed of melons, cucumbers, and lettuces! Needless to say, however, under such circumstances melon, cucumber, and lettuce would soon be exterminated: they would be promptly eaten up at discretion without leaving a descendant to represent them in the second generation. In the ceaseless war between herbivore and plant, which is waged every day and all day long the whole world over with far greater persistence than the war between carnivore and prey, only those species of plant can survive in such exposed situations which happen to develop spines, thorns, or prickles as a means of defence against the mouths of hungry and desperate assailants.

Nor is this so difficult a bit of evolution as it looks at first sight. Almost all plants are more or less covered with hairs, and it needs but a slight thickening at the base, a slight woody deposit at the point, to turn them forthwith into the stout prickles of the rose or the bramble. Most leaves are more or less pointed at the end or at the summits of the lobes; and it needs but a slight intensification of this pointed tendency to produce forthwith the sharp defensive foliage of gorse, thistles, and holly. Often one can see all the intermediate stages still surviving under one's very eyes. The thistles, themselves, for example, vary from soft and unarmed species which haunt out-of-the-way spots beyond the reach of browsing herbivores, to such trebly-mailed types as that enemy of the agricultural interest, the creeping thistle, in which the leaves continue themselves as prickly wings down every side of the stem, so that the whole plant is amply clad from head to foot in a defensive coat of fierce and bristling spearheads. There is a common little English meadow weed, the rest-harrow, which in rich and uncropped fields produces no defensive armour of any sort; but on the much-browsed-over suburban commons and in similar exposed spots, where only gorse and blackthorn stand a chance for their lives against the cows and donkeys, it has developed a protected variety in which some of the branches grow abortive, and end abruptly in stout spines like a hawthorn's. Only those rest-harrows have there survived in the sharp struggle for existence which happened most to baffle their relentless pursuers.

Desert plants naturally carry this tendency to its highest point of development. Nowhere else is the struggle for life so fierce; nowhere else is the enemy so goaded by hunger and thirst to desperate measures. It is a place for internecine warfare Hence, all desert plants are quite absurdly prickly. The starving herbivores will attack and devour under such circumstances even thorny weeds, which tear or sting their tender tongues and palates, but which supply them at least with a little food and moisture: so the plants are compelled in turn to take almost extravagant precautions. Sometimes the leaves end in a stout dagger-like point, as with the agave, or so-called American aloe; sometimes they are reduced to mere prickles or bundles of needle-like spikes; sometimes they are suppressed altogether, and the work of defence is undertaken in their stead by irritating hairs intermixed with caltrops of spines pointing outward from a common centre in every direction. When one remembers how delicately sensitive are the tender noses of most browsing herbivores, one can realize what an excellent mode of defence these irritating hairs must naturally constitute. I have seen cows in Jamaica almost maddened by their stings, and even savage bulls will think twice in their rage before they attempt to make their way through the serried spears of a dense cactus hedge. To put it briefly, plants have survived under very arid or sandy conditions precisely in proportion as they displayed this tendency towards the production of thorns, spines, bristles, and prickles.

It is a marked characteristic of the cactus tribe to be very tenacious of life, and when hacked to pieces, to spring afresh in full vigour from every scrap or fragment. True vegetable hydras, when you cut down one, ten spring in its place: every separate morsel of the thick and succulent stem has the power of growing anew into a separate cactus. Surprising as this peculiarity seems at first sight, it is only a special desert modification of a faculty possessed in a less degree by almost all plants and by many animals. If you cut off the end of a rose branch and stick it in the ground under suitable conditions, it grows into a rose tree. If you take cuttings of scarlet geraniums or common verbenas, and pot them in moist soil, they bud out apace into new plants like their parents. Certain special types can even be propagated from fragments of the leaf; for example, there is a particularly vivacious begonia off which you may snap a corner of one blade, and hang it up by a string from a peg or the ceiling, when, hi, presto! little begonia plants begin to bud out incontinently on every side from its edges. A certain German professor went even further than that; he chopped up a liverwort very fine into vegetable mincemeat, which he then spread thin over a saucerful of moist sand, and lo! in a few days the whole surface of the mess was covered with a perfect forest of sprouting little liverworts. Roughly speaking, one may say that every fragment of every organism has in it the power to rebuild in its entirety another organism like the one of which it once formed a component element.

Similarly with animals. Cut off a lizard's tail, and straightway a new tail grows in its place with surprising promptitude. Cut off a lobster's claw, and in a very few weeks that lobster is walking about airily on his native rocks, with two claws as usual. True, in these cases the tail and the claw don't bud out in turn into a new lizard or a new lobster. But that is a penalty the higher organisms have to pay for their extreme complexity. They have lost that plasticity, that freedom of growth, which characterizes the simpler and more primitive forms of life; in their case the power of producing fresh organisms entire from a single fragment, once diffused equally over the whole body, is now confined to certain specialized cells which, in their developed form, we know as seeds or eggs. Yet, even among animals, at a low stage of development, this original power of reproducing the whole from a single part remains inherent in the organism; for you may chop up a fresh-water hydra into a hundred little bits, and every bit will be capable of growing afresh into a complete hydra.

Now, desert plants would naturally retain this primitive tendency in a very high degree; for they are specially organized to resist drought, being the survivors of generations of drought-proof ancestors, and, like the camel, they have often to struggle on through long periods of time without a drop of water. Exactly the same thing happens at home to many of our pretty little European stone-crops. I have a rockery near my house overgrown with the little white sedum of our gardens. The birds often peck off a tiny leaf or branch; it drops on the dry soil, and remains there for days without giving a sign of life. But its thick epidermis effectually saves it from withering; and as soon as rain falls, wee white rootlets sprout out from the under side of the fragment as it lies, and it grows before long into a fresh small sedum plant. Thus, what seem like destructive agencies themselves, are turned in the end by mere tenacity of life into a secondary means of propagation.

That is why the prickly pear is so common in all countries where the climate suits it, and where it has once managed to gain a foothold. The more you cut it down, the thicker it springs; each murdered bit becomes the parent in due time of a numerous offspring. Man, however, with his usual ingenuity, has managed to best the plant, on this its own ground, and turn it into a useful fodder for his beasts of burden. The prickly pear is planted abundantly on bare rocks in Algeria, where nothing else would grow, and is cut down when adult, divested of its thorns by a rough process of hacking, and used as food for camels and cattle. It thus provides fresh moist fodder in the African summer when the grass is dried up and all other pasture crops have failed entirely.

The flowers of the prickly pear, as of many other cactuses, grow apparently on the edge of the leaves, which alone might give the observant mind a hint as to the true nature of those thick and flattened expansions. For whenever what look like leaves bear flowers or fruit on their edge or midrib, as in the familiar instance of butcher's broom, you may be sure at a glance they are really branches in disguise masquerading as foliage. The blossoms in the prickly pear are large, handsome, and yellow; at least, they would be handsome if one could ever see them, but they are generally covered so thick in dust that it is difficult properly to appreciate their beauty. They have a great many petals in numerous rows, and a great many stamens in a rosette in the centre; and, to the best of my knowledge and belief, as lawyers put it, they are fertilized for the most part by tropical butterflies; but on this point, having observed them but little in their native habitats, I speak under correction.

The fruit itself, to which the plant owes its popular name, is botanically a berry, though a very big one, and it exhibits in a highly specialized degree the general tactics of all its family. As far as their leaf-like stems go, the main object in life of the cactuses is, not to get eaten. But when it comes to the fruit, this object in life is exactly reversed; the plant desires its fruit to be devoured by some friendly bird or adapted animal, in order that the hard little seeds buried in the pulp within may be dispersed for germination under suitable conditions. At the same time, true to its central idea, it covers even the pear itself with deterrent and prickly hairs, meant to act as a defence against useless thieves or petty depredators, who would eat the soft pulp on the plant as it stands (much as wasps do peaches) without benefiting the species in return by dispersing its seedlings. This practice is fully in accordance with the general habit of tropical or sub-tropical fruits, which lay themselves out to deserve the kind offices of monkeys, parrots, toucans, hornbills, and other such large and powerful fruit-feeders. Fruits which arrange themselves for a clientèle, of this character have usually thick or nauseous rinds, prickly husks, or other deterrent integuments; but they are full within of juicy pulp, embedding stony or nutlike seeds, which pass undigested through the gizzards of their swallowers.

For a similar reason, the actual prickly pears themselves are attractively coloured. I need hardly point out, I suppose, at the present time of day, that such tints in the vegetable world act like the gaudy posters of our London advertisers. Fruits and flowers which desire to attract the attention of beasts, birds, or insects, are tricked out in flaunting hues of crimson, purple, blue, and yellow; fruits and flowers which could only be injured by the notice of animals are small and green, or dingy and inconspicuous.

## PRETTY POLL

It is an error of youth to despise parrots for their much talking. Loquacity isn't always a sign of empty-headedness, nor is silence a sure proof of weight and wisdom. Biologists, for their part, know better than that. By common consent, they rank the parrot group as the very head and crown of bird creation. Not, of course, because pretty Poll can talk (in a state of nature, parrots only chatter somewhat meaninglessly to one another), but because the group display on the whole, all round, a greater amount of intelligence, of cleverness, and of adaptability to circumstances than any other birds, including even their cunning and secretive rivals, the ravens, the jackdaws, the crows, and the magpies.

What are the efficient causes of this exceptionally high intelligence in parrots? Well, Mr. Herbert Spencer, I believe, was the first to point out the intimate connection that exists throughout the animal world between mental development and the power of grasping an object all round so as to know exactly its shape and its tactile properties. The possession of an effective prehensile organ, a hand or its equivalent, seems to be the first great requisite for the evolution of a high order of intellect. Man and the monkeys, for example, have a pair of hands; and in their case one can see at a glance how dependent is their intelligence upon these grasping organs. All human arts base themselves ultimately upon the human hand; and even the apes approach nearest to humanity in virtue of their ever-active and busy little fingers. The elephant, again, has his flexible trunk, which, as we have all heard over and over again, usque ad nauseam, is equally well adapted to pick up a pin or to break the great boughs of tropical forest trees. (That pin, in particular, is now a well-worn classic.) The squirrel, once more, celebrated for his unusual intelligence when judged by a rodent standard, uses his pretty little paws as veritable hands, by which he can grasp a nut or fruit all round, and so gain in his small mind a clear conception of its true shape and properties. Throughout the animal kingdom generally, indeed, this correspondence, or rather this chain of causation, makes itself everywhere felt; no high intelligence without a highly developed prehensile and grasping organ.

Perhaps the opossum is the very best and most crucial instance that could possibly be adduced of the intimate connection which exists between touch and intellect. For the opossum is a marsupial; it belongs to the same group of lowly-organized, antiquated, and pouch-bearing animals as the kangaroo, the wombat, and the other belated Australian mammals. Now everybody knows the marsupials as a class are nothing short of preternaturally stupid. They are just about the very dullest and silliest of all existing quadrupeds. And this is reasonable enough, when one comes to think of it, for they represent a very antique and early type, the first rough sketch of the mammalian idea, if I may so describe them, with wits unsharpened as yet by contact with the world in the fierce competition of the struggle for life as it displays itself on the crowded stage of the great continents. They stand, in short, to the lions and tigers, the elephants and horses, the monkeys and squirrels, of Europe and America, as the Australian blackfellow stands to the Englishman or the Yankee. They are the last relic of the original secondary quadrupeds, stranded for ages in a remote southern island, and still keeping up among Australian forests the antique type of life that went out of fashion in Europe, Asia, and America before the chalk was laid down or the London Clay deposited on the bed of our northern oceans. Hence they have still very narrow brains, and are so extremely stupid that a kangaroo, it is said, though I don't vouch for it myself, when struck a smart blow, will turn and bite the stick that hurts him instead of expending his anger on the hand that holds it.

Now, every Girton girl is well aware that the opossum, though it is a marsupial too, differs inexpressibly in psychological development from the kangaroo and the wombat. Your opossum, in short, is active, sly, and extremely intelligent. He knows his way about the world he lives in. 'A 'possum up a gum-tree' is accepted by the observant American mind as the very incarnation of animal cleverness, cunning, and duplicity. In negro folk-lore the resourceful 'possum takes the place of Reynard the Fox in European stories: he is the Macchiavelli of wild beasts: there is no ruse on earth of which he isn't amply capable, no artful trick which he can't design and execute, no wily manoeuvre which he can't contrive and carry to an end successfully. All guile and intrigue, the 'possum can circumvent even Uncle Remus himself by his crafty diplomacy. And what is it that makes all the difference between this 'cute Yankee marsupial and his backward and belated Australian cousins? Why, nothing but the possession of a prehensile hand and tail. Therein lies the whole secret. The opossum's hind foot has a genuine opposable thumb; and he also uses his tail in climbing as a supernumerary hand, almost as much as do any of the monkeys. He often suspends himself by it, like an acrobat, swings his body to and fro to get up steam, then lets go suddenly, and flies away to a distant branch, which he clutches by means of his hand-like hind feet. If the toes play him false, he can 'recover his tip,' as circus-folk put it, with his prehensile tail. The consequence is that the opossum, being able to form for himself clear and accurate conceptions of the real shapes and relations of things by these two distinct grasping organs, has acquired an unusual amount of general intelligence. And further, in the keen competition of the American continent, he has been forced to develop an amount of cleverness and low cunning which leaves his Australian poor relations far behind in the Middle Ages of evolution.

At the risk of seeming to run off at a tangent and forsake our ostensible subject, pretty Poll, altogether, I must just pause for one moment more to answer an objection which I know has been trembling on the tip of your tongue any time the last five minutes. You've been waiting till you could get a word in edgeways to give me a friendly nudge and remark very wisely, 'But look here, I say; how about the dog and the horse in your argument? They've got no prehensile organ that ever I heard of, and yet they're universally allowed to be the cleverest and most intelligent of all earthly quadrupeds.' True, O most sapient and courteous objector. I grant it you at once. But observe the difference. The cleverness of the horse and the dog is acquired, not original. It has probably arisen in the course of their long hereditary intercourse and companionship with man, the cleverest and most serviceable individuals being deliberately selected from generation to generation, as dams and sires to breed from. We can't fairly compare these artificial human products, therefore, with wild races whose intelligence is all native and self-evolved. Moreover, the horse at least has to some slight extent a prehensile organ in his very mobile and sensitive lip, which he uses like an undeveloped or rudimentary proboscis to feel things all over with. So that the dog alone remains as a contradictory instance; and even the dog derives his cleverness indirectly from man, whose hand and thumb in the last resort are really at the bottom of his vicarious wisdom.

We may conclude, then, I believe, that touch, as Mr. Herbert Spencer admirably words it, is 'the mother-tongue of the senses;' and that in proportion as animals have or have not highly developed and serviceable tactile organs will they rank high or low in the intellectual hierarchy of nature. Now, how does this bear upon the family of parrots? Well, in the first place, everybody who has ever kept a cockatoo or a macaw in domestic slavery is well aware that in no other birds do the claws so closely resemble a human or simian hand, not indeed in outer form or appearance, but in opposability of the thumbs and in perfection of grasping power. The toes on each foot are arranged in opposite pairs, two turning in front and two backward, which gives all parrots their peculiar firmness in clinging on a perch or on the branch of a tree with one foot only, while they extend the other to grasp a fruit or to clutch at any object they desire to take possession of. True, this peculiarity isn't entirely confined to the parrots alone, as such. They share the division of the foot into two thumbs and two fingers with a whole large group of allied birds, called, in the charmingly concise and poetical language of technical ornithology, the Scansorial Picarians, and more generally, known to the unlearned herd (meaning you and me) by their several names of woodpeckers, cuckoos, toucans, and plantain-eaters. All the members of this great group, of which the parrots proper are only the most advanced and developed family, possess the same arrangement of the digits into front-toes and back-toes. But in none is the arrangement so perfect as in the parrots, and in none is the power of grasping an object all round so completely developed and so pregnant in moral and intellectual consequences.

All the Scansorial Picarians, however (if the reader with his proverbial courtesy will kindly pardon me the inevitable use of such very bad words), are essentially tree-haunters; and the tree-haunting and climbing habit, as is well beknown, seems particularly favourable to the growth of intelligence. Thus schoolboys climb trees, but I forgot: this is a scientific article, and such levity is inconsistent with the dignity of science. Let us be serious! Well, at any rate, monkeys, squirrels, opossums, wild cats, are all of them climbers, and all of them, in the act of clinging, jumping, and balancing themselves on boughs, gain such an accurate idea of geometrical figure, perspective, distance, and the true nature of space-relations, as could hardly be acquired in any other manner. In one word, they thoroughly understand space of three dimensions, and the tactual realities that answer to and underlie each visible appearance. This is the very substratum of all intelligence; and the monkeys, possessing it more profoundly than any other animals, have accordingly taken the top of the form in the competitive examination perpetually conducted by survival of the fittest.

So, too, among birds, the parrots and their allies climb trees and rocks with exceptional ease and agility. Even in their own department they are the great feathered acrobats. Anybody who watches a woodpecker, for example, grasping the bark of a tree with its crooked and powerful toes, while it steadies itself behind by digging its stiff tail-feathers into the crannies of the outer rind, will readily understand how clear a notion the bird must gain into the practical action of the laws of gravity. But the true parrots go a step further in the same direction than the woodpeckers or the toucans; for, in addition to prehensile feet, they have also a highly-developed prehensile bill, and within it a tongue which acts in reality as an organ of touch. They use their crooked beaks to help them in climbing from branch to branch; and being thus provided alike with wings, legs, hands, fingers, bill and tongue, they are in fact the most truly arboreal of all known animals, and present in the fullest and highest degree all the peculiar features of the tree-haunting existence.

Nor is that all. Alone among birds or mammals, the parrots have the curious peculiarity of being able to move the upper as well as the lower jaw. It is this strange mobility of both the mandibles together, combined with the crafty effect of the sideways glance from those artful eyes, that gives the characteristic air of intelligence and wisdom to the parrot's face. We naturally expect so clever a bird to speak. And when it turns upon us suddenly with a copy-book maxim, we are in no way astonished at its surpassing smartness.

Parrots are vegetarians; with a single degraded exception to whom I shall recur hereafter, Sir Henry Thompson himself couldn't find fault with their regimen. They live chiefly upon a light but nutritious diet of fruit and seeds, or upon the abundant nectar of rich tropical flowers. And it is mainly for the sake of getting at their chosen food that they have developed the large and powerful bills which characterise the family. You may have perhaps noted that most tropical fruit-eaters, like the hornbills and the toucans, are remarkable for the size and strength of their beaks: if you haven't, I dare say you will generously take my word for it. And, per contra, it may also have struck you that most tropical fruits have thick or hard or nauseous rinds, which need to be torn off before the monkeys or birds for whose use they are intended, can get at them and eat them. Our little northern strawberries, and raspberries, and currants, and whortleberries, developed with a single eye to the petty robins and finches of temperate climates, can be popped into, the mouth whole and eaten as they stand: they are meant for small birds to devour, and to disperse the tiny undigested nut-like seeds in return for the bribe of the soft pulp that surrounds them. But it is quite otherwise with oranges, shaddocks, bananas, plantains, mangoes, and pine-apples: those great tropical fruits can only be eaten properly with a knife and fork, after stripping off the hard and often acrid rind that guards and preserves them. They lay themselves out for dispersion by monkeys, toucans, and other relatively large and powerful fruit-eaters; and the rind is put there as a barrier against small thieves who would rob the sweet pulp, but be absolutely incapable of carrying away and dispersing the large and richly-stored seeds it covers.

Parrots and toucans, however, have no knives and forks to cut off the rind with; but as monkeys use their fingers, so the birds use for the same purpose their sharp and powerful bills. No better nut-crackers and fruit-parers could possibly be found. The parrot, in particular, has developed for the purpose his curved and inflated beak, a wonderful weapon, keen as a tailor's scissors, and moved by powerful muscles on either side of the face which bring together the cutting edges with extraordinary energy. The way the bird holds the fruit gingerly in one claw, while he strips off the rind dexterously with his under-hung lower mandible, and keeps a sharp look-out meanwhile on either side with those sly and stealthy eyes of his for a possible intruder, suggests to the observing mind the whole living drama of his native forest. One sees in that vivid world the watchful monkey ever ready to swoop down upon the tempting tail-feathers of his hereditary foe: one sees the canny parrot ever prepared for his rapid attack, and ever eager to make him pay with five joints of his tail for his impertinent interference with an unoffending fellow-citizen of the arboreal community.

Still, there are parrots and parrots, of course. Not all this vast family are in all things of like passions one with another. The great black cockatoo, for example, the largest of the tribe, lives almost entirely off the central shoot or 'cabbage' of palm-trees: an expensive kind of food, for when once the 'cabbage' is eaten the tree dies forthwith, so that each black cockatoo must have killed in his time whole groves of cabbage-palms. Others, again, feed off fruits and seeds; and not a few are entirely adapted for flower-haunting and honey-sucking.

As a group, the parrots are comparatively modern birds. Indeed, they could have no place in the world till the big tropical fruits and nuts were beginning to be developed. And it is now pretty certain that fruits and nuts are for the most part of very recent and special evolution. To put it briefly, the monkeys and parrots developed the fruits and nuts, while the fruits and nuts returned the compliment by developing conversely the monkeys and parrots. In other words, both types grew up side by side in mutual dependence, and evolved themselves pari passu for one another's benefit. Without the fruits there could be no fruit-eaters; and without the fruit-eaters to disperse their seeds, there could just to the same extent be no fruits to speak of.

Most of the parrots very much resemble the monkeys and other tropical fruit-feeders in their habits and manners. They are gregarious, mischievous, noisy, and irresponsible. They have no moral sense, and are fond of practical jokes and other schoolboy horseplay. They move about in flocks, screeching aloud as they go, and alight together on some tree well covered with berries. No doubt, they herd together for the sake of protection and screech both to keep the flock in a body and to strike alarm and consternation into the breasts of their enemies. When danger threatens, the first bird that perceives it sounds a note of warning; and in a moment the whole troop is on the wing at once, vociferous and eager, roaring forth a song in their own tongue which may be roughly interpreted as stating in English that they don't want to fight, but by Jingo, if they do, they'll tear their enemy to shreds and drink his blood up too.

The common grey parrot, the best known in confinement of all his kind, and unrivalled as an orator for his graces of speech, is a native of West Africa; so that he shares with other West Africans that perfect command of language which has always been a marked characteristic of the negro race. He feeds in a general way upon palm-nuts, bananas, mangoes, and guavas, but he is by no means averse, if opportunity offers, to the Indian corn of the industrious native. His wife accompanies him in his solitary rambles, for they are not gregarious. In her native haunts, indeed, Polly is an unsociable bird. It is only in confinement that her finer qualities come out, and that she develops into a speech-maker of distinguished attainments.

A very peculiar and exceptional offshoot of the parrot group is the brush-tongued lory, several species of which are common in Australia, India, and the Molucca Islands. These pretty and interesting creatures are in point of fact parrots which have practically made themselves into humming-birds by long continuance in the poetical habit of visiting flowers for food. Like Mr. Oscar Wilde in his æsthetic days, they breakfast off a lily. Flitting about from tree to tree with great rapidity, they thrust their long extensible tongues, pencilled with honey-gathering hairs, into the tubes of many big tropical blossoms. The lories, indeed, live entirely on nectar, and they are so common in the region they have made their own that all the larger flowers there have been developed with a special view to their tastes and habits, as well as to the structure of their peculiar brush-like honey-collector. In most parrots the mouth is dry and the tongue horny; but in the lories it is moist and much more like the same organ in the humming-birds and sun-birds. The prevalence of very large and brilliantly coloured flowers in the Malayan region must be set down for the most part to the selective action of these æsthetic and colour-loving little brush-tongued parrots.

Australia and New Zealand, as everybody knows, are the countries where everything goes by contraries. And it is here that the parrot group has developed some of its strangest and most abnormal offshoots. One would imagine beforehand that no two birds could be more unlike in every respect than the gaudy, noisy, gregarious cockatoos and the sombre, nocturnal, solitary owls. Yet the New Zealand owl-parrot is, to put it plainly, a lory which has assumed all the outer appearance and habits of an owl. A lurker in the twilight or under the shades of night, burrowing for its nest in holes in the ground, it has dingy brown plumage like the owls, with an undertone of green to bespeak its parrot origin: while its face is entirely made up of two great disks, surrounding the eyes, which succeed in giving it a most marked and unmistakable owl-like appearance.

Now, why should a parrot so strangely disguise itself and belie its ancestry? The reason is plain. It found a place for it ready made in nature. New Zealand is a remote and sparsely-stocked island, peopled by mere casual waifs and strays of life from adjacent but still very distant continents. There are no dangerous enemies there. Here, then, was a clear chance for a nightly prowler. The owl-parrot with true business instinct saw the opening thus clearly laid before it, and took to a nocturnal and burrowing life, with the natural consequence that it acquired in time the dingy plumage, crepuscular eyes, and broad disk-like reflectors of other prowling night-fliers. Unlike the owls, however, the owl-parrot, true to the vegetarian instincts of the whole lory race, lives almost entirely upon sprigs of mosses and other creeping plants. It is thus essentially a ground bird; and as it feeds at night in a country possessing no native beasts of prey, it has almost lost the power of flight, and uses its wings only as a sort of parachute to break its fall in descending from a rock or tree to its accustomed feeding-ground. To get up again, it climbs, parrot-like, with its hooked claws, up the surface of the trunk or the face of a precipice.

Even more aberrant in its ways, however, than the burrowing owl-parrot, is that other strange and hated New Zealand lory, the kea, which, alone among its kind, has abjured the gentle ancestral vegetarianism of the cockatoos and macaws, in favour of a carnivorous diet of singular ferocity. And what is odder still, this evil habit has been developed in the kea since the colonization of New Zealand by the English, those most demoralizing of new-comers. The settlers have taught the Maori to wear tall hats and to drink strong liquors: and they have thrown temptation in the way of even the once innocent native parrot. Before the white man came, in fact, the kea was a mild-mannered fruit-eating or honey-sucking bird. But as soon as sheep-stations were established in the island these degenerate parrots began to acquire a distinct taste for raw mutton. At first, to be sure, they ate only the sheep's heads and offal that were thrown out from the slaughter-houses picking the bones as clean of meat as a dog or a jackal. But in process of time, as the taste for blood grew upon them, a still viler idea entered into their wicked heads. The first step on the downward path suggested the second. If dead sheep are good to eat, why not also living ones? The kea, pondering deeply on this abstruse problem, solved it at once with an emphatic affirmative. And he straightway proceeded to act upon his convictions, and invent a really hideous mode of procedure. Perching on the backs of the living sheep he has now learnt the exact spot where the kidneys are to be found; and he tears open the flesh to get at these dainty morsels, which he pulls out and devours, leaving the unhappy animal to die in miserable agony. As many as two hundred ewes have thus been killed in a night at a single station. I need hardly add that the sheep-farmer naturally resents this irregular proceeding, so opposed to all ideals of good grazing, and that the days of the kea are now numbered in New Zealand. But from the purely psychological point of view the case is an interesting one, as being the best recorded instance of the growth of a new and complex instinct actually under the eyes of human observers.

One word as to the general colouring of the parrot group as a whole. Tropical forestine birds have usually a ground tone of green because that colour enables them best to escape notice among the monotonous verdure of equatorial woodland scenery. In the north, to be sure, green is a very conspicuous colour; but that is only because for half the year our trees are bare, and even during the other half they lack that 'breadth of tropic shade' which characterises the forests of all hot countries. Therefore, in temperate climates, the common ground-tone of birds is brown, to harmonise with the bare boughs and leafless twigs, the clods of earth and dead turf or stubble. But in the evergreen tropics green is the right hue for concealment or defence. Therefore the parrots, the most purely tropical family of birds on earth, are mostly greenish; and among the smaller and more defenceless sorts, like the familiar little love-birds, where the need for protection is greatest, the green of the plumage is almost unbroken. Of the tiny Pigmy Parrots of New Guinea, for instance, Mr. Bowdler Sharpe says: 'Owing to their small size and the resemblance of their green colouring to the forests they inhabit, they are not easily seen, and until recent years were very hard to procure.' And of the green parrot of Jamaica, Mr. Gosse remarks: 'Often we hear their voices proceeding from a certain tree, or else have marked the descent of a flock on it; but on proceeding to the spot, though the eye has not wandered from it, we cannot discover an individual. We go close to the tree, but all is silent and still as death. We institute a careful survey of every part with the eye, to detect the slightest motion, or the form of a bird among the leaves, but all in vain. We begin to think they have stolen off unperceived; but on throwing a stone into the tree, a dozen throats burst forth into a cry, and as many green birds rush forth upon the wing. Green may thus be regarded as the normal or basal parrot tint, from which all other colours are special decorative variations.

But fruit-eating and flower-feeding creatures, like butterflies and humming-birds, seeking their food ever among the bright berries and brilliant flowers, almost invariably acquire in the long run an æsthetic taste for pure and varied colouring, and by the aid of sexual selection this taste stereotypes itself at last in their own wings and plumage. They choose their mates for colour as they choose their foodstuffs. Hence all the larger and more gregarious parrots, in which the need for concealment is less, tend to diversify the fundamental green of their coats with crimson, yellow, or blue, which in some cases take possession of the entire body. The largest kinds of all, like the great blue and yellow or crimson macaws, are as gorgeous as Solomon in all his glory: and they are also the species least afraid of enemies; for in Brazil you may often see them wending their way homeward openly in pairs every evening, with as little attempt at concealment as rooks in England. In the Moluccas and New Guinea, says Mr. Wallace, white cockatoos and gorgeous lories in crimson and blue are the very commonest objects in the local fauna. Even the New Zealand owl-parrot, however, still retains many traces of his original greenness, mixed with the dirty brown and dingy yellow of his acquired nocturnal and burrowing nature.

If fruit-eaters are fine, flower-haunters are magnificent. And the brush-tongued lories, that search for nectar among the bells of Malayan blossoms, are the brightest-coloured of all the parrot tribes. Indeed, no group of birds, according to Mr. Alfred Russel Wallace (who ought to know, if anybody does), exhibits within the same limited number of types so extraordinary a diversity and richness of colouring as the parrots. 'As a rule,' he says, 'parrots may be termed green birds, the majority of the species having this colour as the basis of their plumage, relieved by caps, gorgets, bands and wing-spots of other and brighter hues. Yet this general green tint sometimes changes into light or deep blue, as in some macaws; into pure yellow or rich orange, as in some of the American macaw-parrots; into purple, grey or dove-colour, as in some American, African, and Indian species; into the purest crimson, as in some of the lories; into rosy-white and pure white, as in the cockatoos; and into a deep purple, ashy or black, as in several Papuan, Australian, and Mascarene species. There is in fact hardly a single distinct and definable colour that cannot be fairly matched among the 390 species of known parrots. Their habits, too, are such as to bring them prominently before the eye. They usually feed in flocks; they are noisy, and so attract attention; they love gardens, orchards, and open sunny places; they wander about far in search of food, and towards sunset return homeward in noisy flocks, or in constant pairs. Their forms and motions are often beautiful and attractive. The immensely long tails of the macaws and the more slender tails of the Indian parroquets, the fine crest of the cockatoos, the swift flight of many of the smaller species, and the graceful motions of the little love-birds and allied forms, together with their affectionate natures, aptitude for domestication, and power of mimicry, combine to render them at once the most conspicuous and the most attractive of all the specially tropical forms of bird life.'

I have purposely left to the last the one point about parrots which most often attracts the attention of the young, the gay, the giddy, and the thoughtless: I mean their power of mimicry in human language. And I believe I am justified in passing it over lightly. For in fact this power is but a very incidental result of the general intelligence of parrots, combined with the other peculiarities of their social life and forestine character. Dominant woodland animals, indeed, like monkeys, parrots, toucans, and hornbills, at least if vegetarian in their habits, are almost always gregarious, noisy, mischievous, and imitative. And the imitation results directly from the unusual intelligence; for, after all, what is the power of learning itself, at least, in all save its very highest phases, but the faculty of accurately imitating another? Monkeys for the most part imitate action only, because they haven't very varied or flexible voices. Parrots and many other birds, on the contrary, like the starling and still more markedly the American mocking-bird, being endowed with considerable flexibility of voice, imitate either songs or spoken words with great distinctness. In the parrot the power of attention is also very considerable, for the bird will often try over with itself repeatedly the lesson it has set itself to learn. But people too generally forget that at best the parrot knows only the general application of a sentence, not the separate meanings of its component words. It knows, for example, that 'Polly wants a lump of sugar' is a phrase often followed by a present of food. But to believe it can understand an abstract expression, like the famous 'By Jove! what a beastly lot of parrots!' is to confound learning by rote with genuine comprehension. A careful review of all the evidence makes almost every scientific observer conclude that at most a parrot knows a word of command as a horse knows 'Whoa!' or a dog knows the order to hunt for rats in the wainscot.

## HIGH LIFE

Everybody knows mountain flowers are beautiful. As one rises up any minor height in the Alps or the Pyrenees below snow-level, one notices at once the extraordinary brilliancy and richness of the blossoms one meets there. All nature is dressed in its brightest robes. Great belts of blue gentian hang like a zone on the mountain slopes; masses of yellow globe-flower star the upland pastures; nodding heads of soldanella lurk low among the rugged boulders by the glacier's side. No lowland blossoms have such vividness of colouring, or grow in such conspicuous patches. To strike the eye from afar, to attract and allure at a distance, is the great aim and end in life of the Alpine flora.

Now, why are Alpine plants so anxious to be seen of men and angels? Why do they flaunt their golden glories so openly before the world, instead of shrinking in modest reserve beneath their own green leaves, like the Puritan primrose and the retiring violet? The answer is, Because of the extreme rarity of the mountain air. It's the barometer that does it. At first sight, I will readily admit, this explanation seems as fanciful as the traditional connection between Goodwin Sands and Tenterden Steeple. But, like the amateur stories in country papers, it is 'founded on fact,' for all that. (Imagine, by the way, a tale founded entirely on fiction! How charmingly aerial!) By a roundabout road, through varying chains of cause and effect, the rarity of the air does really account in the long run for the beauty and conspicuousness of the mountain flowers.

For bees, the common go-betweens of the loves of the plants, cease to range about a thousand or fifteen hundred feet below snow-level. And why? Because it's too cold for them? Oh, dear, no: on sunny days in early English spring, when the thermometer doesn't rise above freezing in the shade, you will see both the honey-bees and the great black bumble as busy as their conventional character demands of them among the golden cups of the first timid crocuses. Give the bee sunshine, indeed, with a temperature just about freezing-point, and he'll flit about joyously on his communistic errand. But bees, one must remember, have heavy bodies and relatively small wings: in the rarefied air of mountain heights they can't manage to support themselves in the most literal sense. Hence their place in these high stations of the world is taken by the gay and airy butterflies, which have lighter bodies and a much bigger expanse of wing-area to buoy them up. In the valleys and plains the bee competes at an advantage with the butterflies for all the sweets of life: but in this broad sub-glacial belt on the mountain-sides the butterflies in turn have things all their own way. They flit about like monarchs of all they survey, without a rival in the world to dispute their supremacy.

And how does the preponderance of butterflies in the upper regions of the air affect the colour and brilliancy of the flowers? Simply thus. Bees, as we are all aware on the authority of the great Dr. Watts, are industrious creatures which employ each shining hour (well-chosen epithet, 'shining') for the good of the community, and to the best purpose. The bee, in fact, is the bon bourgeois of the insect world: he attends strictly to business, loses no time in wild or reckless excursions, and flies by the straightest path from flower to flower of the same species with mathematical precision. Moreover, he is careful, cautious, observant, and steady-going, a model business man, in fact, of sound middle-class morals and sober middle-class intelligence. No flitting for him, no coquetting, no fickleness. Therefore, the flowers that have adapted themselves to his needs, and that depend upon him mainly or solely for fertilisation, waste no unnecessary material on those big flaunting coloured posters which we human observers know as petals. They have, for the most part, simple blue or purple flowers, tubular in shape and, individually, inconspicuous in hue; and they are oftenest arranged in long spikes of blossom to avoid wasting the time of their winged Mr. Bultitudes. So long as they are just bright enough to catch the bee's eye a few yards away, they are certain to receive a visit in due season from that industrious and persistent commercial traveller. Having a circle of good customers upon whom they can depend with certainty for fertilisation, they have no need to waste any large proportion of their substance upon expensive advertisements or gaudy petals.

It is just the opposite with butterflies. Those gay and irrepressible creatures, the fashionable and frivolous element in the insect world, gad about from flower to flower over great distances at once, and think much more of sunning themselves and of attracting their fellows than of attention to business. And the reason is obvious, if one considers for a moment the difference in the political and domestic economy of the two opposed groups. For the honey-bees are neuters, sexless purveyors of the hive, with no interest on earth save the storing of honey for the common benefit of the phalanstery to which they belong. But the butterflies are full-fledged males and females, on the hunt through the world for suitable partners: they think far less of feeding than of displaying their charms: a little honey to support them during their flight is all they need:—'For the bee, a long round of ceaseless toil; for me,' says the gay butterfly, 'a short life and a merry one.' Mr. Harold Skimpole needed only 'music, sunshine, a few grapes.' The butterflies are of his kind. The high mountain zone is for them a true ball-room: the flowers are light refreshments laid out in the vestibule. Their real business in life is not to gorge and lay by, but to coquette and display themselves and find fitting partners.

So while the bees with their honey-bags, like the financier with his money-bags, are storing up profit for the composite community, the butterfly, on the contrary, lays himself out for an agreeable flutter, and sips nectar where he will, over large areas of country. He flies rather high, flaunting his wings in the sun, because he wants to show himself off in all his airy beauty: and when he spies a bed of bright flowers afar off on the sun-smitten slopes, he sails off towards them lazily, like a grand signior who amuses himself. No regular plodding through a monotonous spike of plain little bells for him: what he wants is brilliant colour, bold advertisement, good honey, and plenty of it. He doesn't care to search. Who wants his favours must make himself conspicuous.

Now, plants are good shopkeepers; they lay themselves out strictly to attract their customers. Hence the character of the flowers on this beeless belt of mountain side is entirely determined by the character of the butterfly fertilisers. Only those plants which laid themselves out from time immemorial to suit the butterflies, in other words, have succeeded in the long run in the struggle for existence. So the butterfly-plants of the butterfly-zone are all strictly adapted to butterfly tastes and butterfly fancies. They are, for the most part, individually large and brilliantly coloured: they have lots of honey, often stored at the base of a deep and open bell which the long proboscis of the insect can easily penetrate: and they habitually grow close together in broad belts or patches, so that the colour of each reinforces and aids the colour of the others. It is this cumulative habit that accounts for the marked flowerbed or jam-tart character which everybody must have noticed in the high Alpine flora.

Aristocracies usually pride themselves on their antiquity: and the high life of the mountains is undeniably ancient. The plants and animals of the butterfly-zone belong to a special group which appears everywhere in Europe and America about the limit of snow, whether northward or upward. For example, I was pleased to note near the summit of Mount Washington (the highest peak in New Hampshire) that a large number of the flowers belonged to species well known on the open plains of Lapland and Finland. The plants of the High Alps are found also, as a rule, not only on the High Pyrenees, the Carpathians, the Scotch Grampians, and the Norwegian fjelds, but also round the Arctic Circle in Europe and America. They reappear at long distances where suitable conditions recur: they follow the snow-line as the snow-line recedes ever in summer higher north toward the pole or higher vertically toward the mountain summits. And this bespeaks in one way to the reasoning mind a very ancient ancestry. It shows they date back to a very old and cold epoch.

Let me give a single instance which strikingly illustrates the general principle. Near the top of Mount Washington, as aforesaid, lives to this day a little colony of very cold-loving and mountainous butterflies, which never descend below a couple of thousand feet from the wind-swept summit. Except just there, there are no more of there sort anywhere about: and as far as the butterflies themselves are aware, no others of their species exist on earth: they never have seen a single one of their kind, save of their own little colony. One might compare them with the Pitcairn Islanders in the South Seas, an isolated group of English origin, cut off by a vast distance from all their congeners in Europe or America. But if you go north some eight or nine hundred miles from New Hampshire to Labrador, at a certain point the same butterfly reappears, and spreads northward toward the pole in great abundance. Now, how did this little colony of chilly insects get separated from the main body, and islanded, as it were, on a remote mountain-top in far warmer New Hampshire?

The answer is, they were stranded there at the end of the Glacial epoch.

A couple of hundred thousand years ago or thereabouts, don't let us haggle, I beg of you, over a few casual centuries, the whole of northern Europe and America was covered from end to end, as everybody knows, by a sheet of solid ice, like the one which Frithiof Nansen crossed from sea to sea on his own account in Greenland. For many thousand years, with occasional warmer spells, that vast ice-sheet brooded, silent and grim, over the face of the two continents. Life was extinct as far south as the latitude of New York and London. No plant or animal survived the general freezing. Not a creature broke the monotony of that endless glacial desert. At last, as the celestial cycle came round in due season, fresh conditions supervened. Warmer weather set in, and the ice began to melt. Then the plants and animals of the sub-glacial district were pushed slowly northward by the warmth after the retreating ice-cap. As time went on, the climate of the plains got too hot to hold them. The summer was too much for the glacial types to endure. They remained only on the highest mountain peaks or close to the southern limit of eternal snow. In this way, every isolated range in either continent has its own little colony of arctic or glacial plants and animals, which still survive by themselves, unaffected by intercourse with their unknown and unsuspected fellow-creatures elsewhere.

Not only has the Glacial epoch left these organic traces of its existence, however; in some parts of New Hampshire, where the glaciers were unusually thick and deep, fragments of the primæval ice itself still remain on the spots where they were originally stranded. Among the shady glens of the white mountains there occur here and there great masses of ancient ice, the unmelted remnant of primæval glaciers; and one of these is so large that an artificial cave has been cleverly excavated in it, as an attraction for tourists, by the canny Yankee proprietor. Elsewhere the old ice-blocks are buried under the débris of moraine-stuff and alluvium, and are only accidentally discovered by the sinking of what are locally known as ice-wells. No existing conditions can account for the formation of such solid rocks of ice at such a depth in the soil. They are essentially glacier-like in origin and character: they result from the pressure of snow into a crystalline mass in a mountain valley: and they must have remained there unmelted ever since the close of the Glacial epoch, which, by Dr. Croll's calculations, must most probably have ceased to plague our earth some eighty thousand years ago. Modern America, however, has no respect for antiquity: and it is at present engaged in using up this palæocrystic deposit, this belated storehouse of prehistoric ice, in the manufacture of gin slings and brandy cocktails.

As one scales a mountain of moderate height, say seven or eight thousand feet, in a temperate climate, one is sure to be struck by the gradual diminution as one goes in the size of the trees, till at last they tail off into mere shrubs and bushes. This diminution, an old commonplace of tourists, is a marked characteristic of mountain plants, and it depends, of course, in the main upon the effect of cold, and of the wind in winter. Cold, however, is by far the more potent factor of the two, though it is the least often insisted upon: and this can be seen in a moment by anyone who remembers that trees shade off in just the self-same manner near the southern limit of permanent snow in the Arctic regions. And the way the cold acts is simply this: it nips off the young buds in spring in exposed situations, as the chilly sea-breeze does with coast plants, which, as we commonly but incorrectly say, are "blown sideways" from seaward.

Of course, the lower down one gets, and the nearer to the soil, the warmer the layer of air becomes, both because there is greater radiation, and because one can secure a little more shelter. So, very far north, and very near the snow-line on mountains, you always find the vegetation runs low and stunted. It takes advantage of every crack, every cranny in the rocks, every sunny little nook, every jutting point or wee promontory of shelter. And as the mountain plants have been accustomed for ages to the strenuous conditions of such cold and wind-swept situations, they have ended, of course, by adapting themselves to that station in life to which it has pleased the powers that be to call them. They grow quite naturally low and stumpy and rosette-shaped: they are compact of form and very hard of fibre: they present no surface of resistance to the wind in any way; rounded and boss-like, they seldom rise above the level of the rooks and stones, whose interstices they occupy. It is this combination of characters that makes mountain plants such favourites with florists: for they possess of themselves that close-grown habit and that rich profusion of clustered flowers which it is the grand object of the gardener by artificial selection to produce and encourage.

When one talks of the 'limit of trees' on a mountain side, however, it must be remembered that the phrase is used in a strictly human or Pickwickian sense, and that it is only the size, not the type, of the vegetation that is really in question. For trees exist even on the highest hill-tops: only they have accommodated themselves to the exigencies of the situation. Smaller and ever smaller species have been developed by natural selection to suit the peculiarities of these inclement spots. Take, for example, the willow and poplar group. Nobody would deny that a weeping willow by an English river, or a Lombardy poplar in an Italian avenue, was as much of a true tree as an oak or a chestnut. But as one mounts towards the bare and wind-swept mountain heights one finds that the willows begin to grow downward gradually. The 'netted willow' of the Alps and Pyrenees, which shelters itself under the lee of little jutting rocks, attains the height of only a few inches; while the 'herbaceous willow,' common on all very high mountains in Western Europe, is a tiny creeping weed, which nobody would ever take for a forest tree by origin at all, unless he happened to see it in the catkin-bearing stage, when its true nature and history would become at once apparent to him.

Yet this little herb-like willow, one of the most northerly and hardy of European plants, is a true tree at heart none the less for all that. Soft and succulent as it looks in branch and leaf, you may yet count on it sometimes as many rings of annual growth as on a lordly Scotch fir-tree. But where? Why, underground. For see how cunning it is, this little stunted descendant of proud forest lords: hard-pressed by nature, it has learnt to make the best of its difficult and precarious position. It has a woody trunk at core, like all other trees; but this trunk never appears above the level of the soil: it creeps and roots underground in tortuous zigzags between the crags and boulders that lie strewn through its thin sheet of upland leaf-mould. By this simple plan the willow manages to get protection in winter, on the same principle as when we human gardeners lay down the stems of vines: only the willow remains laid down all the year and always. But in summer it sends up its short-lived herbaceous branches, covered with tiny green leaves, and ending at last in a single silky catkin. Yet between the great weeping willow and this last degraded mountain representative of the same primitive type, you can trace in Europe alone at least a dozen distinct intermediate forms, all well marked in their differences, and all progressively dwarfed by long stress of unfavourable conditions.

From the combination of such unfavourable conditions in Arctic countries and under the snow-line of mountains there results a curious fact, already hinted at above, that the coldest floras are also, from the purely human point of view, the most beautiful. Not, of course, the most luxuriant: for lush richness of foliage and 'breadth of tropic shade' (to quote a noble lord) one must go, as everyone knows, to the equatorial regions. But, contrary to the common opinion, the tropics, hoary shams, are not remarkable for the abundance or beauty of their flowers. Quite otherwise, indeed: an unrelieved green strikes the keynote of equatorial forests. This is my own experience, and it is borne out (which is far more important) by Mr. Alfred Russel Wallace, who has seen a wider range of the untouched tropics, in all four hemispheres, northern, southern, eastern, western, than any other man, I suppose, that ever lived on this planet. And Mr. Wallace is firm in his conviction that the tropics in this respect are a complete fraud. Bright flowers are there quite conspicuously absent. It is rather in the cold and less favoured regions of the world that one must look for fine floral displays and bright masses of colour. Close up to the snow-line the wealth of flowers is always the greatest.

In order to understand this apparent paradox one must remember that the highest type of flowers, from the point of view of organisation, is not at the same time by any means the most beautiful. On the contrary, plants with very little special adaptation to any particular insect, like the water-lilies and the poppies, are obliged to flaunt forth in very brilliant hues, and to run to very large sizes in order to attract the attention of a great number of visitors, one or other of whom may casually fertilise them; while plants with very special adaptations, like the sage and mint group, or the little English orchids, are so cunningly arranged that they can't fail of fertilisation at the very first visit, which of course enables them to a great extent to dispense with the aid of big or brilliant petals. So that, where the struggle for life is fiercest, and adaptation most perfect, the flora will on the whole be not most, but least, conspicuous in the matter of very handsome flowers.

Now, the struggle for life is fiercest, and the wealth of nature is greatest, one need hardly say, in tropical climates. There alone do we find every inch of soil 'encumbered by its waste fertility,' as Comus puts it; weighed down by luxuriant growth of tree, shrub, herb, creeper. There alone do lizards lurk in every hole; beetles dwell manifold in every cranny; butterflies flock thick in every grove; bees, ants, and flies swarm by myriads on every sun-smitten hillside. Accordingly, in the tropics, adaptation reaches its highest point; and tangled richness, not beauty of colour, becomes the dominant note of the equatorial forests. Now and then, to be sure, as you wander through Brazilian or Malayan woods, you may light upon some bright tree clad in scarlet bloom, or some glorious orchid drooping pendant from a bough with long sprays of beauty: but such sights are infrequent. Green, and green, and ever green again, that is the general feeling of the equatorial forest: as different as possible from the rich mosaic of a high alp in early June, or a Scotch hillside deep in golden gorse and purple heather in broad August sunshine.

In very cold countries, on the other hand, though the conditions are severe, the struggle for existence is not really so hard, because, in one word, there are fewer competitors. The field is less occupied; life is less rich, less varied, less self-strangling. And therefore specialisation hasn't gone nearly so far in cold latitudes or altitudes. Lower and simpler types everywhere occupy the soil; mosses, matted flowers, small beetles, dwarf butterflies. Nature is less luxuriant, yet in some ways more beautiful. As we rise on the mountains the forest trees disappear, and with them the forest beasts, from bears to squirrels; a low, wind-swept vegetation succeeds, very poor in species, and stunted in growth, but making a floor of rich flowers almost unknown elsewhere. The humble butterflies and beetles of the chillier elevation produce in the result more beautiful bloom than the highly developed honey-seekers of the richer and warmer lowlands. Luxuriance is atoned for by a Turkey carpet of floral magnificence.

How, then, has the world at large fallen into the pardonable error of believing tropical nature to be so rich in colouring, and circumpolar nature to be so dingy and unlovable? Simply thus, I believe. The tropics embrace the largest land areas in the world, and are richer by a thousand times in species of plants and animals than all the rest of the earth in a lump put together. That richness necessarily results from the fierceness of the competition. Now among this enormous mass of tropical plants it naturally happens that some have finer flowers than any temperate species; while as to the animals and birds, they are undoubtedly, on the whole, both larger and handsomer than the fauna of colder climates. But in the general aspect of tropical nature an occasional bright flower or brilliant parrot counts for very little among the mass of lush green which surrounds and conceals it. On the other hand, in our museums and conservatories we sedulously pick out the rarest and most beautiful of these rare and beautiful species, and we isolate them completely from their natural surroundings. The consequence is that the untravelled mind regards the tropics mentally as a sort of perpetual replica of the hot-houses at Kew, superimposed on the best of Mr. Bull's orchid shows. As a matter of fact, people who know the hot world well can tell you that the average tropical woodland is much more like the dark shade of Box Hill or the deepest glades of the Black Forest. For really fine floral display in the mass, all at once, you must go, not to Ceylon, Sumatra, Jamaica, but to the far north of Canada, the Bernese Oberland, the moors of Inverness-shire, the North Cape of Norway. Flowers are loveliest where the climate is coldest; forests are greenest, most luxuriant, least blossoming, where the conditions of life are richest, warmest, fiercest. In one word, High Life is always poor but beautiful.


## EIGHT-LEGGED FRIENDS

A singular opportunity was afforded me last summer for making myself thoroughly at home with the habits and manners of the common English geometrical spider. By the pure chance of circumstance, two ladies of that intelligent and interesting species were kind enough to select for their temporary residence a large pane of glass just outside my drawing-room window. Now, it so happened that this particular pane was constructed not to open, being, in fact, part of a big bow-window, the alternate sashes of which were alone intended for ventilation. Hence it came to pass that by diligent care I was enabled to preserve my two eight-legged acquaintances from the devouring broom of the British housemaid, and to keep them constantly under observation at all times and seasons during a whole summer. Of course this result was only obtained by a distinct exercise of despotic authority, for I know those poor spiders were a constant eyesore in Ellen's sight, the housemaid of the moment bore the name of Ellen, but I persisted in my prohibition of any forcible ejectment, and I carried my point in the end in the very teeth of that constituted domestic authority. So successful was I, indeed, that when at last we flitted southwards ourselves with the swallows on our annual migration to the Mediterranean shores, we left Lucy and Eliza, those were the names we had given them, in undisturbed possession of their prescriptive rights in the drawing-room windows. This year they are gone, and our home is left spiderless.

They were curious and uninviting pets, I'm bound to admit, those great juicy-looking creatures. Nobody could say that any form of spider is precisely what our Italian friends prettily describe in their liquid way as simpatico. At times, indeed, the conduct of Lucy and Eliza was so peculiarly horrible and blood-curdling in its atrocity, that even I, their best friend, who had so often interceded for their lives and saved them from the devastating duster of the aggressive housemaid, even I myself, I say, more than once debated in my own mind whether I was justified in letting them go on any longer in their career of crime unchecked, or whether I ought not rather to rush out at once, avenging rag in hand, and sweep them away at one fell swoop from the surface of a world they disgraced with their unbridled wickedness. Eliza, in particular, I'm constrained to allow, was a perfect monster of vice, a sort of undeveloped arachnid Borgia, quick to slay and relentless in pursuit; a mass of eight-legged sins, stained with the colourless gore of ten thousand struggling victims, and absolutely without a single redeeming point in her hateful character. And yet, whenever any more than usually horrible massacre of some pretty and innocent fly almost moved me in my righteous wrath to rush out into the garden in hot haste and put an end at once to the cruel wretch's existence with a judicial antimacassar, a number of moral scruples, such as could only be adequately resolved by the editor of the Spectator, always occurred spontaneously to my mind and conscience just in time to ensure that wicked Eliza a fresh spell of life in which to continue unabashed her atrocious behaviour.

Has man, I asked myself at such moments, mere human man, any right to set himself up in the place of earthly providence, as so much better and more moral than insentient nature? If the spider cruelly devours living flies and intelligent or highly sensitive bees, we must at least remember that she has no choice in the matter, and that, as the poet justly remarks, ''tis her nature to.' But then, on the other hand, it might be plausibly argued that 'tis our nature equally to kill the creature that we see so hatefully fulfilling the law of its own cruel being. And yet again it might be pleaded by any able counsel who undertook the defence of Lucy or Eliza on her trial for her life against her human accusers, that she was impelled to all these evil deeds by maternal affection, one of the noblest and most unselfish of animal instincts. Moreover, if the spider didn't prey, it would obviously die; and it seems rather hard on any creature to condemn it to death for no better reason than because it happens to have been born a member of its own kind, and not of any other and less morally objectionable species. Jedburgh justice of that sort rather savours of the method pursued by the famous countryman who was found cutting a harmless amphibian into a hundred pieces with his murderous spade, and saying spitefully as he did so, at every particularly savage cut: 'I'll larn ye to be a twoad, I will; I'll larn ye to be a twoad!'

Nevertheless, in spite of all this my vaunted philosophy, I will frankly confess that more than once Eliza and Lucy sorely tried my patience, and that I was often a good deal better than half-minded in my soul to rush out in a feverish fit of moral indignation and put an end to their ghastly career of crime without waiting to hear what they had to say in their own favour, showing cause why sentence of death should not be executed upon them. And I would have done it, I believe, had it not been for that peculiar arrangement of the drawing-room windows, which made it impossible to get at the culprits direct, without going out into the garden and round the house; which, of course, is a severe strain in wet or windy weather to put upon anybody's moral enthusiasm. In the end, therefore, I always gave the evil-doers the benefit of the doubt; and I only mention my ethical scruples in the matter here lest scoffers should say, when they come to read what manner of things

Lucy and Eliza did: 'Oh yes, that's just like those scientific folks; they're always so cold-blooded. He could stand by and see these poor helpless flies tortured slowly to death, without a chance for their lives, and never put out a helping hand to save them!' Well, I would only ask you one question, my sapient friend, who talk like that: Has it ever occurred to you that, if you kill one spider, you merely make room in the overflowing economy of nature for another to pick up a dishonest livelihood? Have you ever reflected that the prime blame of spiderhood rests with Nature herself (if we may venture to personify that impersonal entity); and that she has provided such a constant supply or relay of spiders as will amply suffice to fill up all the possible vacancies that can ever occur in insect-eating circles? Unless you have considered all these points carefully, and have an answer to give about them, you are not in a position to pronounce upon the subject, and you had better be referred for six months longer, as the medical examiners gracefully put it, to your ethical, psychological, and biological studies. The great point about the position in which Eliza and Lucy had placed themselves was simply this. They stood full against the light, so that we could see right through their translucent bodies, which were almost liquid to look upon, and beautifully dappled with dark spots on a grey ground in a very pretty and effective pattern. So favourable was the opportunity for observation, indeed, that we could clearly make out with the naked eye even the joints of their legs, the hairs on their tarsi, excuse the phrase, and the very shape of their cruel tigerlike claws, as they rushed forth upon their prey in a sort of carnivorous frenzy. At all hours of the day we could notice exactly what they were doing or suffering; and so familiar did we become with them individually and personally, that before the end of the season we recognized in detail all the differences of their characters almost as one might do with cats or dogs, and spoke of them by their Christian names like old and well-known acquaintances.

As the webs which Lucy and Eliza spun were several times broken or mutilated during the year, either by accident or the gardener, we had plenty of chances for seeing how they proceeded in making them. The lines were in both cases stretched between a white rose-bush that climbed up one side of the window, and a purple clematis that occupied and draped the opposite mullion. But Lucy and Eliza didn't live in the webs, those were only their snares or traps for prey; each of them had in addition a private home or apartment of her own under shelter of a rose-leaf at some distance from the treacherous geometrical structure. The house itself consisted merely of a silken cell, built out from the rose-leaf, and connected with the snare by a single stout cord of very solid construction. On this cord the spider kept one foot, I had almost said one hand, constantly fixed. She poised it lightly by her claws, and whenever an insect got entangled in the web, a subtle electric message, so to speak, seemed to run along the line to the ever-watchful carnivore. In one short second Lucy or Eliza, as the case might be, had darted out upon her quarry, and was tackling it might main, according to the particular way its size and strength rendered then and there advisable. The method of procedure, which I shall describe more fully by-and-by, differed considerably from case to case, as these very large and strong spiders have sometimes to deal with mere tiny midges, and sometimes with extremely big and dangerous creatures, like bumble-bees, wasps, and even hornets.

In building their webs, as in many other small points, Lucy and Eliza showed from the first no inconsiderable personal differences. Lucy began hers by spinning a long line from her spinnerets, and letting the wind carry it wherever it would; while Eliza, more architectural in character, preferred to take her lines personally from point to point, and see herself to their proper fastening. In either case, however, the first thing done was to stretch some eight or ten stout threads from place to place on the outside of the future web, to act as points d'appuy for the remainder of the structure. To these outer threads, which the spiders strengthened so as to bear a considerable strain by doubling and trebling them, other thinner single threads were then carried radially at irregular distances, like the spokes of a wheel, from a point in the centre, where they were all made fast and connected together. As soon as this radiating framework or scaffolding was finished, like the woof on a loom, the industrious craftswoman started at the middle, and began the task of putting in the cross-pieces or weft which were to complete and bind together the circular pattern. These she wove round and round in a continuous spiral, setting out at the centre, and keeping on in ever-widening circlets, till she arrived at last at the exterior or foundation threads. How she fastened these cross-pieces to the ray-lines I could never quite make out, though I often followed the work closely from inside through the pane of glass with a platyscopic lens; for, strange to say, the spiders were not in the least disturbed by being watched at their work, and never took the slightest notice of anything that went on at the other side of the window. My impression is, however, that she gummed them together, letting them harden into one as they dried; for the thread itself is always semi-liquid when first exuded.

The cross-pieces, we observed from the very beginning, were invariably covered by little sparkling drops of something wet and beadlike, which at first in our ignorance we took for dew; for until I began systematically observing Lucy and Eliza, I will frankly confess I had never paid any particular attention to the spider-kind with the solitary exception of my old winter friends, the trap-door spiders of the Mediterranean shores. But, after a little experience, we soon found out that these pearly drops on the web were not dew at all, but a sticky substance, akin, to that of the web, secreted by the animals themselves from their own bodies. We also quickly discovered, coming to the observation as we did with minds unbiased by previous knowledge, that the viscid liquid in question was of the utmost importance to the spiders in securing their prey, and that unfortunate insects were not merely entangled but likewise gummed down or glued by it, like birds in bird-lime or flies in treacle. So necessary is the sticky stuff, indeed, to the success of the trap, that Lucy and Eliza used to renew the entire set of cross-pieces in the web every morning, and thus ensure from day to day a perfectly fresh supply of viscid fluid; but, so far as I could see, they only renewed the rays and the foundation-threads under stress of necessity, when the snare had been so greatly injured by large insects struggling in it, or by the wind or the gardener, as to render repairs absolutely unavoidable. The whole structure, when complete, is so beautiful and wonderful a sight, with its geometrical regularity and its beaded drops, that if it were produced by a rare creature from Madagascar or the Cape, in the insect-house at the Zoo, all the world, I'm convinced, would rush to look at it as a nine-days' wonder. But since it's only the trap of the common English garden spider, why, we all pass it by without deigning even to glance at it.

At night my eight-legged friends slept always in their own homes or nests under shelter of the rose-leaves. But during the day they alternated between the nest and the centre of the web, which last seemed to serve them as a convenient station where they waited for their prey, standing head downward with legs wide spread on the rays, on the look-out for incidents. Whether at the centre or in the nest, however, they kept their feet constantly on the watch for any disturbance on the webs; and the instant any unhappy little fly got entangled in their meshes, the ever-watchful spider was out like a flash of lightning, and down at once in full force upon that incautious intruder. I was convinced after many observations that it is by touch alone the spider recognizes the presence of prey in its web, and that it hardly derives any indications worth speaking of from its numerous little eyes, at least as regards the arrival of booty. If a very big insect has got into the web, then a relatively large volume of disturbance is propagated along the telegraphic wire that runs from the snare to the house, or from the circumference to the centre; if a small one, then a slight disturbance; and the spider rushes out accordingly, either with an air of caution or of ferocious triumph.

Supposing the booty in hand was a tiny fly, then Lucy or Eliza would jump upon it at once with that strange access of apparently personal animosity with seems in some mysterious way a characteristic of all hunting carnivorous animals. She would then carelessly wind a thread or two about it, in a perfunctory way, bury her jaws in its body, and in less than half a minute suck out its juices to the last drop, leaving the empty shell unhurt, like a dry skeleton or the slough of a dragon-fly larva. But when wasps or other large and dangerous insects got entangled in the webs, the hunters proceeded with far greater caution. Lucy, indeed, who was a decided coward, would stand and look anxiously at the doubtful intruder for several seconds, feeling the web with her claws, and running up and down in the most undecided manner, as if in doubt whether or not to tackle the uncertain customer. But Eliza, whose spirits always rose like Nelson's before the face of danger, and whose motto seemed to be 'De l'audace, de l'audace, et toujours de l'audace,' would rush at the huge foe in a perfect transport of wild fury, and go to work at once to enclose him in her toils of triple silken cables. I always fancied, indeed, that Eliza was in a thoroughly housewifely tantrum at seeing her nice new web so ruthlessly torn and tattered by the unwelcome visitor, and that she said to herself in her own language: 'Oh well, then, if you will have it, you shall have it; so here goes for you.' And go for him she did, with most unladylike ferocity. Indeed, Eliza's best friend, I must fain admit, could never have said of her that she was a perfect lady.

The chawing-up of that wasp was a sight to behold. I have no great sympathy with wasps, they have done me so many bad turns in my time that I don't pretend to regard them as deserving of exceptional pity, but I must say Eliza's way of going at them was unduly barbaric. She treated them for all the world as if they were entirely devoid of a nervous system. I wouldn't treat a Saturday Reviewer myself as that spider treated the wasps when once she was sure of them. She went at them with a sort of angry, half-contemptuous dash, kept cautiously out of the way of the protruded sting, began in most business-like fashion at the head, and rolling the wasp round and round with her legs and feelers, swathed him rapidly and effectually, with incredible speed, in a dense network of web poured forth from her spinnerets. In less than half a minute the astonished wasp, accustomed rather to act on the offensive than the defensive, found himself helplessly enclosed in a perfect coil of tangled silk, which confined him from head to sting without the possibility of movement in any direction. The whole time this had been going on the victim, struggling and writhing, had been pushing out its sting and doing the very best it knew to deal the wily Eliza a poisoned death-blow. But Eliza, taught by ancestral experience, kept carefully out of the way; and the wasp felt itself finally twirled round and round in those powerful hands, and tied about as to its wings by a thousand-fold cable. Sometimes, after the wasp was secured, Eliza even took the trouble to saw off the wings so as to prevent further struggling and consequent damage to the precious web; but more often she merely proceeded to eat it alive without further formality, still avoiding its sting as long as the creature had a kick left in it, but otherwise entirely ignoring its character as a sentient being in the most inhuman fashion. And all the time, till the last drop of his blood was sucked out, the wasp would continue viciously to stick out his deadly sting, which the spider would still avoid with hereditary cunning. It was a horrid sight, a duel à outrance between two equally hateful and poisonous opponents; a living commentary on the appalling but o'er-true words of the poet, that 'Nature is one with rapine, a harm no preacher can heal.' Though these were the occasions when one sometimes felt as if the cup of Eliza's iniquities was really full, and one must pass sentence at last, without respite or reprieve, upon that life-long murderess.

One insect there was, however, before which even Eliza herself, hardened wretch as she seemed, used to cower and shiver; and that was the great black bumble-bee, the largest and most powerful of the British bee-kind. When one of these dangerous monsters, a burly, buzzing bourgeois, got entangled in her web, Eliza, shaking in her shoes (I allow her those shoes by poetical licence) would retire in high dudgeon to her inmost bower, and there would sit and sulk, in visible bad temper, till the clumsy big thing, after many futile efforts, had torn its way by main force out of the coils that surrounded it. Then, the moment the telegraphic communication told her the lines in the web were once more free, Eliza would sally forth again with a smiling face, oh yes, I assure you, we could tell by her look when she was smiling, and would repair afresh with cheerful alacrity the damage done to her snare by the unwelcome visitor. Hummingbird hawk-moths, on the other hand, though so big and quick, she would kill immediately. As for Lucy, craven soul, she had so little sense of proper pride and arachnid honour, that she shrank even from the wasps which Eliza so bravely and unhesitatingly tackled; and more than once we caught her in the very act of cutting them out entire, with the whole piece of web in which they were immeshed, and letting them drop on to the ground beneath, merely as a short way of getting rid of them from her premises. I always rather despised Lucy. She hadn't even the one redeeming virtue of most carnivorous or predatory races, an insensate and almost automatic courage.

I need hardly say, however, that the spider does not kill her prey by a mere fair-and-square bite alone. She has recourse to the art of the Palmers and Brinvilliers. All spiders, as far as known, are provided with poison-fangs in the jaws, which sometimes, as in the tarantula and many other large tropical kinds, well known to me in Jamaica and elsewhere, are sufficiently powerful to produce serious effects upon man himself; while even much smaller spiders, like Eliza and Lucy, have poison enough in their falces, as the jawlike organs are called, to kill a good big insect, such as a wasp or a bumble-bee. These channelled poison-glands, combined with their savage tigerlike claws, make the spiders as a group extremely formidable and dominant creatures, the analogues in their own smaller invertebrate world of the serpents and wolves in the vertebrate creation.

Lucy and Eliza's family relations, I am sorry to say, were not, we found, of a kind to endear them to a critical public already sufficiently scandalized by their general mode of behaviour to their inoffensive neighbours. As mothers, indeed, gossip itself had not a word of blame to whisper against them; but as wives, their conduct was distinctly open to the severest animadversion. The males of the garden spider, as in many other instances, are decidedly smaller than their big round mates; so much so is this the case, indeed, in certain species that they seem almost like parasites of the immensely larger sack-bodied females. Now, just as the worker bees kill off the drones as soon as the queen-bee has been duly fertilized, regarding them as of no further importance or value to the hive, so do the lady-spiders not only kill but eat their husbands as soon as they find they have no further use for them. Nay, if a female spider doesn't care for the looks of a suitor who is pressing himself too much upon her fond attention, her way of expressing her disapprobation of his appearance and manners is to make a murderous spring at him, and, if possible, devour him. Under these painful circumstances the process of courtship is necessarily to some extent a difficult and delicate one, fraught with no small danger to the adventurous swain who has the boldness to commend himself by personal approach to these very fickle and irascible fair ones. It was most curious and exciting, accordingly, to watch the details of the strange courtship, which we could only observe in the case of the cruel Eliza, the rather gentler Lucy having been already mated, apparently, before she took up her quarters in our climbing white rose-bush. One day, however, a timid-looking male spider, with inquiry and doubt in every movement of his tarsi, strolled tentatively up on the neat round web where Eliza was hanging, head downward as usual, all her feet on the thread, on the look-out for house-flies. We knew he was a male at once by his longer and thinner body, and by his natural modesty. He walked gingerly on all eights, like an arachnid Agag, in the direction of the object of his ardent affections, with a most comic uncertainty in every step he took towards her. His claws felt the threads as he moved with anxious care; and it was clear he was ready at a moment's notice to jump away and flee for his life with headlong speed to his native obscurity if Eliza showed the slightest disposition, by gesture or movement, to turn and rend him. Now and again, as he approached, Eliza, half coquettish, moved her feet a short step, and seemed to debate within her own mind in which spirit she should meet his flattering advances, whether to accept him or to eat him. At each such hesitation, the unhappy male, fearing the worst, and sore afraid, would turn on his heel and fly for dear life as fast as eight trembling legs would carry him. Then, after a minute or two, he would evidently come to the conclusion that he had wronged his lady-love, and that her movement was one of true, true love rather than of carnivorous and cannibalistic appetite. At last, as I judged, his constancy was rewarded, though his ominous disappearance very shortly afterwards made me fear for the worst as to his final adventures.

In the end, Eliza laid a large number of eggs in a silken cocoon, in shape a balloon, and secreted, like the web, by her invaluable spinnerets. Indeed, the real reason, I won't say excuse, for the rapacity and Gargantuan appetite of the spider lies, no doubt, in the immense amount of material she has to supply for her daily-renewed webs, her home, and her cocoon, all which have actually to be spun out of the assimilated food-stuffs in her own body; to say nothing of the additional necessity imposed upon her by nature for laying a trifle of six or seven hundred eggs in a single summer. And, to tell the truth, Lucy and Eliza seemed to us to be always eating. No matter at what hour one looked in upon them, they were pretty constantly engaged in devouring some inoffensive fly, or weaving hateful labyrinths of hasty cord round some fiercely-struggling wasp or some unhappy beetle.

We weren't fortunate enough, I regret to say, to see Eliza's eggs hatch out from the cocoon; but in other instances, especially in Southern Europe, I have noticed the little heap of well-covered ova, glued together into a mass, and attached to a branch or twig by stout silken cables. If you open the cocoon when the young spiders are just hatched, they begin to run about in the most lively fashion, and look like a living and moving congeries of little balls or seedlets. The common garden spider lays some seven hundred or more such eggs at a sitting, and out of those seven hundred only two on an average reach maturity and once more propagate their kind. For if only four lived and throve, then clearly, in the next generation, there would be twice as many spiders as in this; and in the generation after that again, four times as many; and then eight times; and so on ad infinitum, until the whole world was just one living and seething mass of common garden spiders.

What keeps them down, then, in the end to their average number? What prevents the development of the whole seven hundred? The simple answer is, continuous starvation. As usual, nature works with cruel lavishness. There are just as many spiders at any given minute as there are insects enough in the world or in their area to feed upon. Every spider lays hundreds of eggs, so as to make up for the average infant mortality by starvation, or by the attacks of ichneumon flies, or by being eaten themselves in the young stage, or by other casualties. And so with all other species. Each produces as many young on the average as will allow for the ordinary infant mortality of their kind, and leave enough over just to replace the parents in the next generation. And that's one of the reasons why it's no use punishing Lucy and Eliza for their misdeeds in this world. Kill them off if you will, and before next week a dozen more like them will dispute with one another the vacant place you have thus created in the balanced economy of that microcosm the garden.

Our observations upon Lucy and Eliza, however, had the effect of making us take an increased interest thenceforth in spiders in general, which till that time we had treated with scant courtesy, and set us about learning something as to the extraordinary variety of life and habit to be found within the range of this single group of arthropods, at first sight so extremely alike in their shapes, their appearance, their morals, and their manners. It's perfectly astonishing, though, when one comes to look into it in detail, how exceedingly diverse spiders are in their mode of life, their structure, and the variety of uses to which they put their one extremely distinctive structural organ, the spinnerets. I will only say here that some spiders use these peculiar glands to form light webs by whose aid, though wingless, they float balloon-wise through the air; that others employ them to line the sides of their underground tunnels, and to make the basis of their marvellously ingenious earthen trap-doors; that yet others have learnt how to adapt these same organs to a subaquatic existence, and to fill cocoons with air, like miniature diving bells; while others, again, have taught themselves to construct webs thick enough to catch and hold even creatures so superior to themselves in the scale of being as humming-birds and sunbirds. This extraordinary variety in the utilization of a single organ teaches once more the same lesson which is impressed upon us elsewhere by so many other forms of organic evolution: whatever enables an animal or plant to gain an advantage over others in the struggle for life, no matter in what way, is sure to survive, and to be turned in time to every conceivable use of which its structure is capable, in the infinite whirligig of ever-varying nature.


## MUD

Even a prejudiced observer will readily admit that the most valuable mineral on earth is mud. Diamonds and rubies are just nowhere by comparison. I don't mean weight for weight, of course, mud is 'cheap as dirt,' to buy in small quantities, but aggregate for aggregate. Quite literally, and without hocus-pocus of any sort, the money valuation of the mud in the world must outnumber many thousand times the money valuation of all the other minerals put together. Only we reckon it usually not by the ton, but by the acre, though the acre is worth most where the mud lies deepest. Nay, more, the world's wealth is wholly based on mud. Corn, not gold, is the true standard of value. Without mud there would be no human life, no productions of any kind: for food stuffs of every description are raised on mud; and where no mud exists, or can be made to exist, there, we say, there is desert or sand-waste. Land, without mud, has no economic value. To put it briefly, the only parts of the world that count much for human habitation are the mud deposits of the great rivers, and notably of the Nile, the Euphrates, the Ganges, the Indus, the Irrawaddy, the Hoang Ho, the Yang-tse-Kiang; of the Po, the Rhone, the Danube, the Rhine, the Volga, the Dnieper; of the St. Lawrence, the Mississippi, the Missouri, the Orinoco, the Amazons, the La Plata. A corn-field is just a big mass of mud; and the deeper and purer and freer from stones or other impurities it is the better.

But England, you say, is not a great river-mud field; yet it supports the densest population in the world. True; but England is an exceptional product of modern civilization. She can't feed herself: she is fed from Odessa, Alexandria, Bombay, New York, Montreal, Buenos Ayres, in other words, from the mud fields of the Russian, the Egyptian, the Indian, the American, the Canadian, the Argentine rivers. Orontes, said Juvenal, has flowed into Tiber; Nile, we may say nowadays, with equal truth, has flowed into Thames.

There is nothing to make one realize the importance of mud, indeed, like a journey up Nile when the inundation is just over. You lounge on the deck of your dahabieh, and drink in geography almost without knowing it. The voyage forms a perfect introduction to the study of mudology, and suggests to the observant mind (meaning you and me) the real nature of mud as nothing else on earth that I know of can suggest it. For in Egypt you get your phenomenon isolated, as it were, from all disturbing elements. You have no rainfall to bother you, no local streams, no complex denudation: the Nile does all, and the Nile does everything. On either hand stretches away the bare desert, rising up in grey rocky hills. Down the midst runs the one long line of alluvial soil, in other words, Nile mud, which alone allows cultivation and life in that rainless district. The country bases itself absolutely on mud. The crops are raised on it; the houses and villages are built of it; the land is manured with it; the very air is full of it. The crude brick buildings that dissolve in dust are Nile mud solidified; the red pottery of Assiout is Nile mud baked hard; the village mosques and minarets are Nile mud whitewashed. I have even seen a ship's bulwarks neatly repaired with mud. It pervades the whole land, when wet, as mud undisguised; when dry, as dust-storm.

Egypt, says Herodotus, is a gift of the Nile. A truer or more pregnant word was never spoken. Of course it is just equally true, in a way, that Bengal is a gift of the Ganges, and that Louisiana and Arkansas are gifts of the Mississippi; but with this difference, that in the case of the Nile the dependence is far more obvious, far freer from disturbing or distracting details. For that reason, and also because the Nile is so much more familiar to most English-speaking folk than the American rivers, I choose Egypt first as my type of a regular mud-land. But in order to understand it fully you mustn't stop all your time in Cairo and the Delta; you mustn't view it only from the terrace of Shepheard's Hotel or the rocky platform of the Great Pyramid at Ghizeh: you must push up country early, under Mr. Cook's care, to Luxor and the First Cataract. It is up country that Egypt unrolls itself visibly before your eyes in the very process of making: it is there that the full importance of good, rich black mud first forces itself upon you by undeniable evidence.

For remember that, from a point above Berber to the sea, the dwindling Nile never receives a single tributary, a single drop of fresh water. For more than fifteen hundred miles the ever-lessening river rolls on between bare desert hills and spreads fertility over the deep valley in their midst, just as far as its own mud sheet can cover the barren rocky bottom, and no farther. For the most part the line of demarcation between the grey bare desert and the cultivable plain is as clear and as well-defined as the margin of sea and land: you can stand with one foot on the barren rock and one on the green soil of the tilled and irrigated mud-land. For the water rises up to a certain level, and to that level accordingly it distributes both mud and moisture: above it comes the arid rock, as destitute of life, as dead and bare and lonely as the centre of Sahara. In and out, in waving line, up to the base of the hills, cultivation and greenery follow, with absolute accuracy, the line of highest flood-level; beyond it the hot rock stretches dreary and desolate. Here and there islands of sandstone stand out above the green sea of doura or cotton; here and there a bay of fertility runs away up some lateral valley, following the course of the mud; but one inch above the inundation-mark vegetation and life stop short all at once with absolute abruptness. In Egypt, then, more than anywhere else, one sees with one's own eyes that mud and moisture are the very conditions of mundane fertility.

Beyond Cairo, as one descends seaward, the mud begins to open out fan-wise and form a delta. The narrow mountain ranges no longer hem it in. It has room to expand and spread itself freely over the surrounding country, won by degrees from the Mediterranean. At the mouths the mud pours out into the sea and forms fresh deposits constantly on the bottom, which are gradually silting up still newer lands to seaward. Slow as is the progress of this land-forming action, there can be no doubt that the Nile has the intention of filling up by degrees the whole eastern Mediterranean, and that in process of time, say in no more than a few million years or so, a mere bagatelle to the geologist, with the aid of the Po and some other lesser streams, it will transform the entire basin of the inland sea into a level and cultivable plain, like Bengal or Mesopotamia, themselves (as we shall see) the final result of just such silting action.

It is so very important, for those who wish to see things "as clear as mud," to understand this prime principle of the formation of mud-lands, that I shall make no apology for insisting on it further in some little detail; for when one comes to look the matter plainly in the face, one can see in a minute that almost all the big things in human history have been entirely dependent upon the mud of the great rivers. Thebes and Memphis, Rameses and Amenhotep, based their civilisation absolutely upon the mud of Nile. The bricks of Babylon were moulded of Euphrates mud; the greatness of Nineveh reposed on the silt of the Tigris. Upper India is the Indus; Agra and Delhi are Ganges and Jumna mud; China is the Hoang Ho and the Yang-tse-Kiang; Burmah is the paddy field of the Irrawaddy delta. And so many great plains in either hemisphere consist really of nothing else but mud-banks of almost incredible extent, filling up prehistoric Baltics and Mediterraneans, that a glance at the probable course of future evolution in this respect may help us to understand and to realize more fully the gigantic scale of some past accumulations.

As a preliminary canter I shall trot out first the valley of the Po, the existing mud flat best known by personal experience to the feet and eyes of the tweed-clad English tourist. Everybody who has looked down upon the wide Lombard plain from the pinnacled roof of Milan Cathedral, or who has passed by rail through that monotonous level of poplars and vines between Verona and Venice, knows well what a mud flat due to inundation and gradual silting up of a valley looks like. What I want to do now is to inquire into its origin, and to follow up in fancy the same process, still in action, till it has filled the Adriatic from end to end with one great cultivable lowland.

Once upon a time (I like to be at least as precise as a fairy tale in the matter of dates) there was no Lombardy. And that time was not, geologically speaking, so very remote; for the whole valley of the Po, from Turin to the sea, consists entirely of alluvial deposits, or, in other words, of Alpine mud, which has all accumulated where it now lies at a fairly recent period. We know it is recent, because no part of Italy has ever been submerged since it began to gather there. To put it more definitely, the entire mass has almost certainly been laid down since the first appearance of man on our earth: the earliest human beings who reached the Alps or the Apennines, black savages clad in skins of extinct wild beasts, must have looked down from their slopes, with shaded eyes, not on a level plain such as we see to-day, but on a great arm of the sea which stretched like a gulf far up towards the base of the hills about Turin and Rivoli. Of this ancient sea the Adriatic forms the still unsilted portion. In other words, the great gulf which now stops short at Trieste and Venice once washed the foot of the Alps and the Apennines to the Superga at Turin, covering the sites of Padua, Ferrara, Bologna, Ravenna, Mantua, Cremona, Modena, Parma, Piacenza, Pavia, Milan, and Novara. The industrious reader who gets out his Baedeker and looks up the shaded map of North Italy which forms its frontispiece will be rewarded for his pains by a better comprehension of the district thus demarcated. The idle must be content to take my word for what follows. I pledge them my honour that I'll do my best not to deceive their trustful innocence.

It may sound at first hearing a strange thing to say so, but the whole of that vast gulf, from Turin to Venice, has been entirely filled up within the human period by the mud sheet brought down by mountain torrents from the Alps and the Apennines.

A parallel elsewhere will make this easier of belief. You have looked down, no doubt, from the garden of the hotel at Glion upon the lake of Geneva and the valley of the Rhone about Villeneuve and Aigle. If so, you can understand from personal knowledge the first great stage in the mud-filling process; for you must have observed for yourself from that commanding height that the lake once extended a great deal farther up country towards Bex and St. Maurice than it does at present. You can still trace at once on either side the old mountainous banks, descending into the plain as abruptly and unmistakably as they still descend to the water's edge at Montreux and Vevey. But the silt of the Rhone, brought down in great sheets of glacier mud (about which more anon) from the Furca and the Jungfrau and the Monte Rosa chain, has completely filled in the upper nine miles of the old lake basin with a level mass of fertile alluvium. There is no doubt about the fact: you can see it for yourself with half an eye from that specular mount (to give the Devil his due, I quote Milton's Satan): the mud lies even from bank to bank, raised only a few inches above the level of the lake, and as lacustrine in effect as the veriest geologist on earth could wish it. Indeed, the process of filling up still continues unabated at the present day where the mud-laden Rhone enters the lake at Bouveret, to leave it again, clear and blue and beautiful, under the bridge at Geneva. The little delta which the river forms at its mouth shows the fresh mud in sheets gathering thick upon the bottom. Every day this new mud-bank pushes out farther and farther into the water, so that in process of time the whole basin will be filled in, and a level plain, like that which now spreads from Bex and Aigle to Villeneuve, will occupy the entire bed from Montreux to Geneva.

Turn mentally to the upper feeders of the Po itself, and you find the same causes equally in action. You have stopped at Pallanza, Garoni's is so comfortable. Well, then, you know how every Alpine stream, as it flows, full-gorged, into the Italian lakes, is busily engaged in filling them up as fast as ever it can with turbid mud from the uplands. The basins of Maggiore, Como, Lugano, and Garda are by origin deep hollows scooped out long since during the Great Ice Age by the pressure of huge glaciers that then spread far down into what is now the poplar-clad plain of Lombardy. But ever since the ice cleared away, and the torrents began to rush headlong down the deep gorges of the Val Leventina and the Val Maggia, the mud has been hard at work, doing its level best to fill those great ice-worn bowls up again. Near the mouth of each main stream it has already succeeded in spreading a fan-shaped delta. I will not insult you by asking you at the present time of day whether you have been over the St. Gothard. In this age of trains de luxe I know to my cost everybody has been everywhere. No chance of pretending to superior knowledge about Japan or Honolulu; the tourist knows them. Very well, then; you must remember as you go past Bellinzona, revolutionary little Bellinzona with its three castled crags, you look down upon a vast mud flat by the mouth of the Ticino. Part of this mud flat is already solid land, but part is mere marsh or shifting quicksand. That is the first stage in the abolition of the lakes: the mud is annihilating them.

Maggiore, indeed, least fortunate of the three main sheets, is being attacked by the insidious foe at three points simultaneously. At the upper end, the Ticino, that furious radical river, has filled in a large arm, which once spread far away up the valley towards Bellinzona. A little lower down, the Maggia near Locarno carries in a fresh contribution of mud, which forms another fan-shaped delta, and stretches its ugly mass half across the lake, compelling the steamers to make a considerable detour eastward. This delta is rapidly extending into the open water, and will in time fill in the whole remaining space from bank to bank, cutting off the upper end of the lake about Locarno from the main basin by a partition of lowland. This upper end will then form a separate minor lake, and the Ticino will flow out of it across the intervening mud flat into the new and smaller Maggiore of our great-great-grandchildren. If you doubt it, look what the torrent of the Toce, the third assailing battalion of the persistent mud force, has already done in the neighbourhood of Pallanza. It has entirely cut off the upper end of the bay, that turns westward towards the Simplon, by a partition of mud; and this isolated upper bit forms now in our own day a separate lake, the Lago di Mergozzo, divided from the main sheet by an uninteresting mud bank. In process of time, no doubt, the whole of Maggiore will be similarly filled in by the advancing mud sheet, and will become a level alluvial plain, surrounded by mountains, and greatly admired by the astute Piedmontese cultivator.

What is going on in Maggiore is going on equally in all the other sub-Alpine lakes of the Po valley. They are being gradually filled in, every one of them, by the aggressive mud sheet. The upper end of Lugano, for example, has already been cut off, as the Lago del Piano, from the main body; and the piano itself, from which the little isolated tarn takes its name, is the alluvial mud fiat of a lateral torrent, the mud flat, in fact, which the railway from Porlezza traverses for twenty minutes before it begins its steep and picturesque climb by successive zigzags over the mountains to Menaggio. Similarly the influx of the Adda at the upper end of Como has cut off the Lago di Mezzola from the main lake, and has formed the alluvial level that stretches so drearily all around Colico. Slowly the mud fiend encroaches everywhere on the lakes; and if you look for him when you go, there you can see him actually at work every spring under your very eyes, piling up fresh banks and deltas with alarming industry, and preparing (in a few hundred thousand years) to ruin the tourist trade of Cadenabbia and Bellagio.

If we turn from the lakes themselves to the Lombard plain at large, which is an immensely older and larger basin, we see traces of the same action on a vastly greater scale. A glance at the map will show the intelligent and ever courteous reader that the 'wandering Po', I drop into poetry after Goldsmith, flows much nearer the foot of the Apennines than of the Alps in the course of its divagations, and seems purposely to bend away from the greater range of mountains. Why is this, since everything in nature must needs have a reason? Well, it is because, when the mud first began to accumulate in the old Lombard bay of the Adriatic, there was no Po at all, whether wandering or otherwise: the big river has slowly grown up in time by the union of the lateral torrents that pour down from either side, as the growth of the mud flat brought them gradually together. Careful study of a good map will show how this has happened, especially if it has the plains and mountains distinctively tinted after the excellent German fashion. The Ticino, the Adda, the Mincio, if you look at them close, reveal themselves as tributaries of the Po, which once flowed separately into the Lombard bay; the Adige, the Piave, the Tagliamento farther along the coast, reveal themselves equally as tributaries of the future Po, when once the great river shall have filled up with its mud the space between Trieste and Venice, though for the moment they empty themselves and their store of detritus into the open Adriatic.

Fix your eyes for a moment on Venetia proper, and you will see how this has all happened and is still happening. Each mountain torrent that leaps from the Tyrolese Alps bring down in its lap a rich mass of mud, which has gradually spread over a strip of sea some forty or fifty miles wide, from the base of the mountains to the modern coast-line of the province. Near the sea, or, in other words, at the temporary outlet, it forms banks and lagoons, of which those about Venice are the best known to tourists, though the least characteristic. For miles and miles between Venice and Trieste the shifting north shore of the Adriatic consists of nothing but such accumulating mud banks. Year after year they push farther seaward, and year after year fresh islets and shoals grow out into the waves beyond the temporary deltas. In time, therefore, the gathering mud banks of these Alpine torrents must join the greater mud bank that runs rapidly seaward at the delta of the Po. As soon as they do so the rivers must rush together, and what was once an independent stream, emptying itself into the Adriatic, must become a tributary of the Po, helping to swell the waters of that great united river. The Adige has now just reached this state: its delta is continuous with the delta of the Po, and their branches interosculate. The Mincio and the Adda reached it ages since: the Piave and the Livenia will not reach it for ages. In Roman days Hatria was still on the sea: it is now some fifteen miles inland.

From all this you can gather why the existing Po flows far from the Alps and nearer the base of the Apennines. The Alpine streams in far distant days brought down relatively large floods of glacial mud; formed relatively large deltas in the old Lombard bay; filled up with relative rapidity their larger half of the basin. The Apennines, less lofty, and free from glaciers, sent down shorter and smaller torrents, laden with far less mud, and capable therefore of doing but little alluvial work for the filling in of the future Lombardy. So the river was pushed southward by the Alpine deposits of the northern streams, leaving the great plains of Cisalpine Gaul spread away to the north of it.

And this land-making action is ceaseless and continuous. About Venice, Chioggia, Maestra, Comacchio, the delta of the Po is still spreading seaward. In the course of ages, if nothing unforeseen occurs meanwhile to prevent it, the Alpine mud will have filled in the entire Adriatic; and the Ionian Isles will spring like isolated mountain ridges from the Adriatic plain, as the Euganean hills, those 'mountains Euganean' where Shelley 'stood listening to the pæan with which the legioned rocks did hail the sun's uprise majestical', spring in our own time from the dead level of Lombardy. Once they in turn were the Euganean islands, and even now to the trained eye of the historical observer they stand up island-like from the vast green plain that spreads flat around them.

Perhaps it seems to you a rather large order to be asked to believe that Lombardy and Venetia are nothing more than an outspread sheet of deep Alpine mud. Well, there is nothing so good for incredulity, don't you know, as capping the climax. If a man will not swallow an inch of fact, the best remedy is to make him gulp down an ell of it. And, indeed, the Lombard plain is but an insignificant mud flat compared with the vast alluvial plains of Asiatic and American rivers. The alluvium of the Euphrates, of the Mississippi, of the Hoang Ho, of the Amazons would take in many Lombardies and half-a-dozen Venetias without noticing the addition. But I will insist upon only one example, the rivers of India, which have formed the gigantic deep mud flat of the Ganges and the Jumna, one of the very biggest on earth, and that because the Himalayas are the highest and newest mountain chain exposed to denudation. For, as we saw foreshadowed in the case of the Alps and Apennines, the bigger the mountains on which we can draw the greater the resulting mass of alluvium. The Rocky Mountains give rise to the Missouri (which is the real Mississippi); the Andes give rise to Amazons and the La Plata; the Himalayas give rise to the Ganges and the Indus. Great mountain, great river, great resulting mud sheet.

At a very remote period, so long ago that we cannot reduce it to any common measure with our modern chronology, the southern table-land of India, the Deccan, as we call it, formed a great island like Australia, separated from the continent of Asia by a broad arm of the sea which occupied what is now the great plain of Bengal, the North-West, and the Punjaub. This ancient sea washed the foot of the Himalayas, and spread south thence for 600 miles to the base of the Vindhyas. But the Himalayas are high and clad with gigantic glaciers. Much ice grinds much mud on those snow-capped summits. The rivers that flowed from the Roof of the World carried down vast sheets of alluvium, which formed fans at their mouths, like the cones still deposited on a far smaller scale in the Lake of Geneva by little lateral torrents. Gradually the silt thus brought down accumulated on either side, till the rivers ran together into two great systems, one westward, the Indus, with its four great tributaries, Jhelum, Chenab, Ravee, Sutlej; one eastward, the Ganges, reinforced lower down by the sister streams of the Jumna and the Brahmapootra. The colossal accumulation of silt thus produced filled up at last all the great arm of the sea between the two mountain chains, and joined the Deccan by slow degrees to the continent of Asia. It is still engaged in filling up the Bay of Bengal on one side by the detritus of the Ganges, and the Arabian Sea on the other by the sand-banks of the Indus.

In the same way, no doubt, the silt of the Thames, the Humber, the Rhine, and the Meuse tend slowly (bar accidents) to fill up the North Sea, and anticipate Sir Edward Watkin by throwing a land bridge across the English Channel. If ever that should happen, then history will have repeated itself, for it is just so that the Deccan was joined to the mainland of Asia.

One question more. Whence comes the mud? The answer is, Mainly from the detritus of the mountains. There it has two origins. Part of it is glacial, part of it is leaf-mould. In order to feel we have really got to the very bottom of the mud problem, and we are nothing if not thorough, we must examine in brief these two separate origins.

The glacier mud is of a very simple nature. It is disintegrated rock, worn small by the enormous millstone of ice that rolls slowly over the bed, and deposited in part as 'terminal moraine' near the summer melting-point. It is the quantity of mud thus produced, and borne down by mountain torrents, that makes the alluvial plains collect so quickly at their base. The mud flats of the world are in large part the wear and tear of the eternal hills under the planing action of the eternal glaciers.

But let us be just to our friends. A large part is also due to the industrious earth-worm, whose place in nature Darwin first taught us to estimate at its proper worth. For there is much detritus and much first-rate soil even on hills not covered by glaciers. Some of this takes its origin, it is true, from disintegration by wind or rain, but much more is caused by the earth-worm in person. That friend of humanity, so little recognized in his true light, has a habit of drawing down leaves into his subterranean nest, and there eating them up, so as to convert their remains into vegetable mould in the form of worm-casts. This mould, the most precious of soils, gets dissolved again by the rain, and carried off in solution by the streams to the sea or the lowlands, where it helps to form the future cultivable area. At the same time the earthworms secrete an acid, which acts upon the bare surface of rock beneath, and helps to disintegrate it in preparation for plant life in unfavourable places. It is probable that we owe almost more on the whole to these unknown but conscientious and industrious annelids than even to those 'mills of God' the glaciers, of which the American poet justly observes that though they grind slowly, yet they grind exceedingly small.

In the last resort, then, it is mainly on mud that the life of humanity in all countries bases itself. Every great plain is the alluvial deposit of a great river, ultimately derived from a great mountain chain. The substance consists as a rule of the débris of torrents, which is often infertile, owing to its stoniness and its purely mineral character; but wherever it has lain long enough to be covered by earth-worms with a deep black layer of vegetable mould, there the resulting soil shows the surprising fruitfulness one gets (for example) in Lombardy, where twelve crops a year are sometimes taken from the meadows. Everywhere and always the amount and depth of the mud is the measure of possible fertility; and even where, as in the Great American Desert, want of water converts alluvial plains into arid stretches of sand-waste, the wilderness can be made to blossom like the rose in a very few years by artificial irrigation. The diversion of the Arkansas River has spread plenty over a vast sage scrub; the finest crops in the world are now raised over a tract of country which was once the terror of the traveller across the wild west of America.


## THE GREENWOOD TREE

It is a common, not to say a vulgar error, to believe that trees and plants grow out of the ground. And of course, having thus begun by calling it bad names, I will not for a moment insult the intelligence of my readers by supposing them to share so foolish a delusion. I beg to state from the outset that I write this article entirely for the benefit of Other People. You and I, O proverbially Candid and Intelligent One, it need hardly be said, are better informed. But Other People fall into such ridiculous blunders that it is just as well to put them on their guard beforehand against the insidious advance of false opinions. I have known otherwise good and estimable men, indeed, who for lack of sound early teaching on this point went to their graves with a confirmed belief in the terrestrial origin of all earthly vegetation. They were probably victims of what the Church in its succinct way describes and denounces as Invincible Ignorance.

Now, the reason why these deluded creatures supposed trees to grow out of the ground, instead of out of the air, is probably only because they saw their roots there.

Of course, when people see a wallflower rooted in the clefts of some old church tower, they don't jump at once to the inane conclusion that it is made of rock, that it derives its nourishment direct from the solid limestone; nor when they observe a barnacle hanging by its sucker to a ship's hull, do they imagine it to draw up its food incontinently from the copper bottom. But when they see that familiar pride of our country, a British oak, with its great underground buttresses spreading abroad through the soil in every direction, they infer at once that the buttresses are there, not, as is really the case, to support it and uphold it, but to drink in nutriment from the earth beneath, which is just about as capable of producing oak-wood as the copper plate on the ship's hull is capable of producing the flesh of a barnacle. Sundry familiar facts about manuring and watering, to which I will return later on, give a certain colour of reasonableness, it is true, to this mistaken inference. But how mistaken it really is for all that, a single and very familiar little experiment will easily show one.

Cut down that British oak with your Gladstonian axe; lop him of his branches; divide him into logs; pile him up into a pyramid; put a match to his base; in short, make a bonfire of him; and what becomes of robust majesty? He is reduced to ashes, you say. Ah, yes, but what proportion of him? Conduct your experiment carefully on a small scale; dry your wood well, and weigh it before burning; weigh your ash afterwards, and what will you find? Why, that the solid matter which remains after the burning is a mere infinitesimal fraction of the total weight: the greater part has gone off into the air, from whence it came, as carbonic acid. Dust to dust, ashes to ashes; but air to air, too, is the rule of nature.

It may sound startling, to Other People, I mean, but the simple truth remains, that trees and plants grow out of the atmosphere, not out of the ground. They are, in fact, solidified air; or to be more strictly correct, solidified gas—carbonic acid.

Take an ordinary soda-water syphon, with or without a wine-glassful of brandy, and empty it till only a few drops remain in the bottom. Then the bottle is full of gas; and that gas, which will rush out with a spurt when you press the knob, is the stuff that plants eat, the raw material of life, both animal and vegetable. The tree grows and lives by taking in the carbonic acid from the air, and solidifying its carbon; the animal grows and lives by taking the solidified carbon from the plant, and converting it once more into carbonic acid. That, in its ideally simple form, is the Iliad in a nutshell, the core and kernel of biology. The whole cycle of life is one eternal see-saw. First the plant collects its carbon compounds from the air in the oxidized state; it deoxidizes and rebuilds them: and then the animal proceeds to burn them up by slow combustion within his own body, and to turn them loose upon the air, once more oxidized. After which the plant starts again on the same round as before, and the animal also recommences da capo. And so on ad infinitum.

But the point which I want particularly to emphasize here is just this: that trees and plants don't grow out of the ground at all, as most people do vainly talk, but directly out of the air; and that when they die or get consumed, they return once more to the atmosphere from which they were taken. Trees undeniably eat carbon.

Of course, therefore, all the ordinary unscientific conceptions of how plants feed are absolutely erroneous. Vegetable physiology, indeed, got beyond these conceptions a good hundred years ago. But it usually takes a hundred years for the world at large to make up its leeway. Trees don't suck up their nutriment by the roots, they don't derive their food from the soil, they don't need to be fed, like babies through a tube, with terrestrial solids. The solitary instance of an orchid hung up by a string in a conservatory on a piece of bark, ought to be sufficient at once to dispel for ever this strange illusion, if people thought; but of course they don't think, I mean Other People. The true mouths and stomachs of plants are not to be found in the roots, but in the green leaves; their true food is not sucked up from the soil, but is inhaled through tiny channels from the air; the mass of their material is carbon, as we can all see visibly to the naked eye when a log of wood is reduced to charcoal: and that carbon the leaves themselves drink in, by a thousand small green mouths, from the atmosphere around them.

But how about the juice, the sap, the qualities of the soil, the manure required? is the incredulous cry of Other People. What is the use of the roots, and especially of the rootlets, if they are not the mouths and supply-tubes of the plants? Well, I plainly perceive I can get 'no forrarder,' like the farmer with his claret, till I've answered that question, provisionally at least; so I will say here at once, without further ado, the plant requires drink as well as food, and the roots are the mouths that supply it with water. They also suck up a few other things as well, which are necessary indeed, but far from forming the bulk of the nutriment. Many plants, however, don't need any roots at all, while none can get on without leaves as mouths and stomachs. That is to say, no true plantlike plants, for some parasitic plants are practically, to all intents and purposes, animals. To put it briefly, every plant has one set of aerial mouths to suck in carbon, and many plants have another set of subterranean mouths as well, to suck up water and mineral constituents.

Have you ever grown mustard and cress in the window on a piece of flannel? If so, that's a capital practical example of the comparative unimportance of soil, except as a means of supplying moisture. You put your flannel in a soup-plate by the dining-room window; you keep it well wet, and you lay the seeds of the cress on top of it. The young plants, being supplied with water by their roots, and with carbon by the air around, have all the little they need below, and grow and thrive in these conditions wonderfully. But if you were to cover them up with an air-tight glass case, so as to exclude fresh air, they'd shrivel up at once for want of carbon, which is their solid food, as water is their liquid.

The way the plant really eats is little known to gardeners, but very interesting. All over the lower surface of the green leaf lie scattered dozens of tiny mouths or apertures, each of them guarded by two small pursed-up lips which have a ridiculously human appearance when seen through a simple microscope. When the conditions of air and moisture are favourable, these lips open visible to admit gases; and then the tiny mouths suck in carbonic acid in abundance from the air around then. A series of pipes conveys the gaseous food thus supplied to the upper surface of the leaf, where the sunlight falls full upon it. Now, the cells of the leaf contain a peculiar green digestive material, which I regret to say has no simpler or more cheerful name than chlorophyll; and where the sunlight plays upon this mysterious chlorophyll, it severs the oxygen from the carbon in the carbonic acid, turns the free gas loose upon the atmosphere once more through the tiny mouths, and retains the severed carbon intact in its own tissues. That is the whole process of feeding in plants: they eat carbonic acid, digest it in their leaves, get rid of the oxygen with which it was formerly combined, and keep the carbon stored up for their own purposes.

Life as a whole depends entirely upon this property of chlorophyll; for every atom of organic matter in your body or mine was originally so manufactured by sunlight in the leaves of some plant from which, directly or indirectly, we derive it.

To be sure, in order to make up the various substances which compose their tissues, to build up their wood, their leaves, their fruits, their blossoms, plants require hydrogen, nitrogen, and even small quantities of oxygen as well; but these various materials are sufficiently supplied in the water which is taken up by the roots, and they really contribute very little indeed to the bulk of the tree, which consists for the most part of almost pure carbon. If you were to take a thoroughly dry piece of wood, and then drive off from it by heat these extraneous matters, you would find that the remainder, the pure charcoal, formed the bulk of the weight, the rest being for the most part very light and gaseous. Briefly put, plants are mostly carbon and water, and the carbon which forms their solid part is extracted direct from the air around them.

How does it come about then that a careless world in general, and more especially the happy-go-lucky race of gardeners and farmers in particular, who have to deal so much with plants in their practical aspect, always attach so great importance to root, soil, manure, minerals, and so little to the real gaseous food stuff of which their crops are, in fact, composed? Why does Hodge, who is so strong on grain and guano, know absolutely nothing about carbonic acid? That seems at first sight a difficult question to meet. But I think we can meet it with a simple analogy.

Oxygen is an absolute necessary of human life. Even food itself is hardly so important an element in our daily existence; for Succi, Dr. Tanner, the prophet Elijah, and other adventurous souls too numerous to mention, have abundantly shown us that a man can do without food altogether for forty days at a stretch, while he can't do without oxygen for a single minute. Cut off his supply of that life-supporting gas, choke him, or suffocate him, or place him in an atmosphere of pure carbonic acid, or hold his head in a bucket of water, and he dies at once. Yet, except in mines or submarine tunnels, nobody ever takes into account practically this most important factor in human and animal life. We toil for bread, but we ignore the supply of oxygen. And why? Simply because oxygen is universally diffused everywhere. It costs nothing. Only in the Black Hole of Calcutta or in a broken tunnel shaft do men ever begin to find themselves practically short of that life-sustaining gas, and then they know the want of it far sooner and far more sharply than they know the want of food on a shipwreck raft, or the want of water in the thirsty desert. Yet antiquity never even heard of oxygen. A prime necessary of life passed unnoticed for ages in human history, only because there was abundance of it to be had everywhere.

Now it isn't quite the same, I admit, with the carbonaceous food of plants. Carbonic acid isn't quite so universally distributed as oxygen, nor can every plant always get as much as it wants of it. I shall show by-and-by that a real struggle for food takes place between plants, exactly as it takes place between animals; and that certain plants, like Oliver Twist in the workhouse, never practically get enough to eat. Still, carbonic acid is present in very large quantities in the air in most situations, and is freely brought by the wind to all the open spaces which alone man uses for his crops and his gardening. The most important element in the food of plants is thus in effect almost everywhere available, especially from the point of view of the mere practical everyday human agriculturist. The wind that bloweth where it listeth brings fresh supplies of carbon on its wings with every breeze to the mouths and throats of the greedy and eager plants that long to absorb it.

It is quite otherwise, however, with the soil and its constituents. Land, we all know, or if we don't, it isn't the fault of Mr. George and Mr. A.R. Wallace, land is 'naturally limited in quantity.' Every plant therefore struggles for a foothold in the soil far more fiercely and far more tenaciously than it struggles for its share in the free air of heaven. Your plant is a land-grabber of Rob Roy proclivities; it believes in a fair fight and no favour. A sufficient supply of food it almost takes for granted, if only it can once gain a sufficient ground-space. But other plants are competing with it, tooth and nail (if plants may be permitted by courtesy those metaphorical adjuncts), for their share of the soil, like crofters or socialists; every spare inch of earth is permeated and pervaded with matted fibres; and each is striving to withdraw from each the small modicum of moisture, mineral matter, and manure for which all alike are eagerly battling.

Now, what the plant wants from the soil is three things. First and foremost it wants support; like all the rest of us it must have its pou sto, its pied-à-terre, its locus standi. It can't hang aloft, like Mahomet's coffin, miraculously suspended on an aerial perch between earth and heaven. Secondly, it wants water, and this it can take in, as a rule, only or mainly by means of the rootlets, though there are some peculiar plants which grow (not parasitically) on the branches of trees, and absorb all the moisture they need by pores on their surface. And thirdly, it wants small quantities of nitrogenous matter, in the simpler language of everyday life called manure, as well as of mineral matter, in the simpler language of everyday life called ashes. It is mainly the first of these three, support, that the farmer thinks of when he calculates crops and acreage; for the second, he depends upon rainfall or irrigation; but the third, manure, he can supply artificially; and as manure makes a great deal of incidental difference to some of his crops, especially corn, which requires abundant phosphates, he is apt to over-estimate vastly its importance from a theoretical point of view.

Besides, look at it in another light. Over large areas together, the conditions of air, climate, and rainfall are practically identical. But soil differs greatly from place to place. Here it's black; there it's yellow; here it's rich loam; there it's boggy mould or sandy gravel. And some soils are better adapted to growing certain plants than others. Rich lowlands and oolites suit the cereals; red marl produces wonderful grazing grass; bare uplands are best for gorse and heather. Hence everything favours for the practical man the mistaken idea that plants and trees grow mainly out of the soil. His own eyes tell him so; he sees them growing, he sees the visible result undeniable before his face; while the real act of feeding off the carbon in the air is wholly unknown to him, being realizable only by the aid of the microscope, aided by the most delicate and difficult chemical analysis.

Nevertheless French chemists have amply proved by actual experiment that plants can grow and produce excellent results without any aid from the soil at all. You have only to suspend the seeds freely in the air by a string, and supply the rootlets of the sprouting seedlings with a little water, containing in solution small quantities of manure-stuffs, and the plants will grow as well as on their native heath, or even better. Indeed, nature has tried the same experiment on a larger scale in many cases, as with the cliff-side plants that root themselves in the naked clefts of granite rocks; the tropical orchids that fasten lightly on the bark of huge forest trees; and the mosses that spread even over the bare face of hard brick walls, with scarcely a chink or cranny in which to fasten their minute rootlets. The insect-eating plants are also interesting examples in their way of the curious means which nature takes for keeping up the manure supply under trying circumstances. These uncanny things are all denizens of loose, peaty soil, where they can root themselves sufficiently for purposes of foothold and drink, but where the water rapidly washes away all animal matter. Under such conditions the cunning sundews and the ruthless pitcher-plants set deceptive honey traps for unsuspecting insects, which they catch and kill, absorbing and using up the protoplasmic contents of their bodies, by way of manure, to supply their quota of nitrogenous material.

It is the literal fact, then, that plants really eat and live off carbon, just as truly as sheep eat grass or lions eat antelopes; and that the green leaves are the mouths and stomachs with which they eat and digest it. From this it naturally results that the growth and spread of the leaves must largely depend upon the supply of carbon, as the growth and fatness of sheep depends upon the supply of pasturage. Under most circumstances, to be sure, there is carbon enough and to spare lying about loose for every one of them; but conditions do now and again occur where we can clearly see the importance of the carbon supply. Water, for example, contains practically much less carbonic acid than atmospheric air, especially when the water is stagnant, and therefore not supplied fresh to the plant from moment to moment. As a consequence, almost all water-plants have submerged leaves very narrow and waving, while floating plants, like the water-lilies, have them large and round, owing to the absence of competition from other kinds about, which enables them to spread freely in every direction from the central stalk. Moreover, these leaves, lolling on the water as they do, have their mouths on the upper instead of the under surface. But the most remarkable fact of all is that many water plants have two entirely different types of leaves, one submerged and hair-like, the other floating and broad or circular. Our own English water-crowfoot, for example, has the leaves that spring from its stem, below the surface, divided into endless long waving filaments, which look about in the water for the stray particles of carbon; but the moment it reaches the top of its native pond the foliage expands at once into broad lily-like lobes, that recline on the water like oriental beauties, and absorb carbon from the air to their heart's content, The one type may be likened to gills, that similarly catch the dissolved oxygen diffused in water; the other type may be likened to lungs, that drink in the free and open air of heaven.

Equally important to the plant, however, with the supply of carbonic acid, is the supply of sunshine by whose aid to digest it. The carbon alone is no good to the tree if it can't get something which will separate it from the oxygen, locked in close embrace with it. That thing is sunshine. There is nothing, therefore, for which herbs, trees, and shrubs compete more eagerly than for their fair share of solar energy. In their anxiety for this they jostle one another down most mercilessly, in the native condition, grasses struggling up with their hollow stems above the prone low herbs, shrubs overtopping the grasses in turn, and trees once more killing out the overshadowed undershrubs. One must remember that wherever nature has free play, instead of being controlled by the hand of man, dense forest covers every acre of ground where the soil is deep enough; gorse, whins, and heather, or their equivalents grow wherever the forest fails; and herbs can only hold their own in the rare intervals where these domineering lords of the vegetable creation can find no foothold. Meadows or prairies occur nowhere in nature, except in places where the liability to destructive fires over wide areas together crushes out forest trees, or else where goats, bison, deer, and other large herbivores browse them ceaselessly down in the stage of seedlings. Competition for sunlight is thus even keener perhaps than competition for foodstuffs. Alike on trees, shrubs, and herbs, accordingly the arrangement of the leaves is always exactly calculated so as to allow the largest possible horizontal surface, and the greatest exposure of the blade to the open sunshine. In trees this arrangement can often be very well observed, all the leaves being placed at the extremities of the branches, and forming a great dome-shaped or umbrella-shaped mass, every part of which stands an even chance of catching its fair share of carbonic acid and solar energy.

The shapes of the leaves themselves are also largely due to the same cause, every leaf being so designed in form and outline as to interfere as little as possible with the other leaves on the same stem, as regards supply both of light and of carbonaceous foodstuffs. It is only in rare cases, like that of the water-lily, that perfectly round leaves occur, because the conditions are seldom equal all round, and the incidence of light and the supply of carbon are seldom unlimited. But wherever leaves rise free and solitary into the air, without mutual interference, they are always circular, as may be well seen in the common nasturtium and the English pennywort. On the other hand, among dense hedgerows and thickets, where the silent, invisible struggle for life is fierce indeed, and where sunlight and carbonic acid are intercepted by a thousand competing mouths and arms, the prevailing types of leaf are extremely cut up and minutely subdivided into small lace-like fragments. The plant in such cases can't afford material to fill up the interstices between the veins and ribs which determine its underlying architectural structure. Often indeed species which grow under these hard conditions produce leaves which are, as it were, but skeleton representatives of their large and well filled-out compeers in the open meadows.

It is only by bearing vividly in mind this ceaseless and noiseless struggle between plants for their gaseous food and the sunshine which enables them to digest it that we can ever fully understand the varying forms and habits of the vegetable kingdom. To most people, no doubt, it sounds like pure metaphor to talk of an internecine struggle between rooted beings which cannot budge one inch from their places, nor fight with horns, hoofs, or teeth, nor devour one another bodily, nor tread one another down with ruthless footsteps. But that is only because we habitually forget that competition is just as really a struggle for life as open warfare. The men who try against one another for a clerkship in the City, or a post in a gang of builder's workmen, are just as surely taking away bread and butter out of their fellows' mouths for their own advantage, as if they fought for it openly with fists or six-shooters. The white man who encloses the hunting grounds of the Indian, and plants them with corn, is just as surely dooming that Indian to death as if he scalped or tomahawked him. And so too with the unconscious warfare of plants. The daisy or the plantain that spreads its rosette of leaves flat against the ground is just as truly monopolizing a definite space of land as the noble owner of a Highland deer forest. No blade of grass can spring beneath the shadow of those tightly pressed little mats of foliage; no fragment of carbon, no ray of sunshine can ever penetrate below that close fence of living greenstuff.

Plants, in fact, compete with one another all round for everything they stand in need of. They compete for their food, carbonic acid. They compete for their energy, their fair share of sunlight. They compete for water, and their foothold in the soil. They compete for the favours of the insects that fertilize their flowers. They compete for the good services of the birds or mammals that disseminate their seeds in proper spots for germination. And how real this competition is we can see in a moment, if we think of the difficulties of human cultivation. There, weeds are always battling manfully with our crops or our flowers for mastery over the field or garden. We are obliged to root up with ceaseless toil these intrusive competitors, if we wish to enjoy the kindly fruits of the earth in due season. When we leave a garden to itself for a few short years, we realize at once what effect the competition of hardy natives has upon our carefully tended and unstable exotics. In a very brief time the dahlias and phloxes and lilies have all disappeared, and in their place the coarse-growing docks and nettles and thistles have raised their heads aloft to monopolize air and space and sunshine.

Exactly the same struggle is always taking place in the fields and woods and moors around us, and especially in the spots made over to pure nature. There, the greenwood tree raises its huge umbrella of foliage to the skies, and allows hardly a ray of sunlight to struggle through to the low woodland vegetation of orchid or wintergreen underneath. Where the soil is not deep enough for trees to root securely, bushes and heathers overgrow the ground, and compete with their bell-shaped blossoms for the coveted favour of bees and butterflies. And in open glades, where for some reason or other the forest fails, tall grasses and other aspiring herbs run up apace towards the free air of heaven. Elsewhere, creepers struggle up to the sun over the stems and branches of stronger bushes or trees, which they often choke and starve by monopolizing at last all the available carbon and sunlight. And so throughout; the struggle for life goes on just as ceaselessly and truly among these unconscious combatants as among the lions and tigers of the tropical jungle, or among the human serfs of the overstocked market.

An ounce of example, they say, is worth a pound of precept. So a single concrete case of a fierce vegetable campaign now actually in progress over all Northern Europe may help to make my meaning a trifle clearer. Till very lately the forests of the north were largely composed in places of the light and airy silver birches. But with the gradual amelioration of the climate of our continent, which has been going on for several centuries, the beech, a more southern type of tree, has begun to spread slowly though surely northward. Now, beeches are greedy trees, of very dense and compact foliage; nothing else can grow beneath their thick shade, where once they have gained a foothold; and the seedlings of the silver birch stand no chance at all in the struggle for life against the serried leaves of their formidable rivals. The beech literally eats them out of house and home; and the consequence is that the thick and ruthless southern tree is at this very moment gradually superseding over vast tracts of country its more graceful and beautiful, but far less voracious competitor.

### FISH AS FATHERS

Comparatively little is known as yet, even in this age of publicity, about the domestic arrangements and private life of fishes. Not that the creatures themselves shun the wiles of the interviewer, or are at all shy and retiring, as a matter of delicacy, about their family affairs; on the contrary, they display a striking lack of reticence in their native element, and are so far from pushing parental affection to a quixotic extreme that many of them, like the common rabbit immortalised by Mr. Squeers, 'frequently devour their own offspring.' But nature herself opposes certain obvious obstacles to the pursuit of knowledge in the great deep, which render it difficult for the ardent naturalist, however much he may be so disposed, to carry on his observations with the same facility as in the case of birds and quadrupeds. You can't drop in upon most fish, casually, in their own homes; and when you confine them in aquariums, where your opportunities of watching them through a sheet of plate-glass are considerably greater, most of the captives get huffy under the narrow restrictions of their prison life, and obstinately refuse to rear a brood of hereditary helots for the mere gratification of your scientific curiosity.

Still, by hook and by crook (especially the former), by observation here and experiment there, naturalists in the end have managed to piece together a considerable mass of curious and interesting information of an out-of-the-way sort about the domestic habits and manners of sundry piscine races. And, indeed, the morals of fish are far more varied and divergent than the uniform nature of the world they inhabit might lead an à priori philosopher to imagine. To the eye of the mere casual observer every fish would seem at first sight to be a mere fish, and to differ but little in sentiments and ethical culture from all the rest of his remote cousins. But when one comes to look closer at their character and antecedents, it becomes evident at once that there is a deal of unsuspected originality and caprice about sharks and flat-fish. Instead of conforming throughout to a single plan, as the young, the gay, the giddy, and the thoughtless are too prone to conclude, fish are in reality as various and variable in their mode of life as any other great group in the animal kingdom. Monogamy and polygamy, socialism and individualism, the patriarchal and matriarchal types of government, the oviparous and viviparous methods of reproduction, perhaps even the dissidence of dissent and esoteric Buddhism, all alike are well represented in one family or another of this extremely eclectic and philosophically unprejudiced class of animals.

If you want a perfect model of domestic virtue, for example, where can you find it in higher perfection than in that exemplary and devoted father, the common great pipe-fish of the North Atlantic and the British Seas? This high-principled lophobranch is so careful of its callow and helpless young that it carries about the unhatched eggs with him under his own tail, in what scientific ichthyologists pleasantly describe as a subcaudal pouch or cutaneous receptacle. There they hatch out in perfect security, free from the dangers that beset the spawn and fry of so many other less tender-hearted kinds; and as soon as the little pipe-fish are big enough to look after themselves the sac divides spontaneously down the middle, and allows them to escape, to shift for themselves in the broad Atlantic. Even so, however, the juniors take care always to keep tolerably near that friendly shelter, and creep back into it again on any threat of danger, exactly as baby-kangaroos do into their mother's marsupium. The father-fish, in fact, has gone to the trouble and expense of developing out of his own tissues a membranous bag, on purpose to hold the eggs and young during the first stages of their embryonic evolution. This bag is formed by two folds of the skin, one of which grows out from each side of the body, the free margins being firmly glued together in the middle by a natural exudation, while the eggs are undergoing incubation, but opening once more in the middle to let the little fish out as soon as the process of hatching is fairly finished.

So curious a provision for the safety of the young in the pipe-fish may be compared to some extent, as I hinted above, with the pouch in which kangaroos and other marsupial animals carry their cubs after birth, till they have attained an age of complete independence. But the strangest part of it all is the fact that while in the kangaroo it is the mother who owns the pouch and takes care of the young, in the pipe-fish it is the father, on the contrary, who thus specially provides for the safety of his defenceless offspring. And what is odder still, this topsy-turvy arrangement (as it seems to us) is the common rule throughout the class of fishes. For the most part it must be candidly admitted by their warmest admirer, fish make very bad parents indeed. They lay their eggs anywhere on a suitable spot, and as soon as they have once deposited them, like the ostrich in Job, they go on their way rejoicing, and never bestow another passing thought upon their deserted progeny. But if ever a fish does take any pains in the education and social upbringing of its young, you're pretty sure to find on enquiry it's the father, not as one would naturally expect, the mother, who devotes his time and attention to the congenial task of hatching or feeding them. It is he who builds the nest, and sits upon the eggs, and nurses the young, and imparts moral instruction (with a snap of his jaw or a swish of his tail) to the bold, the truant, the cheeky, or the imprudent; while his unnatural spouse, well satisfied with her own part in having merely brought the helpless eggs into this world of sorrow, goes off on her own account in the giddy whirl of society, forgetful of the sacred claims of her wriggling offspring upon a mother's heart.

In the pipe-fish family, too, the ardent evolutionist can trace a whole series of instructive and illustrative gradations in the development of this instinct and the corresponding pouch-like structure among the male fish. With the least highly-evolved types, like the long-nosed pipe-fish of the English Channel, and many allied forms from European seas, there is no pouch at all, but the father of the family carries the eggs about with him, glued firmly on to the service of his abdomen by a natural mucus. In a somewhat more advanced tropical kind, the ridges of the abdomen are slightly dilated, so as to form an open groove, which loosely holds the eggs, though its edges do not meet in the middle as in the great pipe-fish. Then come yet other more progressive forms, like the great pipe-fish himself, where the folds meet so as to produce a complete sac, which opens at maturity, to let out its little inmates. And finally, in the common Mediterranean sea-horses, which you can pick up by dozens on the Lido at Venice, and a specimen of which exists in the dried form in every domestic museum, the pouch is permanently closed by coalescence of the edges, leaving a narrow opening in front, through which the small hippocampi creep out one by one as soon as they consider themselves capable of buffeting the waves of the Adriatic.

Fish that take much care of their offspring naturally don't need to produce eggs in the same reckless abundance as those dissipated kinds that leave their spawn exposed on the bare sandy bottom, at the mercy of every comer who chooses to take a bite at it. They can afford to lay a smaller number, and to make each individual egg much larger and richer in proportion than their rivals. This plan, of course, enables the young to begin life far better provided with muscles and fins than the tiny little fry which come out of the eggs of the improvident species. For example, the cod-fish lays nine million odd eggs; but anybody who has ever eaten fried cod's-roe must needs have noticed that each individual ovum was so very small as to be almost indistinguishable to the naked eye. Thousands of these infinitesimal specks are devoured before they hatch out by predaceous fish; thousands more of the young fry are swallowed alive during their helpless infancy by the enemies of their species. Imagine the very fractional amount of parental affection which each of the nine million must needs put up with! On the other hand, there is a paternally-minded group of cat-fish known as the genus Arius, of Ceylon, Australia, and other tropical parts, the males of which carry about the ova loose in their mouths, or rather in an enlargement of the pharynx, somewhat resembling the pelican's pouch; and the spouses of these very devoted sires lay accordingly only very few ova, all told, but each almost as big as a hedge-sparrow's egg, a wonderful contrast to the tiny mites of the cod-fish. To put it briefly, the greater the amount of protection afforded the eggs, the smaller the number and the larger the size. And conversely, the larger the size of the egg to start with, the better fitted to begin the battle of life is the young fish when first turned out on a cold world upon his own resources.

This is a general law, indeed, that runs through all nature, from London slums to the deep sea. Wasteful species produce many young, and take but little care of them when once produced. Economical species produce very few young, but start each individual well-equipped for its place in life and look after them closely till they can take care of themselves in the struggle for existence. And on the average, however many or however few the offspring to start with, just enough attain maturity in the long run to replace their parents in the next generation. Were it otherwise, the sea would soon become one solid mass of herring, cod, and mackerel.

These cat-fish, however, are not the only good fathers that carry their young (like woodcock) in their own mouths. A freshwater species of the Sea of Galilee, Chromis Andreæ by name (dedicated by science to the memory of that fisherman apostle, St. Andrew, who must often have netted them), has the same habit of hatching out its young in its own gullet: and here again it is the male fish upon whom this apparently maternal duty devolves, just as it is the male cassowary that sits upon the eggs of his unnatural mate, and the male emu that tends the nest, while the hen bird looks on superciliously and contents herself with exercising a general friendly supervision of the nursery department. I may add parenthetically that in most fish families the eggs are fertilised after they have been laid, instead of before, which no doubt accounts for the seeming anomaly.

Still, good mothers too may be found among fish, though far from frequently. One of the Guiana catfishes, known as Aspredo, very much resembles her countrywoman the Surinam toad in her nursery arrangements. Of course you know the Surinam toad, whom not to know argues yourself unknown, that curious creature that carries her eggs in little pits on her back, where the young hatch out and pass through their tadpole stage in a slimy fluid, emerging at last from the cells of this living honeycomb only when they have attained the full amphibian honours of four-legged maturity. Well, Aspredo among cat-fish manages her brood in much the same fashion; only she carries her eggs beneath her body instead of on her back like her amphibious rival. When spawning time approaches, and Aspredo's fancy lightly turns to thoughts of love, the lower side of her trunk begins to assume, by anticipation, a soft and spongy texture, honeycombed with pits, between which are arranged little spiky protuberances. After laying her eggs, the mother lies flat upon them on the river bottom, and presses them into the spongy skin, where they remain safely attached until they hatch out and begin to manage for themselves in life. It is curious that the only two creatures on earth which have hit out independently this original mode of providing for their offspring should both be citizens of Guiana, where the rivers and marshes must probably harbour some special danger to be thus avoided, not found in equal intensity in other fresh waters.

A prettily marked fish of the Indian Ocean, allied, though not very closely, to the pipe fishes, has also the distinction of handing over the young to the care of the mother instead of the father. Its name is Solenostoma (I regret that no more popular title exists), and it has a pouch, formed in this case by a pair of long broad fins, within which the eggs are attached by interlacing threads that push out from the body. Probably in this instance nutriment is actually provided through these threads for the use of the embryo, in which case we must regard the mechanism as very closely analogous indeed to that which obtains among mammals.

Some few fish, indeed, are truly viviparous; among them certain blennies and carps, in which the eggs hatch out entirely within the body of the mother. One of the most interesting of these divergent types is the common Californian and Mexican silver-fish, an inhabitant of the bays and inlets of sub-tropical America. Its chief peculiarity and title to fame lies in the extreme bigness of its young at birth. The full-grown fish runs to about ten inches in length, fisherman's scale, while the fry measure as much as three inches apiece; so that they lie, as Professor Seeley somewhat forcibly expresses it, 'packed in the body of the parent as close as herrings in a barrel.' This strange habit of retaining the eggs till after they have hatched out is not peculiar to fish among egg-laying animals, for the common little brown English lizard is similarly viviparous, though most of its relatives elsewhere deposit their eggs to be hatched by the heat of the sun in earth or sandbanks.

Mr. Hannibal Chollop, if I recollect aright, once shot an imprudent stranger for remarking in print that the ancient Athenians, that inferior race, had got ahead in their time of the modern Loco-foco ticket. But several kinds of fish have undoubtedly got ahead in this respect of the common reptilian ticket; for instead of leaving about their eggs anywhere on the loose to take care of themselves, they build a regular nest, like birds, and sit upon their eggs till the fry emerge from them. All the sticklebacks, for instance, are confirmed nest-builders: but here once more it is the male, not the female, who weaves the materials together and takes care of the eggs during their period of incubation. The receptacle itself is made of fibres of water-weeds or stalks of grass, and is open at both ends to let a current pass through. As soon as the lordly little polygamist has built it, he coaxes and allures his chosen mates into the entrance, one by one, to lay their eggs; and then when the nest is full, he mounts guard over them bravely, fanning them with his fins, and so keeping up a continual supply of oxygen which is necessary for the proper development of the embryo within. It takes a month's sitting before the young hatch out, and even after they appear, this excellent father (little Turk though he be, and savage warrior for the stocking of his harem) goes out attended by all his brood whenever he sallies forth for a morning constitutional in search of caddis-worms, which shows that there may be more good than we imagine, after all, in the domestic institutions even of people who don't agree with us.

The bullheads or miller's thumbs, those quaint big-headed beasts which divide with the sticklebacks the polite attentions of ingenious British youth, are also nest-builders, and the male fish are said to anxiously watch and protect their offspring during their undisciplined nonage. Equally domestic are the habits of those queer shapeless creatures, the marine lump-suckers, which fasten themselves on to rocks, like limpets, by their strange sucking disks, and defy all the efforts of enemy or fishermen to dislodge them by main force from their well-chosen position. The pretty little tropical walking-fish of the filuroid tribe, those fish out of water, carry the nest-making instinct a point further, for they go ashore boldly at the beginning of the rainy season in their native woods, and scoop out a hole in the beach as a place of safety, in which they make regular nests of leaves and other terrestrial materials to hold their eggs. Then father and mother take turns-about at looking after the hatching, and defend the spawn with great zeal and courage against all intruders.

I regret to say, however, there are other unprincipled fish which display their affection and care for their young in far more questionable and unpleasant manners. For instance, there is that uncanny creature that inserts its parasitic fry as a tiny egg inside the unsuspecting shells of mussels and cockles. Our fishermen are only too well acquainted, again, with one unpleasant marine lamprey, the hag or borer, so called because it lives parasitically upon other fishes, whose bodies it enters, and then slowly eats them up from within outward, till nothing at all is left of them but skin, scales, and skeleton. They are repulsive eel-shaped creatures, blind, soft, and slimy; their mouth consists of a hideous rasping sucker; and they pour out from the glands on their sides a copious mucus, which makes them as disagreeable to handle as they are unsightly to look at. Mackerel and cod are the hag's principal victims; but often the fisherman draws up a hag-eaten haddock on the end of his line, of which not a wrack remains but the hollow shell or bare outer simulacrum. As many as twenty of these disgusting parasites have sometimes been found within the body of a single cod-fish.

Yet see how carefully nature provides nevertheless for the due reproduction of even her most loathsome and revolting creations. The hag not only lays a small number of comparatively large and well-stored eggs, but also arranges for their success in life by supplying each with a bundle of threads at either end, every such thread terminating at last in a triple hook, like those with which we are so familiar in the case of adhesive fruits and seeds, like burrs or cleavers. By means of these barbed processes, the eggs attach themselves to living fishes; and the young borer, as soon as he emerges from his horny covering, makes his way at once into the body of his unconscious host, whom he proceeds by slow degrees to devour alive with relentless industry, from the intestines outward. This beautiful provision of nature enables the infant hag to start in life at once in very snug quarters upon a ready-made fish preserve. I understand, however, that cod-fish philosophers, actuated by purely personal and selfish conceptions of utility, refuse to admit the beauty or beneficence of this most satisfactory arrangement for the borer species.

Probably the best known of all fishes' eggs, however (with the solitary exception of the sturgeon's, commonly observed between brown bread and butter, under the name of caviare), are the queer leathery purse-shaped ova of the sharks, rays, skates, and dog-fishes. Everybody has picked them up on the seashore, where children know them as devil's purses and devil's wheelbarrows. Most of these queer eggs are oblong and quadrangular, with the four corners produced into a sort of handles or streamers, often ending in long tendrils, and useful for attaching them to corallines or seaweeds on the bed of the ocean. But it is worth noticing that in colour the egg-cases closely resemble the common wrack to which they are oftenest fastened; and as they wave up and down in the water with the dark mass around them, they must be almost indistinguishable from the wrack itself by the keenest-sighted of their enemies. This protective resemblance, coupled with the toughness and slipperiness of their leathery envelope or egg-shell, renders them almost perfectly secure from all evil-minded intruders. As a consequence, the dog-fish lay but very few eggs each season, and those few, large and well provided with nutriment for their spotted offspring. It is these purses, and those of the thornback and the edible skate, that we oftenest pick up on the English coast. The larger oceanic sharks are mostly viviparous.

In some few cases, indeed, among the shark and ray family, the mechanism for protection goes a step or two further than in these simple kinds. That well-known frequenter of Australian harbours, the Port Jackson shark, lays a pear-shaped egg, with a sort of spiral staircase of leathery ridges winding round it outside, Chinese pagoda wise, so that even if you bite it (I speak in the person of a predaceous fish) it eludes your teeth, and goes dodging off screw-fashion into the water beyond. There's no getting at this evasive body anywhere; when you think you have it, it wriggles away sideways, and refuses to give any hold for jaws or palate. In fact, a more slippery or guileful egg was never yet devised by nature's unconscious ingenuity. Then, again, the Antarctic chimæra (so called from its very unprepossessing personal appearance) relies rather upon pure deception than upon mechanical means for the security of its eggs. The shell or case in this instance is prolonged at the edge into a kind of broad wing on either side, so that it exactly resembles one of the large flat leaves of the Antarctic fucus in whose midst it lurks. It forms the high-water mark, I fancy, of protective resemblance amongst eggs, for not only is the margin leaf-like in shape, but it is even gracefully waved and fringed with floating hairs, as is the fashion with the expanded fronds of so many among the gigantic far-southern sea-weeds.

A most curious and interesting set of phenomena are those which often occur when a group of fishes, once marine, take by practice to inhabiting freshwater rivers; or, vice-versâ, when a freshwater kind, moved by an aspiration for more expansive surroundings, takes up its residence in the sea as a naturalised marine. Whenever such a change of address happens, it usually follows that the young fry cannot stand the conditions of the new home to which their ancestors were unaccustomed, we all know the ingrained conservatism of children, and so the parents are obliged once a year to undertake a pilgrimage to their original dwelling-place for the breeding season.

Extreme cases of terrestrial animals, once aquatic in habits, throw a flood of lurid light (as the newspapers say) upon the reason why this should be so. For example, frogs and toads develop from tadpoles, which in all essentials are true gill-breathing fish. It is, therefore, obvious that they cannot lay their eggs on dry land, where the tadpoles would be unable to find anything to breathe; so that even the driest and most tree-haunting toads must needs repair to the water once a year to deposit their spawn in its native surroundings. Once more, crabs pass their earlier larval stages as free-swimming crustaceans, somewhat shrimp-like in appearance, and as agile as fleas: it is only by gradual metamorphosis that they acquire their legs and claws and heavy pedestrian habits. Now there are certain kinds of crab, like the West Indian land-crabs (those dainty morsels whose image every epicure who has visited the Antilles still enshrines with regret in a warm corner of his heart), which have taken in adult life to walking bodily on shore, and visiting the summits of the highest mountains, like the fish of Deucalion's deluge in Horace. But once a year, as the land-crabs bask in the sun on St. Catherine's Peak or the Fern Walk, a strange instinctive longing comes over them automatically to return for a while to their native element; and, obedient to that inner monitor of their race, down they march in thousands, velut agmine facto, to lay their eggs at their leisure in Port Royal harbour. On the way, the negroes catch them, all full of rich coral, waiting to be spawned; and Chloe or Dinah, serves them up hot, with breadcrumbs, in their own red shells, neatly nestling between the folds of a nice white napkin. The rest run away, and deposit their eggs in the sea, where the young hatch out, and pass their larval stage once more as free and active little swimming crustaceans.

Well, crabs, I need hardly explain in this age of enlightenment, are not fish; but their actions help to throw a side-light on the migratory instinct in salmon, eels, and so many other true fish which have changed with time their aboriginal habits. The salmon himself, for instance, is by descent a trout, and in the parr stage he is even now almost indistinguishable from many kinds of river-trout that never migrate seaward at all. But at some remote period, the ancestors of the true salmon took to going down to the great deep in search of food, and being large and active fish, found much more to eat in the salt water than ever they had discovered in their native streams. So they settled permanently in their new home, as far as their own lives went at least; though they found the tender young could not stand the brine that did no harm to the tougher constitutions of the elders. No doubt the change was made gradually, a bit at a time, through the brackish water, the species getting further and further seaward down bays and estuaries with successive generations, but always returning to spawn in its native river, as all well-behaved salmon do to the present moment. At last, the habit hardened into an organic instinct, and nowadays the young salmon hatch out like their fathers as parr in fresh water, then go to the sea in the grilse stage and grow enormously, and finally return as full-grown salmon to spawn and breed in their particular birthplace.

Exactly the opposite fate has happened to the eels. The salmonoids as a family are freshwater fish, and by far the greater number of kinds, trout, char, whitefish, grayling, pollan, vendace, gwyniad, and so forth, are inhabitants of lakes, steams, ponds, and rivers, only a very small number having taken permanently or temporarily to a marine residence. But the eels, as a family, are a saltwater group, most of their allies, like the congers and muraenas, being exclusively confined to the sea, and only a very small number of aberrant types having ever taken to invading inland waters. If the life-history of the salmon, however, has given rise to as much controversy as the Mar peerage, the life-history of the eel is a complete mystery. To begin with, nobody has ever so much as distinguished between male and female eels; except microscopically, eels have never been seen in the act of spawning, nor observed anywhere with mature eggs. The ova themselves are wholly unknown: the mode of their production is a dead secret. All we know is this: that eels never reproduce in fresh water; that a certain number of adults descend the rivers to the sea, irregularly, during the winter months; and that some of these must presumably spawn with the utmost circumspection in brackish water or in the deep sea, for in the course of the summer myriads of young eels, commonly called grigs, and proverbial for their merriment, ascend the rivers in enormous bodies, and enter every smaller or larger tributary.

If we know little about the paternity and maternity of eels, we know a great deal about their childhood and youth, or, to speak more eelishly, their grigginess and elverhood. The young grigs, when they do make their appearance, leave us in no doubt at all about their presence or their reality. They wriggle up weirs, walls, and floodgates; they force there way bodily through chinks and apertures; they find out every drain, pipe, or conduit in a given plane rectilinear figure; and when all other spots have been fully occupied, they take to dry land, like veritable snakes, and cut straight across country for the nearest lake, pond, or ornamental waters.

These swarms or migrations are known to farmers as eel-fairs; but the word ought more properly to be written eel-fares, as the eels then fare or travel up the streams to their permanent quarters. A great many eels, however, never migrate seaward at all, and never seem to attain to years of sexual maturity. They merely bury themselves under stones in winter, and live and die as celibates in their inland retreats. So very terrestrial do they become, indeed, that eels have been taken with rats or field-mice undigested in their stomachs.

The sturgeon is another more or less migratory fish, originally (like the salmon) of freshwater habits, but now partially marine, which ascends its parent stream for spawning during the summer season. Incredible quantities are caught for caviare in the great Russian rivers. At one point on the Volga, a hundred thousand people collect in spring for the fishery, and work by relays, day and night continuously, as long as the sturgeons are going up stream. On some of the tributaries, when fishing is intermitted for a single day, the sturgeons have been known to completely fill a river 360 feet wide, so that the backs of the uppermost fish were pushed out of the water. (I take this statement, not from the 'Arabian Nights,' as the scoffer might imagine, but from that most respectable authority, Professor Seeley.) Still, in spite of the enormous quantity killed, there is no danger of any falling off in the supply for the future, for every fish lays from two to three million eggs, each of which, as caviare eaters well know, is quite big enough to be distinctly seen with the naked eye in the finished product. The best caviare is simply bottled exactly as found, with the addition merely of a little salt. No man of taste can pretend to like the nasty sun-dried sort, in which the individual eggs are reduced to a kind of black pulp, and pressed hard with the feet into doubtful barrels.

In conclusion, let me add one word of warning as to certain popular errors about the young fry of sundry well-known species. Nothing is more common than to hear it asserted that sprats are only immature herring. This is a complete mistake. Believe it not. Sprats are a very distinct species of the herring genus, and they never grow much bigger than when they appear, brochés, at table. The largest adult sprat measures only six inches, while full-grown herring may attain as much as fifteen. Moreover, herring have teeth on the palate, always wanting in sprats, by which means the species may be readily distinguished at all ages. When in doubt, therefore, do not play trumps, but examine the palate. On the other hand, whitebait, long supposed to be a distinct species, has now been proved by Dr. Günther, the greatest of ichthyologists, to consist chiefly of the fry or young of herring. To complete our discomfiture, the same eminent authority has also shown that the pilchard and the sardine, which we thought so unlike, are one and the same fish, called by different names according as he is caught off the Cornish coast or in Breton, Portuguese, or Mediterranean waters. Such aliases are by no means uncommon among his class. To say the plain truth, fish are the most variable and ill-defined of animals; they differ so much in different habitats, so many hybrids occur between them, and varieties merge so readily by imperceptible stages into one another, that only an expert can decide in doubtful cases, and every expert carefully reverses the last man's opinion. Let us at least be thankful that whitebait by any other name would eat as nice; that science has not a single whisper to breathe against their connection with lemon; and that whether they are really the young of Clupea harengus or not, the supply at Billingsgate shows no symptom of falling short of the demand.


## AN ENGLISH SHIRE

For the reasons which have determined the existence of Sussex as a county of England, and which have given it the exact boundaries that it now possesses, we must go back to the remote geological history of the secondary ages. Its limits and its very existence as a separate shire were predetermined for it by the shape and consistence of the mud or sand which gathered at the bottom of the great Wealden lake, or filled up the hollows of the old inland cretaceous sea. Paradoxical as it sounds to say so, the Celtic kingdom of the Regni, the South Saxon principality of Ælle the Bretwalda, the modern English county of Sussex, have all had their destinies moulded by the geological conformation of the rock upon which they repose. Where human annals see only the handicraft and interaction of human beings, Euskarian and Aryan, Celt and Roman, Englishman and Norman, a closer scrutiny of history may perhaps see the working of still deeper elements, chalk and clay, volcanic upheaval and glacial denudation, barren upland and forest-clad plain. The value and importance of these underlying facts in the comprehension of history has, I believe, been very generally overlooked; and I propose accordingly here to take the single county of Sussex in detail, in order to show that when the geological and geographical factors of the problem are given, all the rest follows as a matter of course. By such detailed treatment alone can one hope to establish the truth of the general principle that human history is at bottom a result of geographical conditions, acting upon the fundamentally identical constitution of man.

In a certain sense, it is quite clear that human life depends mainly upon soil and conformation, to an extent that nobody denies. You cannot have a dense population in Sahara; and you can hardly fail to have one in the fruitful valley of the Nile. The growth of towns in one district rather than another must be governed largely by the existence of rivers or harbours, of coal or metals, of agricultural lowlands or defensible heights. Glasgow could not spring up in inland Leicestershire, nor Manchester in coalless Norfolk. Insular England must naturally be the greatest shipping country in Europe; while no large foreign trade is possible in any Bohemia except Shakespeare's. So much everybody admits. But it seems to me that these underlying causes have coloured the entire local history of every district to an extent which few people adequately recognise, and that until such recognition becomes more general, our views of history must necessarily be very narrow. We must see not only that something depends upon geographical configuration, not even merely that a great deal depends upon it, but that everything depends upon it. We must unlearn our purely human history, and learn a history of interaction between nature and man instead.

From the great central boss of the chalk system in Salisbury Plain, two long cretaceous horns or projections run out to eastward towards the Channel and the German Sea. These two horns, separated by the deep valley of the Weald, are known as the North and South Downs respectively. The first great spur or ridge passes through the heart of Surrey, and then forms the backbone of Kent, expanding into a fan at its eastward extremity, where it topples over abruptly into the sea in the sheer bluffs which sweep round in a huge arc from the North Foreland in the Isle of Thanet, to Shakespeare's Cliff at Dover. The second or southernmost range, that of the South Downs, parts company from the main boss in Hampshire, and runs eastward in a narrower but bolder line, till the Channel cuts short its progress in the water-worn precipice of Beachy Head. Between these two ranges of Downs lies the low forest region of the Weald, and between the South Downs and the sea stretches a long but very narrow strip of lowland, beginning at Chichester, and ending where the chalk cliffs first meet the shore beside the new Aquarium and Chain Pier at Brighton. Thus the whole of Sussex consists of three well-marked parallel belts: the low coast-line on the south-west, the high chalk Downs in the centre, and the Weald district on the north and north-west. As these three belts determine the whole history and very existence of Sussex as an English shire, I shall make no apology for treating their origin here in some rapid detail.

The oldest geological formation with which we have to deal in Sussex (to any considerable extent) is the Wealden: so that our inquiry need not go any farther back in the history of the world than the later secondary ages. Before that time, and for long æons afterward, the portion of the earth's crust which now forms Sussex had probably never emerged from the ocean. Britain was then wholly represented by the primary regions of Wales, Scotland, and Cornwall, forming a small archipelago or group of rocky islands separated at some distance by a wide passage from the nucleus of the young European continent. But by the Wealden period, the English Channel and the Eastern half of England had been considerably elevated above the level of the sea. Great rivers and lakes existed in this new continental region, much like those which now exist in Sweden, Northern Russia, and Canada; and the deposits of sand or mud formed at their bottoms or in their estuaries compose the chief part of the Wealden formation in England. Without going fully into this question (somewhat complicated by frequent changes of level), it will suffice for our present purpose to say that the Wealden consists, in the main, of two great divisions, which form, so to speak, the floor, or lowest story, of the Sussex formations. The first or bottom division is chiefly composed of a rather soft and friable sandstone, which runs through the whole Forest Ridges, and crops out in the grey cliffs of Hastings and Fairlight. The second or upper division is chiefly composed of a thick greasy clay, which forms the soil in the greater part of the Weald, and glides unobtrusively under the sea in the flat shore on either side of Hastings, giving rise to the lowlands of Pevensey Bay and the Romney Marshes. Why the sandstone, which is really the bottom layer, should appear higher than the clay in these places, we shall see a little later.

After the deposition of the gritty or muddy Wealden beds in the lake and embouchure of the old continental river, there came a second period of considerable depression, during which the whole of south-eastern England was once more covered by a shallow sea. This sea ran, like an early northern Mediterranean, right across the face of Central Europe; and on its bottom was deposited the soft ooze of globigerina shells and siliceous sponge skeletons which has now hardened into chalk and flint. A great cretaceous sheet thus overlay the Wealden beds and the whole face of Sussex to a depth of at least 600 feet; and if it had not been afterwards worn off in places, as the nursery rhyme says of old Pillicock, it would be there still. I need hardly say that the chalk is yet en évidence along the whole range of South Downs, and forms the tall white cliffs between Brighton and Beachy Head.

Finally, during the Tertiary period, another layer of London clay and other soft deposits was spread over the top of the chalk, certainly on the strip between the South Downs and the sea, and probably over the whole district between the Channel and the Thames valley: though in this case, later denudation has proceeded so far that very few traces of the Tertiary formations are preserved anywhere except in the greater hollows.

Such being the original disposition of the strata which compose Sussex, we have next to ask, What are the causes which have produced its existing configuration? If the whole mass had merely been uplifted straight out of the sea, we ought now to find the whole country a flat and level table-land, covered over its entire surface with a uniform coat of Tertiary deposits. On digging or boring below these, we ought to come upon the chalk, and below the chalk again, with its cretaceous congeners the greensand or the gault, we ought to meet the Weald clay and the Hastings sand. Wherever a seaward cliff exhibited a section for our observation, we ought to find these same strata all exposed in regular order, the sandstone at the bottom, the clay above it, the broad belt of chalk halfway up, and the Tertiary muds and rubbles at the top. But in the county as we actually find it, we get a very different state of things. Here, the surface at sea-level is composed of London clay; there, a great mound of chalk rises into a swelling down; and yonder, once more, a steep escarpment leads us down into a broad lowland of the Weald. The causes which have led to this arrangement of surface and conformation must now be considered with necessary brevity.

The North and South Downs, with all the country between them, form part of a great fold or outward bulge of the strata above enumerated, having its centre about the middle line of the Forest Ridge. Imagine these strata bent or pushed upward by an internal upheaving force acting along that line, and you will get a rough picture of the original circumstances which have led to the existing arrangement of the county. You would then have, instead of a flat table-land, as supposed above, a great curved mountain slope, with its centre on top of the Forest Ridge. This gentle slope would rise from the sea between Chichester and a point south of Beachy, would swell slowly upward till it reached a height of two or three thousand feet at the Surrey border, and would fall again gradually towards the Thames valley at London. On the southern side of the Downs this is pretty much what we now get, the Tertiary strata being preserved in the district near Chichester; though farther east, around Newhaven and Beachy Head, the sea has encroached upon the chalk so as to cut out the great white cliffs which bound the view everywhere along the shore from Brighton to Eastbourne. In the central portion of the boss, however, almost all the highest elevated part has been denuded by ice or water action. Between the North and South Downs, where we ought to find the mountain ridge, we find instead the valley of the Weald. Here the chalk has been quite worn away, giving rise to the steep escarpment on the northern side of the South Downs, seen from the Devil's Dyke, so that at the foot of the sudden descent we get the Weald clay exposed; while in the very centre of the upheaved tract the clay itself has been cut through, and the Hastings sand appears upon the surface. Moreover, the sand, being upraised by the central force, stands higher than the clay on either side, which forms the trough of the Weald; and thus the forest ridge, which abuts upon the sea in the cliffs of Hastings Castle, seems to lie above the clay, under which, however, it really glides on either side. I need hardly add that this rough diagrammatic description is only meant as a general indication of the facts, and that it considerably simplifies the real geological changes probably involved in the sculpture of Sussex. Nevertheless, I believe it pretty accurately represents the main formative points in the ante-human history of the county.

So much by way of preface or introduction. These facts of structure form the data for the reconstruction of the Sussex annals during the human period. Upon them as framework all the subsequent development of the county hangs. And first let us observe how, before the advent of man upon the scene, the shire was already strictly demarcated by its natural boundaries. Along the coast, between Chichester Harbour and Brighton, stretched a long, narrow, level strip of clay and alluvium, suitable for the dwelling-place of an agricultural people. Back of this coastwise belt lay the bare rounded range of the South Downs, good grazing land for sheep, but naturally incapable of cultivation. Two rivers, however, flowed in deep valleys through the Downs, and their basins, with the outlying combes and glens, were also the predestined seats of agricultural communities. The one was the Ouse, passing through the fertile country around Lewes, and falling at last into the English Channel at Seaford, not as now at Newhaven; the other was the Cuckmere river, which has cut itself a deep glen in the chalk hills just beneath the high cliffs of Beachy Head. Beyond the Downs again, to the north, the country descended abruptly to the deep trough of the Weald, whose cold and sticky clays or porous sandstones are never of any use for purposes of tillage. Hence, as its very name tells us, the Weald has always been a wild and wood-clad region. The Romans knew it as the Silva Anderida, or forest of Pevensey; the early English as the Andredesweald. Both names are derived from a Celtic root signifying 'The Uninhabited.' Even in our own day, a large part of this tract is covered by the woodlands of Tolgate Forest, St. Leonard's Forest, and Ashdown Forest; while the remainder is only very scantily laid down in pasture-land or hop-fields, with a considerable sprinkling of copses, woods, commons, and parks. From its very nature, indeed, the Weald can never be anything else, in its greater portion, than a wild, uncultivated, and wooded region.

Let us note, too, how the really habitable strip of Sussex, from the point of view of an early people, was quite naturally cut off from all other parts of England by obvious limits. This habitable strip consists, of course, of the coastwise belt from Brighton to the Hampshire border (which belt I shall henceforward take the liberty of designating as Sussex Proper), together with the seaward valleys and combes of the South Downs. To the west, the great tidal flats and swamps about Hayling Island cut off Sussex from Hampshire; and before drainage and reclamation had done their work, these marshy districts must have formed a most impassable frontier. From this point, the great woodland region of the Weald, thickly covered with primæval forest, and tenanted by wolves, bears, wild boars, and red deer, swept round in a long curve from the swamps at Bosham and Havant to the corresponding swamps of the opposite end at Pevensey and Hurstmonceux. The belt of savage wooded country, thick with the lairs of wild beasts, which thus ringed round the greater part of the county, shut off the coastwise strip at once from all possibility of communication with the rest of England. So Sussex Proper and the combes of the Downs were naturally predestined to form a single Celtic kingdom, a single Saxon principality, and a single English shire.

It will be observed that this description leaves wholly out of consideration the strip of country about Hastings, Rye, and Winchelsea. It does so intentionally. That strip of country does not belong to Sussex in the same intimate and strictly necessary manner as the rest of the county. It probably once formed the seat of a small independent community by itself; and though there were good and obvious reasons why it should become finally united to Sussex rather than to Kent, it may be regarded as to some extent a debateable island between them. For an island it practically was in early times. At Pevensey Bay the Weald ran down into the sea by a series of swamps and bogs still artificially drained by dykes and sluices. On the other side, the Romney marshes formed a similar though wider stretch of tidal flats, reclaimed and drained at a far later period, partly through the agency of the long shingle bank thrown up round the low modern spit of Dungeness. Between them, the Hastings cliffs rose high above marsh and sea. In their rear, the Weald forest covered the ridge; so that the Hastings district (still a separate rape or division of the county) formed a sort of smaller Sussex, divided, like the larger one, from all the rest of England by a semicircular belt of marsh, forest, and marsh once more. These are the main elements out of which the history of the county is made up.

How far such conditions may have acted upon the very earliest human inhabitants of Sussex, the palæolithic savages of the drift, before the last Glacial epoch, it is impossible to say, because we know that many of them did not then exist, and that the present configuration of the county is largely due to subsequent agencies. Britain was then united to the continent by a broad belt of land, filling up the bed of the English Channel, and it possessed a climate wholly different from that of the present day; while the position of the drift and the river gravels shows that the sculpture of the surface was then in many respects unlike the existing distribution of hill and valley. We must confine ourselves, therefore, to the later or recent period (subsequent to the last glaciation of Britain), during which man has employed implements of polished stone, of bronze, and of iron.

The Euskarian neolithic population of Britain, a dark white race, like the modern Basques, had settlements in Sussex, at least in the coast district between the Downs and the sea. Here they could obtain in abundance the flints for the manufacture of their polished stone hatchets; while on the alluvial lowlands of Selsea and Shoreham they could grow those cereals upon which they largely depended for their daily bread. Neolithic monuments, indeed, are common along the range of the South Downs, as they are also on the main mass of the chalk in Salisbury Plain; and at Cissbury Hill, near Worthing, we have remains of one of the largest neolithic camp refuges in Britain. The evidence of tumuli and weapons goes to show that the Euskarian people of Sussex occupied the coast belt and the combes of the Downs from the Chichester marshland to Pevensey, but that they did not spread at all into the Weald. In fact, it is most probable that at this early period Sussex was divided into several little tribes or chieftainships, each of which had its own clearing in the lowland cut laboriously out of the forest by the aid of its stone axes; while in the centre stood the compact village of wooden huts, surrounded by a stockade, and girt without by the small cultivated plots of the villagers. On the Downs above rose the camp or refuge of the tribe, an earthwork rudely constructed in accordance with the natural lines of the hills, to which the whole body of people, with their women, children, and cattle, retreated in case of hostile invasion from the villagers on either side. It is not likely that any foreigners from beyond the great forest belt of the Weald would ever come on the war-trail across that dangerous and trackless wilderness; and it is probable, therefore, that the camps or refuges were constructed as places of retreat for the tribes against their immediate neighbours, rather than against alien intruders from without. Hence we may reasonably conclude, as indeed is natural at such an early stage of civilisation, that the whole district was not yet consolidated under a single rule, but that each village still remained independent, and liable to be engaged in hostilities with all others. Even if extended chieftainships over several villages had already been set up, as is perhaps implied by the great tumuli of chiefs and the size of the camps in some parts of Britain, we must suppose them to have been confined for the most part to a single river valley. If so, there may have been petty Euskarian principalities, rude supremacies or chieftainships like those of South Africa, in the Chichester lowlands, in the dale of Arun, in the valleys of the Adur, the Ouse, and the Cuckmere River, and perhaps, too, in the insulated Hastings region, between the Pevensey levels and the Romney marsh. These principalities would then roughly coincide with the modern rapes of Chichester, Arundel, Bramber, Lewes, Pevensey, and Hastings. Each would possess its own group of villages, and tilled lowland, its own boundary of forest, and its own camp of refuge on the hill-tops. Cissbury almost undoubtedly formed such a camp for the fertile valley of the Adur and the coast strip from Worthing to Brighton. On its summit has been discovered an actual manufactory of stone implements from the copious material supplied by the flint veins in the chalk of which it is composed.

Such a society, left to itself in Sussex, could never have got much further than this. It could not discover or use metals, when it had no metal in its soil except the small quantity of iron to be found in the then inaccessible Weald. It had no copper and no tin, and therefore it could not manufacture bronze. But the geographical position of England generally, within sight of the European continent, made it certain that if ever anywhere else bronze should come to be used, the bronze-weaponed people must ultimately cross over and subjugate the stone-weaponed aborigines of the island. Moreover, bronze was certain to be first hit upon in those countries where tin and copper were most easily workable, that is to say, in Asia. From Asia, the secret of its manufacture spread to the outlying peninsula of Europe, where it was quickly adopted by the Aryan Celts, who had already invaded the outlying continent, armed only with weapons of stone. As soon as they had learnt the use of bronze, certain great changes and improvements followed naturally, amongst others, an immense advance in the art of boat-building. The Celts of the bronze age soon constructed vessels which enabled them to cross the narrow seas and invade Britain. Their superior weapons gave them at once an enormous advantage over the Euskarian natives, armed only with their polished flint hatchets, and before long they overran the whole island, save only the recesses of Wales and the north of Scotland. From that moment, the bronze age of Britain set in, say some 1,000 or 1,500 years before the Christian era.

The Celts, however, did not exterminate the whole Euskarian people; they were too few in number and too far advanced in civilisation for such a course. They knew it was better to make them slaves than to destroy them: for the Celts had just reached, but had not yet got beyond, the slave-making stage of culture. To this day, people of mixed Euskarian parentage, and marked by the long skull, dark complexion, and black eyes of the Euskarian type, form a large proportion of the English peasantry; and they are found even in Sussex, which subsequently suffered more than most other parts of Britain from the destructive deluge of Teutonic barbarism in the fifth century. But though the Celts did not exterminate the Euskarians, they completely Celticised them, just as the Teuton is now Teutonising the old population of Scotland, Wales, and Ireland. In South Wales and elsewhere, indeed, the aborigines retained their own language and institutions, as Silures and so forth; but in the conquered districts of southern and eastern Britain they learned the tongue of their masters, and came to be counted as Celtic serfs. Thus, at the time when Britain comes forth into the full historic glare of Roman civilisation, we find the country inhabited by a Celtic aristocracy of Aryan type, round-headed, fair-haired, and blue-eyed; together-with a plebs of Celticised Euskarian or half-caste serfs, retaining, as they still retain, the long skulls and dark complexions of their aboriginal ancestors. This was the ethnical composition of the Sussex population at the date of the first Roman invasions.

Under the bronze-weaponed Celts, a very different type of civilisation became possible. In the first place a more extended chieftainship resulted from the improved weapons and consequent military power; and all Britain (at least, towards the close of the Celtic domination) became amalgamated into considerable kingdoms, some of which seem to have spread over several modern shires. Sussex, however, enclosed by its barrier of forest, would naturally remain a single little principality of itself, held, at least in later times, by a tribe known to the Romans as Regni. Traces of Celtic occupation are mainly confined to the Downs and the seaward slope of Sussex Proper; in the broad expanse of the Weald, they are few and far between. The Celts occupied the fertile valleys and alluvial slopes, cut down the woods by the river sides and on the plains, and built their larger and more regular camps of refuge upon the Downs, for protection against the kindred Cantii beyond the Weald, or the more distantly-related Belgæ across the Hayling tidal flats. Of these hill-forts, Hollingbury Castle, near Brighton, may be taken as a typical example. Bronze weapons and other implements of the bronze age are found in great numbers about Lewes in particular (where the isolated height, now crowned by the Norman Castle, must always have commanded the fertile river vale of the Ouse), as well as at Chichester, Bognor, and elsewhere. But the great forest, inhabited by savage beasts and still more terrible fiends, proved a barrier to their northward extension. Even if they had cleared the land, they could not have cultivated it with their existing methods; and so it is only in a few spots near the upper river valleys that we find any traces of outlying Celtic hamlets in the wilderness of the Weald. Some kind of trade, however, must have existed between the Regni and the other tribes of Britain, in order to supply them with the bronze, whose component elements Sussex does not possess. Woolsonbury, Westburton Hill, Clayton Hill, Wilmington, Hangleton Down, Plumpton Plain, and many other places along the coast have yielded large numbers of bronze implements; while the occurrence of the raw metal in lumps, together with the finished weapons, at Worthing and Beachy Head, as well the discovery of a mould for a socketed celt at Wilmington, shows that the actual foundry work was performed in Sussex itself. A beautiful torque from Hollingbury Castle attests the workmanship of the Sussex founders. No doubt the tin was imported from Cornwall, while the copper was probably brought over from the continent. Glass beads, doubtless of Southern (perhaps Egyptian) manufacture, have also been found in Sussex, with implements of the bronze age.

In the polished stone age, the county had been self-supporting, because of its possession of flint. In the bronze age it was dependent upon other places, through its non-possession of copper or tin. During the former period it may have exported weapons from Cissbury; during the latter, it must have imported the material of weapons from Cornwall and Gaul.

Before the Romans came, the Celts of Britain had learned the use of iron. Whether they ever worked the iron of the Weald, however, is uncertain. But as the ores lie near the surface, as wood (to be made into charcoal) for the smelting was abundant, and as these two facts caused the Weald iron to be extensively employed in later times, it is probable that small clearings would be made in the most accessible spots, and that rude ironworks would be established.

The same geographical causes which made Britain part of the Roman world naturally affected Sussex, as one of its component portions. Even under the Empire, however, the county remained singularly separate. The Romans built two strong fortresses at Anderida and Regnum, Pevensey and Chichester, to guard the two Gwents or lowland plains, where the shore shelves slowly to seaward; and they ran one of their great roads across the coastwise tract, from Dover to the Portus Magnus (now Porchester), near Portsmouth; but they left Sussex otherwise very much to its own devices. We know that the Regni were still permitted to keep their native chief, who probably exercised over his tribesmen somewhat the same subordinate authority which a Rájput raja now exercises under the British government. Here, again, we see the natural result of the isolation of Sussex. The Romans ruled directly in the open plains of the Yorkshire Ouse and the Thames, as we ourselves rule in the Bengal Delta, the Doáb, and the Punjáb; but they left a measure of independence to the native princes of south Wales, of Sussex, and of Cornwall, as we ourselves do to the native rulers in the deserts of Rájputana, the inaccessible mountains of Nipal, and the aboriginal hill districts of Central India.

When the Roman power began to decay, the outlying possessions were the first to be given up. The Romans had enslaved and demoralised the provincial population; and when they were gone, the great farms tilled by slave labour under the direction of Roman mortgagee-proprietors lay open to the attacks of fresh and warlike barbarians from beyond the sea. How early the fertile east coasts of Yorkshire, Lincolnshire, and East Anglia may have fallen a prey to the Teutonic pirates we cannot say. The wretched legends, indeed, retailed to us by Gildas, Bæda, and the English Chronicle, would have us believe that they were colonised at a later period; but as they lay directly in the path of the marauders from Sleswick, as they were certainly Teutonised very thoroughly, and as no real records survive, we may well take it for granted that the long-boats of the English, sailing down with the prevalent north-east winds from the wicks of Denmark, came first to shore on these fertile coasts. After they had been conquered and colonised, the Saxon and Jutish freebooters began to look for settlements, on their part, farther south. One horde, led, as the legend veraciously assures us, by Hengest and Horsa, landed in Thanet; another, composed entirely of Saxons, and under the command of a certain dubious Ælle, came to shore on the spit of Selsea. It was from this last body that the county took its newer name of Suth-Seaxe, Suth Sexe, or Sussex. Let us first frankly narrate the legend, and then see how far it may fairly be rationalised.

In 477, says the English Chronicle, written down, it must be remembered, from traditional sources, four centuries later, at the court of Alfred the West Saxon, in 477, Ælle and his three sons, Cymen, Wlencing, and Cissa, came to Britain in three ships, and landed at the stow that is cleped Cymenes-ora. There that ilk day they slew many Welshmen, and the rest they drave into the wood hight Andredes-leah. In 485, Ælle, fighting the Welsh near Mearcredes Burn, slew many, and the rest he put to flight. In 491, Ælle, with his son Cissa, beset Andredes-ceaster, and slew all that therein were, nor was there after one Welshman left. Such is the whole story, as told in the bald and simple entries of the West Saxon annalist, A more dubious tradition further states that Ælle was also Bretwalda, or overlord, of all the Teutonic tribes in Britain.

And now let us see what we can make of this wholly unhistorical and legendary tale. Whether there ever was a South Saxon king named Ælle we cannot say; but that the earliest English pirate fleet on this coast should have landed near Selsea is likely enough. The marauders would not land near the Romney marshes or the Pevensey flats, where the great fortresses of Lymne and Anderida would block their passage; and they could not beach their keels easily anywhere along the cliff-girt coast between Beachy Head and Brighton; so they would naturally sail along past the marshland and the chalk cliffs till they reached the open champaign shore near Chichester. Cymenes-ora, where they are said to have landed, is now Keynor on the Bill of Selsea; and Selsea itself, as its name (correctly Selsey) clearly shows us, was then an island in the tidal flats. This was just the sort of place which the English pirates loved, for all tradition represents their first settlements as effected on isolated spots like Thanet, Hurst Castle, Holderness, and Bamborough. Thence they would march upon Regnum, the square Roman town at the harbour head, and reduce it by storm, garrisoned as it doubtless was by a handful of semi-Romanised Welshmen or Britons. The town took the English name of Cissanceaster, or Chichester. Moreover, all around the Chichester district, we still find a group of English clan villages, with the characteristic patronymic termination ing. Such are East and West Wittering, Donnington, Funtington, Didling, and others. It is vraisemblable enough that the little strip of very low coast between Hayling Island and the Arun may have been the first original South Saxon colony. Nor is it by any means impossible that the names of Keynor and Chichester Cymenes-ora and Cissanceaster, may still enshrine the memory of two among the old South Saxon freebooters.

The tradition of a battle at Mearcredes Burn, when the Welsh were again defeated, may refer to an advance by which, a few years later, the South Saxon pirates pushed eastward along the coast, and occupied the strip of shore as far as Brighton, together with the fertile valley of the Lewes Ouse. In the first-named district we find a large group of English Clan villages, including Patching, Poling, Angmering, Goring, Worthing, Tarring, Washington, Lullington, Blatchingden, Ovingdean, Rottingdean, and many others. Amongst them is one which has clearly given rise to the name of Ælle's third son, and that is Lancing. Unfortunately for the legend, we must decide that this was really the settlement of an English clan of Lancingas, as Washington was the tun or enclosure of the Weasingas, and Beddingham was the ham or home of the Beddingas. Around Lewes, in like manner, we find Tarring, Malling, Piddinghoe, Bletchington, and others; while in the valley just to the east we have ten or eleven such names as Lullington, Wilmington, Folkington, and Littlington. These districts, I imagine, represent the second advance of the English conquerors.

Finally, fourteen years after the first landing, the South Saxons crossed the Downs and attacked Anderida. The Roman walls of the great fortress were thick and strong, as their remains, built over by the Norman Castle, still show; but they were defended by half-trained Welsh, who could not withstand the English onset. With the fall of Anderida, the native power was broken for ever, 'nor was there after one Welshman left.' The English tribe of the Hastingas settled at Hastings; and the South Saxons were now supreme from marsh to marsh.

But did they really exterminate the native Celt-Euskarian population? I venture to say, no. Some no doubt, especially the men, they slew; but the women and children, as even Mr. Freeman admits, were probably spared in large numbers. Even of the men, many doubtless became slaves to the Saxon lords; while others maintained themselves in isolated bands in the Weald. To this day the Euskarian type of humanity is not uncommon among the Sussex peasantry, and all the rivers still bear the Celtic names of Arun, Adur, Ouse, and Calder. That there was 'no Welshmen left' is only another way of saying that the armed Welsh resistance ceased. The Romanised Britons became English churls and serfs, nay, the very name for a serf in ordinary conversation was Weala or Welshman. The population received a new element, the English Saxons, but it was not completely changed. The Weorthingas and Goringas simply became masters of the lands formerly held by Roman owners; and the cabins of their British serfs still clustered around the wooden hall of the English lords.

Nevertheless, Sussex is one of the most thoroughly Teutonised counties in England. The proportion of Saxon blood is very marked: light hair and blue eyes, together with the broad and short English skull, are common even among the peasantry. The number of English Clan names noticed by Mr. Kemble in the towns and villages of Sussex is 68 as against 60 in almost equally Teutonic Kent, 48 in Essex, 21 in largely Celtic Dorset, 6 in Cumberland, 2 in Cornwall, and none in Monmouth. The size and number of the hundreds into which the county is divided tells us much the same tale. Each hundred was originally a group of one hundred free English families, settled on the soil, and holding in check the native subject population of Anglicised Celt-Euskarian churls. Now, in Sussex we get 61 hundreds, and in Kent 61, as against 13 in Surrey beyond the Weald (where the clan names also sink to 18), and 8 in Hertfordshire. Or, to put it another way, which I borrow from Mr. Isaac Taylor, in Sussex there is one hundred to every 23 square miles; in Kent to every 24; in Dorset to every 30; in Surrey to every 58; in Herts to every 79; in Gloucester to every 97; in Derby to every 162; in Warwick to every 179; and in Lancashire to every 302. In other words, while in Kent, Sussex, and the east the free English inhabitants clustered thickly on the soil, with a relatively small servile population, in Mercia and the west the English population was much more sparsely scattered, with a relatively great servile population. So, as late as the time of Domesday, in Kent and Sussex the slaves mentioned in the great survey (only a small part, probably, of the total) numbered only 10 per cent. of the population, while in Devon and Cornwall they numbered 20 per cent., and in Gloucestershire 33 per cent.

These results are all inevitable. It is obvious that the first attacks must necessarily be made upon the east and south coasts, and that the inland districts and the west must only slowly be conquered afterward. Especially was it easy to found Teutonic kingdoms in the four isolated regions of Lincolnshire, East Anglia, Kent, and Sussex, each of which was cut off from the rest of England in early times by impassable fens, marshes, forests, or rivers. It was easy here to kill off the Welsh fighting population, to drive the remnants into the Fen Country or the Weald, to enslave the captives, the women, and the children, and to secure the Teutonic colony by a mark or border of woodland, swamp, or hill. On the other hand, Wessex, Northumbria, and Mercia, with a vague and ill-defined internal border, had harder work to fight their way in against a united Welsh resistance; and it was only very slowly that they pushed across the central watershed, to dismember the unconquered remnant of the Britons at last into the three isolated bodies of Damnonia (Cornwall and Devon), Wales Proper, and Strathclyde. This is probably why the earliest settlements were made in these isolated coast regions, and why the inward progress of the other colonies was so relatively slow.

The South Saxons, then, at first occupied the three fertile bits of the county, the coast belt of Sussex Proper, the Valley of the Ouse, and the isolated Hastings district, because these were the best adapted for their strictly agricultural life. In spite of the legend of Ælle, I do not suppose that they were all united from the first under a single principality. It seems far more probable that each little clan settlement was at first wholly independent; that afterwards three little chieftainships grew up in the three fertile strips, typified, perhaps, by the story of Ælle's three sons, and that the whole finally coalesced into a single kingdom of the South Saxons, which is the state in which we find the county in Bæda's time. As ever, its boundaries were marked out for it by nature, for the Weald remained as yet an almost unbroken forest; and the names of Selsea, Pevensey, Winchelsea, Romney, and many others, show by their common insular termination (found in all isles round the British coast, as in Sheppey, Walney, Bardsea, Anglesea, Fursey, Wallasey, and so forth) that the marshland was still wholly undrained, and that a few islands alone stood here and there as masses of dry land out of their desolate and watery expanse. The Hastings district, too, fell more naturally to Sussex than to Kent, because the marshes dividing it from the former were far less formidable than those which severed it from the latter. Most probably the South Saxons intentionally aided nature in cutting off their territory from all other parts of Britain; for every English kingdom loved to surround itself with a distinct mark or border of waste, as a defence against invasion from outside. The Romans had brought Sussex within the great network of their road system; but the South Saxons no doubt took special pains to cut off those parts of the roads which led across their own frontier. At any rate, it is quite clear that Sussex did not largely participate in the general life of the new England, and that intercourse with the rest of the world was extremely limited.

The South Saxon kings probably lived for the most part at Chichester, though no doubt they had hams, after the royal Teutonic fashion generally, in many other parts of their territory; and they moved about from one to the other, with their suite of thegns, eating up in each what food was provided by their serfs for their use, and then moving on to the next. The isolation of Sussex is strikingly shown by its long adherence to the primitive paganism. Missionaries from Rome, under the guidance of Augustine, converted Kent as early as 597. For Kent was the nearest kingdom to the continent; it contained the chief port of entry for continental travellers, Richborough, the Dover of those days, and its king, accustomed to continental connections, had married a Christian Frankish princess from Paris. Hence Kent was naturally the first Teutonic principality to receive the faith. Next came Northumbria, Lindsey, East Anglia, Wessex, and even inland Mercia. But Sussex still held out for Thor and Woden as late as 679, three-quarters of a century after the conversion of Kent, and twenty years after Mercia itself had given way to the new faith. Even when Sussex was finally converted, the manner in which the change took place was characteristic. It was not by missionaries from beyond the Weald in Kent or Surrey, nor from beyond the marsh in Wessex. An Irish monk, Bæda tells us, coming ashore on the open coast near Chichester, established a small monastery at Bosham, even then, no doubt, a royal ham, as we know it was under Harold, 'a place,' says the old historian significantly, 'girt round by sea and forest.' (It lies just on the mark between Wessex and the South Saxons.) Æthelwealh, the king, a curious name, for it means 'noble Welshman' (perhaps he was of mixed blood) had already been baptized in Mercia, and his wife was the daughter of a Christian ealdorman of the Worcester-men; but the rest of the principality was heathen. The Irish monk effected nothing; but shortly after Wilfrith, the fiery Bishop of York, on one of his usual flying visits to Rome, got shipwrecked off Selsea. With his accustomed vigour, he went ashore, and began a crusade in the heathen land. He was able at once to baptize the 'leaders and soldiers', that is to say, the free military English population; while his attendant priests, Eappa, Padda, Burghelm, and Oiddi (it is pleasant to preserve these little personal touches) proceeded to baptize the 'plebs'—that is to say, the servile Anglicised Celt-Euskarian substratum—up and down the country villages.

It was to Wilfrith, too, that Sussex owed her first cathedral. Æthelwealh made him a present of Selsea, 'a place surrounded by the sea on every side save one, where an isthmus about as broad as a stone's-throw connects it with the mainland,' and there the ardent bishop founded a regular monastery, in which he himself remained for five years. On the soil were 250 serfs, whom Wilfrith at once set free. After the death of Aldhelm, the West Saxon bishop, in 709, Sussex was made a separate bishopric, with its seat at Selsea; and it was not till after the Norman Conquest that the cathedral was removed to Chichester. It may be noted that all these arrangements were in strict accordance with early English custom. The kings generally gave their bishops a seat near their own chief town, as Cuthbert had his see at Lindisfarne, close to the royal Northumbrian capital of Bamborough; so that the proximity of Selsea to Chichester made it the most natural place for a bishopstool; and, again, it was usual to make over spots in the fens or marshes to the monks, who, by draining and cultivating them, performed a useful secular work. No traces now remain of old Selsea Cathedral, its site having long been swallowed up by incursions of the sea. Bæda has the ordinary number of miracles to record in connection with the monastery.

As time went on, however, the isolation of Sussex became less complete. Æthelwealh had got himself into complications with Wessex by accepting the sovereignty of the Isle of Wight and the Meonwaras about Southhampton from the hands of a Mercian conqueror. Perhaps Æthelwealh then repaired the old Roman roads which led from his own ham at Chichester to Portsmouth in Wessex, and broke down the mark, so as to connect his old and his new dominions with one another. At any rate, shortly after, Cædwalla, the West Saxon, an ætheling at large on the look-out for a kingdom, attacked him suddenly with his host of thegns from this unexpected quarter, killed the King himself, and harried the South Saxons from marsh to marsh. Two South Saxons thegns expelled him for a time, and made themselves masters of the country. But afterwards, Cædwalla, becoming King of the West Saxons, recovered Sussex once more, and handed it on to his successor, Ini. Hence the South Saxons had no bishopric of their own during this period, but were included in the see of the West Saxons at Winchester.

During the hundred years of the Mercian Supremacy, coincident, roughly speaking, with the eighth century, we hear little of Sussex; but it seems to have shaken off the yoke of Wessex, and to have been in subjection to the great Mercian over-lords alone. It had its own under-kings and its own bishops. Early in the ninth century, however, when Ecgberht the West Saxon succeeding in throwing off the Mercian yoke, the other Saxon States of South Britain willingly joined him against the Anglian oppressors. 'The men of Kent and Surrey, Sussex and Essex, gladly submitted to King Ecgberht.' When the royal house of the South Saxons died out, Sussex still retained a sort of separate existence within the West Saxon State, as Wales does in the England of our own day. Æthelwulf made his son under-king of Kent, Essex, Surrey, and Sussex; and so, during the troublous times of the Danish invasion, when all southern England became one in its resistance to the heathen, those old principalities gradually sank into the position of provinces or shires.

From the period of union with the general West Saxon Kingdom (which grew slowly into the Kingdom of England under Eadgar and Cnut), the markland of the Weald seems to have been gradually encroached upon from the south. Most of the names in that district are distinctly 'Anglo-Saxon' in type; by which I mean that they were imposed before the Norman Conquest, and belong to the stage of the language then in use. Even during the Roman period, settlements for iron-mining existed in the Weald, and these clearings would of course be occupied by the English colonists at a comparatively early time. Just at the foot of the Downs, too, on the north side, we find a few clan settlements on the edge of the Weald, which must date from the first period of English colonisation. Such are Poynings, Didling, Ditchling, Chillington, and Chiltington. Farther in, however, the clan names grow rarer; and where we find them they are not hams or tuns, regular communities of Saxon settlers, but they show, by their forestine terminations of hurst, ley, den, and field, that they were mere outlying shelters of hunters or swineherds in the trackless forest. Such are Billinghurst, Warminghurst, Itchingfield, and Ardingley. On the Cuckmere river, the villages in the combes bear names like Jevington and Lullington; but in the upper valley of the little stream, where it flows through the Weald, we find instead Chiddingley and Hellingley. Most of the Weald villages, however, bear still more woodland titles, Midhurst, Farnhurst, Nuthurst, Maplehurst, and Lamberhurst; Cuckfield, Mayfield, Rotherfield, Hartfield, Heathfield, and Wivelsfield; Crawley, Cowfold, Loxwood, Linchmere, and Marden. Hams and tuns, the sure signs of early English colonisation, are almost wholly lacking; in their place we get abundance of such names as Coneyhurst Common, Water Down Forest, Hayward's Heath, Milland Marsh, and Bell's Oak Green. To this day even, the greater part of the Weald is down in park, copse, heath, forest, common, or marshland. Throughout the whole expanse of the woodland region in Sussex, with the outlying portions in Kent, Surrey, and Hants, Mr. Isaac Taylor has collected no fewer than 299 local names with the significant forest terminations in hurst, den, ley, holt, and field. These facts show that, during the later 'Anglo-Saxon' period, the Weald was being slowly colonised in a few favourable spots. Its use as a mark was now gone, and it might be safely employed for the peaceful purposes of the archer and the swineherd. Names referring to pasture and the wild beasts are therefore common.

To the same time must doubtless be assigned the exact delimitation of the Sussex frontiers. During the early periods, the Kentings, the Suthrige, and the West Saxons would all extend on their side as far as the Weald, which would be treated as a sort of neutral zone. But when the Woodland itself began to be occupied, a demarcation would naturally be made between the neighbouring provinces. The boundary follows the most obvious course. It starts on the east from the old mouth of the Rother (now diverted to Rye New Harbour), known as the Kent Ditch, in what was then the central and most impassable part of the marshland. It runs along the Rother to its bifurcation, and then makes for the heaven-water-parting or dividing back of the Forest Ridge, beside two or three lesser streams. Then it passes along the crest of the ridge from Tunbridge Wells, past East Grinstead and Crawley, till it strikes the Hampshire border. There it follows the line between the two watersheds to the sea, which it reaches at Emsworth. There is, however, one long insulated spur of Hampshire running down from Haslemere to Graffham (in apparent defiance of geographical features), whose origin and meaning I do not understand.

With the Norman Conquest, the history of Sussex, and of England generally, for the most part ceases abruptly; all the rest is mere personal gossip about Prince Edward and the battle of Lewes, or about George IV. and the Brighton Pavilion. Not, of course, that there is not real national history here as elsewhere; but it is hard to disentangle from the puerile personalities of historians generally. Nevertheless, some brief attempt to reconstruct the main facts in the subsequent history of Sussex must still be undertaken. The part which Sussex bore passively in the actual Conquest is itself typical of the new relations. England was getting drawn into the general run of European civilisation, and the old isolation of Sussex was beginning to be broken down. Lying so near the Continent, Sussex was naturally the landing-place for an army coming from Normandy or Ponthieu. William's fleet came ashore on the low coast at Pevensey. Naturally he turned towards Hastings, whence a road now led through the Weald to London. On the tall cliffs he threw up an earthwork, and then marched towards the great town. Harold's army met him on the heights of Senlac, part of the solitary ridge between the marshes, by which alone London could be reached. Harold fell on the spot now marked by the ruined high altar of Battle Abbey, a national monument at present in the keeping of an English duke. Once the native army was routed, William marched on resistlessly to London, and Sussex and England were at his feet.

The new feudal organisation of the county is doubtless shadowed forth in the existing rapes. Of these there are six, called respectively after Chichester, Arundel, Bramber, Lewes, Pevensey, and Hastings. It will be noticed at once that these were the seats of the new bishopric and of the five great early castles. In one form or another, more or less modernised, Arundel Castle, Bramber Castle, Lewes Castle, Pevensey Castle, and Hastings Castle all survive to our own day. In accordance with their ordinary policy of removing cathedrals from villages to chief towns, and so concentrating the civil and ecclesiastical government, the Normans brought the bishopstool from Selsea to Chichester. The six rapes are fairly coincident, Chichester with the marsh district; Arundel with the dale of Arun; Bramber with the dale of Adur; Lewes with the western dale of Ouse; Pevensey with the eastern dale of Ouse; and Hastings with the insulated region between the marshes. In other words, Sussex seems to have been cut up into six natural divisions along the sea-shore; while to each division was assigned all the Weald back of its own shore strip as far as the border. Thus the rapes consist of six long longitudinal belts, each with a short sea front and a long stretch back into the Weald.

Increased intercourse with the Continent brought the Cinque Ports into importance; and, as premier Cinque Port, Hastings grew to be one of the chief towns in Sussex. The constant French wars made them prominent in mediæval history. As trade grew up, other commercial harbours gave rise to considerable mercantile towns. Rye and Winchelsea, at the mouth of the Rother, were great ports of entry from France as late as the days of Elizabeth. Seaford, at the mouth of the Ouse, was also an important harbour till 1570, when a terrible storm changed the course of the stream to the town called from that fact Newhaven. Lewes was likewise a port, as the estuary of the Ouse was navigable from the mouth up to the town. Brighthelmstone was still a village; but old Shoreham on the Adur was a considerable place. Arundel Haven and Chichester Harbour recalls the old mercantile importance of their respective neighbourhoods. The only other places of any note in mediæval Sussex were Steyning, under the walls of Bramber Castle; Hurstmonceux, which the Conqueror bestowed upon the lord of Eu; Battle, where he planted his great expiatory abbey; and Hurst Pierpont, which also dates from William's own time. The sole important part of the county was still the strip along the coast between the Weald and the sea.

During the Plantagenet period, England became a wool-exporting country, like Australia at the present day; and therefore the wool-growing parts of the island rose quickly into great importance. Sussex, with its large expanse of chalk downs, naturally formed one of the best wool-producing tracts; and in the reign of Edward III., Chichester was made one of the 'staples' to which the wool trade was confined by statute. Sussex Proper and the Lewes valley were now among the most thickly populated regions of England.

The Weald, too, was beginning to have its turn. English iron was getting to be in request for the cannon, armour, and arms required in the French wars; and nowhere was iron more easily procured, side by side with the fuel for smelting it, than in the Sussex Weald. From the days of the Edwards to the early part of the eighteenth century, the woods of the Weald were cut down in quantities for the iron works. During this time, several small towns began to spring up in the old forest region, of which the chief are Midhurst, Petworth, Billinghurst, Horsham, Cuckfield, and East Grinstead. Many of the deserted smelting-places may still be seen, with their invariable accompaniment of a pond or dam. The wood supply began to fail as early as Elizabeth's reign, but iron was still smelted in 1760. From that time onward, the competition of Sheffield and Birmingham, where iron was prepared by the 'new method' with coal, blew out the Sussex furnaces, and the Weald relapsed once more into a wild heather-clad and wood-covered region, now thickly interspersed with parks and country seats, of which Petworth, Cowdry, and Ashburnham are the best known.

Modern times, of course, have brought their changes. With the northward revolution caused by steam and coal, Sussex, like the rest of southern England, has fallen back to a purely agricultural life. The sea has blocked up the harbours of Rye, Winchelsea, Seaford, and Lewes. Man's hand has drained the marshes of the Rother, of Pevensey, and of Selsea Bill; and railways have broken down the isolation of Sussex from the remainder of the country. Still, as of old, the natural configuration continues to produce its necessary effects. Even now there are no towns of any size in the Weald: few, save Lewes, Arundel, and Chichester, anywhere but on the coast. The Downs are given up to sheep-farming; the Weald to game and pleasure-grounds; the shore to holiday-making. The proximity to London is now the chief cause of Sussex prosperity. In the old coaching days, Brighton was a foregone conclusion. Sixty miles by road from town, it was the nearest accessible spot by the seaside. As soon as people began to think of annual holidays, Brighton must necessarily attract them. Hence George IV. and the Pavilion. The railroad has done more. It has made Brighton into a suburb, and raised its population to over 100,000. At the same time, the South Coast line has begotten watering-places at Worthing, Bognor, and Littlehampton. In the other direction, it has created Eastbourne. Those who do not love chalk (as the Georges did), choose rather the more broken and wooded country round Hastings and St. Leonards, where the Weald sandstone runs down to the sea. The difference between the rounded Downs and saucer-shaped combes of the chalk, and the deep glens traversing the soft friable strata of the Wealden, is well seen in passing from Beachy Head to Ecclesbourne and Fairlight. Shoreham is kept half alive by the Brighton coal trade: Newhaven struggles on as a port for Dieppe. But as a whole, the county is now one vast seaside resort from end to end, so that to-day the flat coasts at Selsea, Pevensey, and Rye, are alone left out in the cold. The iron trade and the wool trade have long since gone north to the coal districts. Brighton and Hastings sum up in themselves all that is vital in the Sussex of 1881.


## THE BRONZE AXE

There is always a certain fascination in beginning a subject at the wrong end and working backward: it has the charm which inevitably attaches to all evil practices; you know you oughtn't, and so you can't resist the temptation to outrage the proprieties and do it. I can't myself resist the temptation of beginning this article where it ought to break off, with Chinese money, which is not the origin, but the final outcome and sole remaining modern representative of that antique and almost prehistoric implement, the Bronze Age hatchet.

Improbable and grotesque as this affiliation sounds at first hearing, it is, nevertheless, about as certain as any other fact in anthropological science, which isn't, perhaps, saying a great deal. The familiar little brass cash, with the square hole for stringing them together on a thread in the centre, well known to the frequenter of minor provincial museums, are, strange to say, the lineal descendants, in unbroken order, of the bronze axe of remote Celestial ancestors. From the regular hatchet to the modern coin one can trace a distinct, if somewhat broken, succession, so that it is impossible to say where the one leaves off and the other begins, where the implement merges into the medium of exchange, and settles down finally into the root of all evil.

Here is how this curious pedigree first worked itself out. In early times, before coin was invented, barter was usually conducted between producer and consumer with metal implements, as it still is in Central Africa at the present day with Venetian glass beads and rolls of red calico. Payments were all made in kind, and bronze was the commonest form of specie. A gentleman desirous of effecting purchases in foreign parts went about the world with a number of bronze axes in his pocket (or its substitute), which he exchanged for other goods with the native traffickers in the country where he did his primitive business. At first, the early Chinese in that unsophisticated age were content to use real hatchets for this commercial purpose; but, after a time, with the profound mercantile instinct of their race, it occurred to some of them that when a man wanted half a hatchet's worth of goods he might as well pay for them with half a hatchet. Still, as it would be a pity to spoil a good working implement by cutting it in two, the worthy Ah Sin ingeniously compromised the matter by making thin hatchets, of the usual size and shape, but far too slender for practical usage. By so doing he invented coin: and, what is more, he invented it far earlier than the rival claimants to that proud distinction, the Lydians, whose electrum staters were first struck in the seventh century, B.C. But, according to Professor Terrien de la Couperie, some of the fancy Chinese hatchets which we still retain date back as far as the year 1000 (a good round number), and are so thin that they could only have been intended to possess exchange value. And when a distinguished Sinologist gives us a date for anything Chinese, it behoves the rest of the unlearned world to open its mouth and shut its eyes, and thankfully receive whatever the distinguished Sinologist may send it.

In the seventh century, then, these mercantile axes, made in the strictest sense to sell and not to use, were stamped with an official stamp to mark their amount, and became thereby converted into true coins, that was the root of the 'root of all evil.' Thence the declension to the 'cash' is easy; the form grew gradually more and more regular, while the square hole in the centre, once used for the handle, was retained by conservatism and practical sense as a convenient means of stringing them together.

So this was the end of the old bronze hatchet, perhaps the most wonderful civilizing agent ever invented by human ingenuity. Let us hark back now, and from the opposite side see what was its first beginning.

'But why,' you ask, 'the most wonderful civilizing agency? What did the bronze axe ever do for humanity?' Well, nearly everything. I believe I have really not said too much. We are apt to talk big nowadays about the steam-engine, and that marvellous electricity which is always going to do wonders for us all—to-morrow; but I don't know whether either ever produced so great a revolution in human life, or so completely metamorphosed human existence, as that simple and commonplace bronze hatchet.

For, consider that before the days of bronze man knew no weapon or implement of any sort save the stone axe, or tomahawk, and the flint-tipped arrow. Consider, that the highest stage of human culture he had then reached was hardly higher than that of the scalp-hunting Red Indian or the seal-spearing Esquimaux. Consider, that in his Stone Age agriculture and grains were almost unknown, the forest uncleared, the soil untilled, and hunting and fishing the sole or principal human activities. It was the bronze axe that first enabled man to make clearings in the woodland on the large scale, and to sow on those clearings in good big fields the wheat and barley which determined the first great upward step in the drama of civilization. All these things depend in ultimate analysis upon that pioneer of culture, the bronze hatchet.

And how did the first Watt or Edison of metallurgy come to make that earliest bronze implement? Well, it seems probable that between the Stone Age and the Bronze Age there intervened everywhere, or nearly everywhere, a very short and transient age of copper. And the reason for thus thinking is threefold. In the first place, bronze is an alloy of tin and copper: and it seems natural to suppose that men would use the simple metals in isolation to begin with, before they discovered that they could harden and temper them by mixing the two together. In the second place, copper occurs in the pure or native state (without the trouble of smelting) in several countries, and was therefore a very natural metal for early man to cast his inquiring glance upon. And in the third place, weapons of unmixed copper, apparently of very antique types, have been found in various parts of the world, both in Asia and America. According to Mr. John Evans, the most learned historian of the Bronze Age, the greatest copper 'find' of the eastern hemisphere was that at Gungeria, in Central India; and the copper implements there found consisted entirely of flat celts of a very early and almost primitive pattern.

The copper weapons of America, however, have greater illustrative and ethnological interest, because the noble red man, at the period when Columbus first discovered him, and when he first discovered Columbus, was still in the Stone Age of his very imperfect culture, or, to speak more correctly, of extreme barbarism. The fact is, the Indians of Lake Superior were only just beginning to employ copper, and were on the eve of independently inaugurating a Bronze Age of their own, when the intrusive white man came and spoiled the fun by the incontinent introduction of iron, firearms, missionaries, whisky, and all the other resources of civilization. On the shores of Lake Superior native copper exists in abundance; and the intelligent Red Indian, finding this handsome red stone in the cliffs by his side, was pretty sure to try his hand at chipping a tomahawk out of the rare material. But, as soon as he did so, Mr. Evans suggests, he would find to his surprise that it yielded to his blows; in short, that he had got that singular phenomenon, a malleable stone, to deal with. Hammering away at his new invention, he must shortly have hammered it into a shapely axe. The new process took his practical fancy at once: vistas of an untold wealth of scalps floated gaily before his fevered brain; and he proceeded to hammer himself various weapons and implements without delay. Amongst others, he produced for himself very neat spear-heads, with sockets adapted for the reception of a shaft, made by hammering out the base flat, and then turning over the edges so as to enclose the wood between them, like a modern hoe-handle. In Wisconsin alone more than a hundred of such copper axes, spear-heads, and knives have been unearthed by antiquaries and duly recorded.

All these weapons, however, are simply hammered, not cast or melted. The Red Indian hadn't yet reached the stage of making a mould when De Champlain and his voyageurs came down upon Canada and interrupted this interesting experiment in industrial development by springing the seventeenth century upon the unsophisticated red man at one fell blow, with all its inherited wealth of European science. Nevertheless, the Indians must have known that fire melted copper; for the heat of the altars was great enough, say Squier and Davis, to fuse the implements and ornaments laid upon them in sacrificial rites; and so the fact of its fusibility could hardly have escaped them. A people who had advanced so far on the road towards the invention of casting could hardly have been prevented from taking the final step, save by the sudden intervention of some social cataclysm like the European invasion of Eastern America. And how awful a calamity that was for the Indians themselves we at this day can hardly even realize.

In some similar way, no doubt, the Asiatic people who first invented bronze must have learned the fact of the fusibility of metals, and have applied it in time, at first, perhaps, by accident, to the manufacture of that hard alloy. I say Asiatic, because there seems good reason to believe that Asia was the original home of the nascent bronze industry. For a Bronze Age almost necessarily implies a brief preceding age of copper; and there is no proof of pure copper implements ever having been largely used in Europe, while there is ample proof of their having been used to a very considerable extent in Asia. Hence we may reasonably infer that the art of bronze-making was developed in Asia by a copper-using people, and that when metallurgy was first introduced into Europe the method of mixing the copper with tin had already been perfected. The abundance of tin in the south-eastern islands of Asia renders this view probable; while in Europe there are no tin mines worth mentioning, except in the remotest part of a remote outlying island—to wit, in Cornwall.

Be this as it may, the earliest and simplest forms of bronze axe with which we are acquainted are profoundly interesting, as casting a flood of light upon the general process of human evolution all the world over. Every new human invention is always at first directly modelled upon the other similar products which have preceded it. There is no really new thing under the sun. For example, the earliest English railway carriages were built on the model of the old stage-coach, only that three stage-coaches, as it were, were telescoped together, side by side, the very first bore the significant motto, Tria juncta in uno, and it was this preconception of the English coachbuilder that has hampered us ever since with our hateful 'compartments,' instead of the commodious and comfortable open American saloon carriages. So, too, the earliest firearms were modelled on the stock of the old cross-bow, and the earliest earthenware pots and pans were shaped like the still more primitive gourds and calabashes. It need not surprise us, therefore, to find that the earliest metal axes of which we have any knowledge were directly moulded on the original shape of the stone tomahawk.

Such a copper hatchet, cast in a mould formed by a polished neolithic stone celt, was found in an early Etruscan tomb, and is still preserved in the Museum at Berlin. See how natural this process would be. For, in the first place, the primitive workman, knowing already only one form of axe, the stone tomahawk, would naturally reproduce it in the new material, without thinking what improvements in shape and design the malleability and fusibility of the metal would render possible or easy. But, more than that, the idea of coating the polished stone axe with plastic clay, and thereby making a mould for the molten metal, would be so very simple that even the neolithic savage, already accustomed to the manufacture of coarse pottery upon natural shapes, could hardly fail to think of it. As a matter of fact, he did think of it: for celts of bronze or copper, cast in moulds made from stone hatchets, have been found in Cyprus by General di Cesnola, on the site of Troy by Dr. Schliemann, and in many other assorted localities by less distinguished but equally trustworthy archæologists.

To the neolithic hunter, herdsman, and villager this progress from the stone to the metal axe probably seemed at first a mere substitution of an easier for a more difficult material. He little knew whither his discovery tended. It was pure human laziness that urged the change. How nice to save yourself all that long trouble of chipping and polishing, with ceaseless toil, in favour of a stone which you could melt at one go and pour while hot into a ready-made mould! It must have looked, by comparison, like weapon-making by magic; for properly to cut and polish a stone axe is the work of weeks and weeks of elbow-grease. Yet here, in a moment, a better hatchet could be turned out all finished! But the implied effects lay deeper far than the neolithic hunter could ever have imagined. The bronze axe was the beginning of civilization; it brought the steam-engine, the telephone, woman's rights, and the county councillor directly in its train. With the eye of faith, had he only possessed that useful optical organ, the Stone Age artizan might doubtless have beheld Pears' soap and the deceased wife's sister looming dimly in the remote future. Till that moment human life had been almost stationary: thenceforth, it proceeded by leaps and bounds, like a kangaroo society, on its upward path towards triumphant democracy and the penny post. The nineteenth century and all its wiles hung by a thread upon the success of his melting pot.

Indeed, the whole history of human civilization has been one of a constantly accelerated progress. The Older Stone Age, when men knew only how to chip flint implements, but hadn't yet invented the art of grinding and polishing them, was one of immense and incalculable duration, to be reckoned perhaps by tens of thousands of years, some bold chronologists would even suggest by hundreds of thousands. Improvement there was, to be sure, during all that long epoch of slow development; but it was improvement at a snail's pace. The very rude chipped axes of the naked drift age give way after thousands and thousands of years to the shapelier chipped lances, javelins, and arrowheads of the skin-clad cavemen. M. Gabriel de Mortillet, indeed, most indefatigable of theorists, has even pointed out four stages of culture, marked by four different types of weapons, into which he subdivides the Older Stone Age. Yet vast epochs elapsed before some prehistoric Stephenson or dusky Morse first, half by accident, smote out the idea of grinding his tomahawk smooth to a sharp cutting edge, instead of merely chipping it sharp, and so initiated the Neolithic Period. This Neolithic Period itself, again, was immensely long as compared with the Bronze Age which followed, though short by comparison with the Palæolithic epoch which preceded it. Then the Bronze Age saw enormous changes come faster and faster, till the use of iron still further accelerated the rate of progress. For each new improvement becomes, in turn, the parent of yet newer triumphs, so that at last, as in the present day, a single century sees vaster changes in the world of man than whole ages before it have done in far longer intervals.

But the invention of bronze, or, in other words, the introduction of hard metal, was really perhaps the very greatest epoch of all, the most distinct turning-point in the whole history of humanity. True, some beginnings of civilisation were already found in the Newer Stone Age. Man did not then live by slaughter alone. Hand-made pottery and rude tissues of flax are found in neolithic lake dwellings in Switzerland. Agriculture was already practised in a feeble way on small open clearings, cautiously cleaved with fire or hewn with the tomahawk in the native forests. The cow, the sheep, and the goat were more or less domesticated, though the horse was yet riderless; and the pastoral had therefore, to some extent, superseded the pure hunting stage. But what inroad could the stone hatchet make unaided upon the virgin forests of those remote days? The neolithic clearing must have been a mere stray oasis in a desert of woodland, like the villages of the New Guinea savages at the present day, lying few and far between among vast stretches of primæval forest.

With the advent of bronze, everything was different; and the difference showed itself with extraordinary rapidity. One may compare the revolution effected by bronze in the early world, indeed, with the revolution effected by railways in our own time; only the neolithic world had been so very simple a one that the change was perhaps even more marvellous in its suddenness and its comprehensiveness. Metal itself implied metal-working; and metal-working brought about, not only the arts of smelting and casting, but also endless incidental arts of design and decoration. The bronze hatchets, for example, to take our typical implement, begin by being mere copies of the stone originals; but, as time goes on, they acquire rapidly innumerable improvements. First, metal is economized in the upper part which fits into the handle, while the lower or cutting edge is widened out sideways, so as to form an elegant and gracefully curved outline for the whole implement. Next come the flanged axes, with projecting ledges on either side; and then the palstaves with loops and ribs, each marking some new improvement in the character of the weapon, which the inventor would no doubt have patented but for the unfortunate fact that patents were as yet wholly unknown to Bronze Age humanity. Later still come the socketed hatchets of many patterns, with endless ingenious little devices for securing some small advantage to the special manufacturer. I can fancy the Bronze Age smith showing them off with pride to his interested customers: 'These are our own patterns, the newest thing out in bronze axes; observe the advantage you gain from the ribs and pellets, and the peculiar character which the octagonal socket gives to the hafting!' Indeed, in this single department of bronze celts alone, Mr. Evans in his great monumental work figures over a hundred and eighty distinct specimens (out of thousands known), each one presenting some well-marked advance in type upon its predecessor. There is almost a Yankee ingenuity of design in many of the dodges thus registered for our inspection.

Many of the celts, I may add, are most beautifully decorated with geometrical patterns, some of which belong to a very high order of ornamental art. This is still more the case with the daggers, swords, and defensive armour, often intended for the use of great chieftains, and executed with an amount of taste and feeling long since dead among the degenerate workmen of our iron age.

But the indirect effects of the introduction of metal working were far more interesting and important in their way than the direct effects. With bronze began the great age of agriculture, of commerce, and of navigation.

Of agriculture first, because the bronze hatchet enabled men to make such openings in the forest as neolithic man had never ever dreamed of. For the first time in the history of our race, whole tracts of country at once began to be cleared and cultivated. Stone Age tillage was the tillage of tiny plots in the forest's depths; Bronze Age tillage was the tillage of fields and wide open spaces in the champaign country. The Stone Age knew no specials implements of agriculture as such; its tomahawk was indiscriminately applied to all purposes alike of war or gardening. You scalped your enemy with it, or you cut up your dinner, or you dug your field, or you planted your seed-corn, according as taste or circumstances directed. But while the Bronze Age men had axes to hew down the wood, they had also sickles and reaping-hooks to cut their crops, and a sort of hoe or scraper to till the soil with. Specialisation reached a very high pitch. All the remains of the Bronze Age show us an agricultural people by no means idyllic in their habits to be sure, and not all disposed to join the Peace Preservation Society, but cultivating large stretches of wheat or barley, grinding their meal in regular mills, and possessed of implements of considerable diversity, some of which I shall proceed to notice later.

The evidences of commerce and of navigation are equally obvious. Bronze itself consists of tin and copper: and there are only two parts of the world from which tin in any large quantities can be procured—namely, Cornwall and the Malay Archipelago. The very existence of bronze, therefore, necessarily implies the existence of a sea-going trade in tin, for which some corresponding benefits must of course have been offered by the early purchaser. As a matter of fact, we know with some probability that it was Cornish tin which first tempted the Phoenicians out of the inland sea, past the Pillars of Hercules, to brave the terrors of the open Atlantic. Long before the days of such advanced navigation, however, the Cornish tin was transported by land across the whole breadth of Southern Britain and shipped for the Continent from the Isle of Thanet. A very old trackway runs along the crest of the Downs from the West Country to Kent, known now as the Pilgrim's Way, because it was followed in far later times by mediæval wayfarers from Somerset and Dorset to the shrine of St. Thomas à Becket at Canterbury. But Mr. Charles Elton has shown conclusively that the Pilgrim's Way is many centuries more ancient than the martyr of King Henry's epoch, and that it was used in the Bronze Age for the transport of tin from the mines in Cornwall to the port of Sandwich. To this day antique ingots of the valuable metal are often dug up in hoards or finds along the line of the ancient track. They were evidently buried there in fear and trembling, long ages since, in what Indian voyageurs still call a cache, by caravans hurriedly surprised by the enemy; and owing to the unfortunate accident of the possessors all getting killed off in the ensuing fray, the ingots have been left undisturbed for centuries for the benefit of antiquaries at the present time. 'It's an ill wind that blows nobody good.' Probably the inhabitants of Herculaneum and Pompeii had very little notion what valuable relics their bodies and houses would prove in the end for curious posterity.

The converse evidence of a return trade in other goods is no less striking. Not only are articles in amber found in Bronze Age tombs all over Europe (though the gum itself belongs to the Baltic and the North Sea alone), but also gold objects of southern workmanship occur in British barrows; while sometimes even ivory from Africa is noticed in the inlaid handles of some Welsh or Brigantian chieftain's sword. Glass beads were likewise imported into Britain, as were also ornaments of Egyptian porcelain. In fact, the Bronze Age clearly marks for us the period when trade routes extended in every direction from the Mediterranean, north and south, and when the world began to be commercially solidified by a primitive theory of foreign exchange. It is a little odd that the basis of all this traffic was tin, and that we still use the name of that same metal as a brief equivalent for coin in general: but persons of serious economical or philological intelligence are particularly requested not to enter into grave correspondence with the author of this paper on any possible levity which they may detect lurking in this innocent remark.

Some small idea of the rapid advance in civilization which marked the Bronze Age may perhaps be formed from a brief enumeration of the principal classes of remains which have come down to us intact from that first epoch of metal. Besides all the various celts, hatchets, and adzes, whose name is legion, and whose patterns are manifold, many other tools or implements occur abundantly in the barrows or caches. Chisels, either plain, tanged, with lugs, or socketed; gouges, hammers, anvils, and tongs; punches, awls, drills, and prickers; tweezers, needles, fish-hooks, and weights; all these are found by dozens in endless variety of design. Knives are common, and the vanity of Bronze Age man made him even put up without a murmur with the pangs of shaving with a bronze razor. Daggers and rapiers naturally abound, many of them of rare and beautiful workmanship. Halberds turn up less frequently, but swords are abundant, and are sometimes tastefully decorated with gold or ivory. Even the scabbards sometimes survive, while the shields, adorned with concentric rings or with knobs and bosses, would put to shame the rank and file of cheap modern metal work. Nay, the very trumpets which sounded the onset often lie buried by the warrior's side, and the bells which adorned his horse's neck bring back to us vividly the Homeric pictures of Bronze Age warfare.

The private life of Bronze Age man and his correlative wife is illustrated for us by another great group of more strictly personal relics. There are pins simple and pins of the infantile safety-pin order: there are brooches which might be worn by modern ladies, and ear-rings so huge that even modern ladies would in all probability object to wearing them, unless, indeed, a princess or an actress made them the fashion. The torques, or necklets, are among the best known male decorations, and are still famous in Ireland, where Malachi (whoever he may have been) wore the collar of gold which he tore from the proud invader. Many of the bracelets are extremely beautiful; but, strange to say, as if on purpose to spite the common prejudice about the degeneracy of modern man, they are all so small in girth as to betoken a race with arms and legs hardly any bigger than the Finns or Laplanders. Of the clasps, buttons, and buckles I will say nothing here. I have enumerated enough to suggest to even the most casual observer the vastness of the revolution which the Bronze Age wrought in the mode of life and the civilisation of ancient man.

Bronze found our early ancestor, in fact, a half-developed savage: it left him a semi-civilized Homeric Greek. It came in upon a world of skin-clad hunters and fishers: it went out upon a world of Phoenician navigators, Egyptian architects, Achæan poets, and Roman soldiers. And all this wide difference was wrought in a period of some eight or ten centuries at the outside, almost entirely by the advent of the simple bronze axe.


THE ISLE OF RUIM

Perhaps you have never heard its name before; yet in the earlier ages of this kingdom of Britain, Ruim Isle, rising dim through the mist of prehistoric oceans, was once in its own way famous and important.

Off the old and obliterated south-eastern promontory of our island, where the land of Kent shelved almost imperceptibly into the Wantsum Strait, Ruim Island, the Holm of the Headland, stood out with its white wall of broken cliffs into the German Sea. The greater part of it consisted of gorse-clad chalk down, the last subsiding spur of that great upland range which, starting from the central boss of Salisbury Plain, runs right across the face of Surrey and Kent, and, bifurcating near Canterbury, falls sheer into the sea at the end of either fork by Ramsgate or Dover. But in earlier days Ruim Isle was not joined as now by flats and marshes to the adjacent mainland; the chalk dipped under the open Wantsum Strait, much as the chalk of Hampshire dips to-day under the Solent Sea, and reappeared again on the other side in the Thanet Downs, as it reappears in the Isle of Wight at the ridge of St. Boniface and the central hills about Newport and Carisbrooke. For now the murder indeed is out, and you have discovered already that Ruim, his dim, mysterious Ruim, is only just the commonplace, vulgarized Isle of Thanet.

Still, it is not without cause that I have ventured to call it by that strange and now almost forgotten old-world name. There is reason, we know, in the roasting of eggs, and, if I have gone out of my way to introduce the ancient isle to you by its title of Ruim, it is in order that we might start clear of the odour of tea and shrimps, the artificial niggers, and cheap excursionists, that the name of Thanet brings up most prominently at the present day before the travelled mind of the modern Londoner. I want to carry you back to a time when Ramsgate was still but a green gap in the long line of chalk cliff, and Margate but the chine of a little trickling streamlet that tumbled seaward over the undesecrated sands; when a broad arm of the sea still cut off Westgate from the Reculver cliffs, and when the tide swept unopposed four times a day over the submerged sands of Minster Level. You must think of Thanet as then greatly resembling Wight in geographical features, and the Wantsum as the equivalent of the Solent Sea.

In the very earliest period of our history, before ever the existing names had been given at all to the towns or villages, nay, when the towns and villages themselves were not, Ruim was already a noteworthy island. For there is now very little doubt indeed that Thanet is the Ictis or 'Channel Island' to which Cornish tin was conveyed across Britain for shipment to the continent. The great harbour of Britain was then the Wantsum Sea, known afterwards as the Rutupine Port, and later still as Sandwich Haven. To that port came Gaulish and Phoenician vessels, or possibly even at times some belated Phocæan galley from Massilia. But the trade in tin was one of immense antiquity, long antedating these almost modern commercial nations: for tin is a necessary component of bronze, and the bronze age of Europe was entirely dependent for its supply of that all-important metal upon the Cornish mines. From a very early date, therefore, we may be sure that ingots of tin were exported by this route to the continent, and then transported overland by the Rhone valley to the shores of the Mediterranean.

The tin road, to give it its more proper name, followed the crest of the Hog's Back and the Guildford downs, crossing the various rivers at spots whose very names still attest the ancient passages, the Wey at Shalford, the Mole at Burford, the Medway at Aylesford, and the Wantsum Strait at Wade, in which last I seem to hear the dim echo to this day of the Roman Vada. Ruim itself, as less liable to attack than an inland place, formed the depôt for the tin trade, and the ingots were no doubt shipped near the site of Richborough. We may regard it, in fact, as a sort of prehistoric Hong-Kong or Zanzibar, a trading island, where merchants might traffic at ease with the shy and suspicious islanders.

Ruim at that time must have consisted almost entirely of open down, sloping upward from the tidal Wantsum, and extending a little farther out to sea than at the present moment. Pegwell Bay was then a wide sea-mouth; Sandwich flats did not yet exist; and the Stour itself fell into the Wantsum Strait at the place which still bears the historic name of Stourmouth. Round the outer coast only a few houseless gaps marked the spots where 'long lines of cliff, breaking, had left a chasm', the gaps that afterwards bore the familiar names of Ramsgate, that is to say Ruim's Gate, or 'the Door of Thanet;' Margate, that is to say, Mere Gate, the gap of the mere (Kentish for a brook), Broadstairs, Kingsgate, Newgate, and Westgate. The present condition of Dumpton Gap (minus the telegraph) will give some idea of what these Gates looked like in their earliest days; only, instead of seeing the cultivated down, we must imagine it wildly clad with primæval undergrowth of yew and juniper, like the beautiful tangled district near Guildford, still known as Fairyland. Thanet is now all sea-front, it turns its face, freckled with summer resorts, towards the open German Ocean. Ruim had then no sea-front at all, save the bare and inaccessible white cliffs; it turned, such as it was, not toward the sea, but toward the navigable Wantsum. Even until late in the middle ages Minster was the most important place in the whole island; and after it ranked Monkton, St. Nicholas, and Birchington, villages, all of them, on the flat western slope. The growth in importance of the seaward escarpment dates only from the days when Thanet became practically a London suburb.

With the Roman invasion Ruim saw a new epoch begin. A great organization took hold of Britain. Roads were made and colonies established. Verulam and Camulodun gave place in part as centres of life and trade to York and London. Even in the native days, I believe, the Thames must always have been a great commercial focus, and the Pool by Tower Hill must always have been what Bede called it many centuries later, 'a mart of many nations.' But under the Romans London grew into a considerable city; and as the regular sea highway to the Thames lay through the Wantsum, in the rear of Thanet, that strip of estuary became of immense importance. In those days of coasting navigation, indeed, the habit was to avoid headlands, and take advantage everywhere of shallow short cuts. Ships from the continent, therefore, avoided the North Foreland by running through the Wantsum at the back of Thanet; as they avoided Shellness and Warden Point by running through the Swale, at the back of Sheppey.

To protect this main navigable channel, accordingly, the Romans built the two great guardian fortresses of the coast, Rutupiæ, or Richborough, at the southern entrance, and Regulbium, or Reculver, at the northern exit. Under the walls of these powerful strongholds, whose grim ruins still frown upon the dry channel at their feet, ships were safe from piracy, while Ruim itself sheltered them from the heavy sea that now beats with north-east winds upon the Foreland beyond. In fact, the Wantsum was an early Spithead: it stood to Rutupiæ as the Solent stands to Portsmouth and Southampton. But Thanet Isle hardly shared at all in this increased civilisation; on the contrary, Rutupiæ (the precursor of Sandwich Haven) seems to have diverted all its early commerce. For Rutupiæ became clearly the naval capital of our island, the seat of that vir spectabilis, the Count of Saxon Shore, and the rendezvous of the fleets of those British 'usurpers' Maximus and Carausius. It was also the Dover of its own day, the favourite landing place for continental travellers; while its famous oysters, the true natives, now driven by the silting up of their ancient beds to Whitstable, were as much in repute with Roman epicures as their descendants are to-day with the young Luculluses of the Gaiety and the Criterion.

I have ventured by this time to speak of Ruim as Thanet; and indeed that was already one of the names by which the island was known to its own inhabitants. The ordinary history books, to be sure, will tell you in their glib way that Thanet is 'Saxon' for Ruim; but, when they say so, believe not the fond thing, vainly imagined. The name is every day as old as the Roman occupation. Solinus, writing in the third century, calls it Thanaton, and in the torn British fragment of the Peutinger Tables, that curious old map of the later empire, it is marked as Tenet. Indeed, it is a matter of demonstration that every spot which had a known name in Roman Britain retained that name after the English conquest. Kent itself is a case in point, and every one of its towns bears out the law, from Dover and Lymne to Reculver and Richborough, which last is spelt 'Ratesburg' by Leland, Henry the Eighth's commissioner.

In some ways, however, Thanet, under the Romans, must have shared in the general advance of the country. Solinus says it was 'glad with corn-fields', felix frumentariis campis, but this could only have been on the tertiary slope facing Kent, as agriculture had not yet attempted to scale the flanks of the chalk downs. As lying so near Rutupiæ, too, villas must certainly have occupied the soil in places, as we know they did in the Isle of Wight; while the immense number of Roman coins picked up in the island appears to betoken a somewhat dense provincial population.

The advent of the English brings Thanet itself, as distinct from its ancient port, the Wantsum, into the full glare of legendary history. According to tradition, it was at Ebb's Fleet, a little side creek near Minster, that Hengest and Horsa first disembarked in Britain. As a matter of fact, there is reason to suppose that at a very early time an English colony did really settle down in peace in Thanet. On Osengal Hill, not far from Ebb's Fleet, the cemetery of these earliest English pioneers in England was laid bare by the building of the South Eastern Railway. The graves are dug very shallow in the chalk, seldom as deep as four feet; and in them lie the remains of the old heathen pirates, buried with their arms and personal ornaments, their amber beads and strings of glass, and the coins that were to pay their way in the other world. But, what is oddest of all, a few of the graves in this earliest English cemetery are Roman in character, and in them the interment is made in the Roman fashion. The inference is almost irresistible that the first settlement of Thanet by the English was a purely friendly one, and that Roman and Jute lived on side by side as neighbours and allies on the Kentish island.

I don't doubt, myself, that the whole settlement of Kent was equally friendly, and that the population of the county contains throughout an almost balanced mixture of Celtic and Teutonic elements.

However, the century and a half that succeeded the English colonization of south-eastern Britain were, no doubt, a time of great retrogression towards barbarism, as everywhere else in Romanised Europe. The villas that must have covered the gentle slopes towards the Wantsum fell into decay; the fortresses were destroyed; the roads ran wild; and the sea and river began slowly to slit up the central part of the great navigable backwater. A hundred and fifty years after Hengest and Horsa, if those excellent gentlemen ever really existed, another famous landing took place in Thanet. Augustine and his companions disembarked at Ebb's Fleet, and held close by (on the hill behind Prospect House) their first interview with Æthelberht. But though this epoch-making event happened to occur in Thanet, it has no special connection with the history of the island, any further than as a component of England generally. And indeed, even through the garbled version of Bede, it is plain enough to see that British Christendom was not yet wholly wiped out in eastern Britain. The conversion of Kent was essentially a conversion of the king and nobles to the Roman communion; it brought back once more the part of Britain most in connection with the continent into the broad fold of continental Christendom. It is quite clear, in fact, that Rutupiæ and Durovernum, Richborough and Canterbury, had never ceased to hold close intercourse with the opposite shore, whose cliffs still shine so distinctly from the hills about Ramsgate. For Æthelberht himself was married to a Christian Frankish princess of the house of the Merwings; and coins of the Frankish kings and of the Byzantine emperors have been found on the surface or in contemporary Jutish graves in Kent.

It is interesting to observe, too, that of the monks whom Gregory chose to accompany Augustine on his easy mission, one was Lawrence, who succeeded his leader as second Archbishop of Canterbury, and another was Peter, the first Abbot of St. Augustine's monastery. Out of compliment to these pioneer missionaries, or to their Roman house of St. Andrew's, almost every old church in that part of Kent is dedicated accordingly, either to St. Augustine, St. Lawrence, St. Peter, St. Gregory, St. Andrew, or St. Martin (patron of Bertha's first church at Canterbury). Thus, as we shall see hereafter, St. Lawrence was the mother church of Ramsgate, and St. Peter's of Broadstairs, while the entire lathe bears the name of St. Augustine.

In Thanet, too, the first evidence of the new order of things was the foundation in the island of that great civilizing agency of mediæval England, a monastery. The site chosen for its home was still, however, characteristic of the old point of view of Thanet. It was the place that yet bears the name of Minster, situated on a little creek of the Wantsum sea, where some slight remains of an ancient pier may even now be traced among the silt of the marshes. The island still looked towards the narrow seas and the port of Rutupiæ, not, as now, towards the tall cliffs and the German Ocean. Ecgberht, fourth Christian king of Kent, by the advice of Theodore, the monk of Tarsus who became Archbishop of Canterbury, made over to the lady whose name is conveniently Latinised as Dompneva, first abbess, some forty-eight plough-lands in the Isle of Thanet. This cultivated district, bounded by the ancient earthwork known (from the name of the second abbess) as St. Mildred's Lynch, lay almost entirely within the westward-sloping and mainly tertiary lands; the higher chalk country was as yet apparently considered unfit for tillage. The existing remains of Minster Abbey are, of course, of comparatively late Plantagenet date; but as parts of a great grange, whose still larger granary was burnt down only in the last century, they serve well to show the importance of the monastic system as a civilizing agency in the country districts of England.

Already in Bede's time the Wantsum was beginning to get silted up, mainly by the muddy deposits brought down by the Stour. It was then only three furlongs wide, and could be forded at two points, near Sarr and at Wade. The seaward mouth was also beginning to be encumbered with sand, and the first indication we get of this important impending change is the fact that we now hear less of Richborough, and more of Sandwich, the new port a little nearer the sea, whose very name of the Wick or haven on the Sand, in itself sufficiently tells the history of its origin. As the older port got progressively silted up, the newer one grew into ever greater importance, exactly as Norwich ousted Caister, or as Portsmouth has taken the place of Porchester. Nevertheless, the central channel still remained navigable for the vessels of that age, they can only have drawn a very few feet of water, and this made the Wantsum in time the great highway for the Danish pirates on their way to London, and exposed Thanet exceptionally to their relentless incursions.

In fact, the Danes and Northmen were just what they loved to call themselves, vik-ings or wickings, men of the viks, wicks, bays, or estuaries. What they loved was a fiord, a strait, a peninsula, an island. Everywhere round the coast of Britain they seized and fortified the projecting headlands. But in the neighbourhood of the Thames, the high road to the great commercial port of London, the mementoes of their presence are particularly frequent. The whole nomenclature of the lower Thames navigation, as Canon Isaac Taylor has pointed out, is Scandinavian to this day. Deptford (the deep fiord), Greenwich (the green reach), and Woolwich (the hill reach) all bear good Norse names. So do the Foreness, the Whiteness, Shellness, Sheerness, Shoeburyness, Foulness, Wrabness, and Orfordness. Walton-on-the-Naze near Harwich in like manner still recalls the time when a Danish 'wall', that is to say, a vallum, or earthwork, ran across the isthmus to defend the Scandinavian peninsula from its English enemies.

At such a time Sandwich, with its shallow fiord, was sure to afford good shelter to the northern long ships; and isolated Thanet, overlooking the navigable strait, was a predestined depôt for the northern pirates, as four centuries earlier it had been for the followers of those mythical personifications, Hengest and Horsa. Long before the unification of England under a single West Saxon overlordship the Danes used to land in the island every year, to plunder the crops, and in 851, when Æthelwulf was lord of Wessex at Winchester, 'heathen men,' says the Winchester Chronicle, with its usual charming conciseness, 'first sat over winter in Tenet.' From that time forward the 'heathen men' continually returned to the island, which they used apparently as a base of operations, with their ships lying in Sandwich Haven; in fact, Thanet must long have been a sort of irregular Danish colony. Still, St. Mildred's nuns appear to have lived on somehow at Minster through the dark time, for in 988 the Danes landed and burnt the abbey, as they did again under Swegen in 1011, killing at the same time the abbess and all the inmates. On the whole, it is probable that life and property in Thanet were far from secure any time in the ninth, tenth, and early eleventh centuries.

At least as late as the Norman conquest the Wantsum remained a navigable channel, and the usual route to London by sea was in at Sandwich and out at Northmouth. It was thus that King Harold's fleet sailed on its plundering expedition round the coast of Kent (a small unexplained incident of the early English type, only to be understood by the analogies of later Scotch history), and thus too, that many other expeditions are described in the concise style of our unsophisticated early historians. But from the eleventh century onward we hear little of the Wantsum as a navigable channel; it has dwindled down almost entirely to Sandwich Haven, 'the most famous of English ports,' says the writer of the life of Emma of Normandy, about 1050. Sandwich is indeed the oldest of the Cinque Ports, succeeding in this matter to the honours of Rutupiæ, and all through the middle ages it remained the great harbour for continental traffic. Edward III. sailed thence for France or Flanders, and as late as 1446 it is still spoken of by a foreign ambassador as the resort of ships from all quarters of Europe.

Still, the Wantsum was all this while gradually silting up, a grain at a time, and the Isle of Ruim was slowly becoming joined to the opposite mainland. When Leland visited it, in Henry VIII.'s reign, the change was almost complete. 'At Northmouth,' says the royal commissioner, in his quaint dry way, 'where the estery of the se was, the salt water swelleth yet up at a Creeke a myle or more toward a place called Sarre, which was the commune fery when Thanet was fulle iled.' Sandwich Haven itself began to be difficult of access about 1500 (Henry VII. being king), and in 1558 (under Mary) a Flemish engineer, 'a cunning and expert man in waterworks,' was engaged to remedy the blocking of the channel. By a century later it was quite closed, and the Isle of Thanet had ceased to exist, except in name, the Stour now flowing seaward by a long bend through Minster Level, while hardly a relic of the Wantsum could be traced in the artificial ditches that intersect the flat and banked-up surface of the St. Nicholas marshes.

Meanwhile, Thanet had been growing once more into an agricultural country. Minster, untenable by its nuns, had been made over after the Danish invasions to the monks of St. Augustine at Canterbury, and it was they who built the great barn and manor house which were the outer symbol of its new agricultural importance. Monkton, close by, belonged to the rival house of Christ Church at Canterbury (the cathedral monastery), as did also St. Nicholas at Wade, remarkable for its large and handsome Early English church. All these ecclesiastical lands were excellently tilled. After the Reformation, however, things changed greatly. The silting up of the Wantsum and the decay of Sandwich Haven left Thanet quite out of the world, remote from all the main highroads of the new England. Ships now went past the North Foreland to London, and knew it only as a dangerous point, not without a sinister reputation for wrecking. On the other hand, on the land side, the island lay off the great highways, surrounded by marsh or half-reclaimed levels; and it seems rapidly to have sunk into a state resembling that of the more distant parts of Cornwall. The inhabitants degenerated into good wreckers and bad tillers. They say an Orkney man is a farmer who owns a boat, while a Shetlander is a fisherman who owns a farm. In much the same spirit, Camden speaks of the Elizabethan Thanet folks as 'a sort of amphibious creatures, equally skilled in holding helm and plough'; while Lewis, early in the last century, tells us they made 'two voyages a year to the North Seas, and came home soon enough for the men to go to the wheat season.' With genial tolerance the Georgian historian adds, 'It's a thousand pities they are so apt to pilfer stranded ships.' Piracy, which ran in the Thanet blood, seemed to their good easy local annalist a regrettable peccadillo.

In all this, however, we begin to catch the first faintly-resounding note of modern Thanet. The intelligent reader will no doubt have observed, with his usual acuteness, that up to date we have heard practically nothing of Ramsgate, Margate, and Broadstairs, which now form the real centres of population in the nominal island. Its relations have all been with Rutupiæ, Sandwich, Canterbury, and the mainland. But the silting up of the Wantsum turned the new Thanet seaward, by the chalky cliffs; and the gaps or gates in that natural sea-wall now began to be of comparative importance as fishing stations and small havens. Ebb's Fleet was no longer the port of Ruim. The centre of gravity of the island shifts at this point, accordingly, from Minster to Ramsgate. The change is well marked by certain interesting ecclesiastical facts. Neither Ramsgate nor Broadstairs had originally churches of their own. The first formed part of the parish of St. Lawrence, which was itself a mere chapelry of Minster till late in the thirteenth century. The old village lies half a mile inland, and Ramsgate itself was throughout the middle ages nothing more than a mere gap and cove where the fishermen of St. Lawrence kept their boats. The first church in the town proper was not erected till 1791. Similarly, Broadstairs formed part of the parish of St. Peter's, the village of which lies back at about the same distance from the sea as St. Lawrence; and St Peter's, too, was at first a chapelry of Minster. The cliffs were then nothing; the inward slope was everything.

Margate seems to have been the first place in the new Thanet to attain the honour of a place in history. As in two previous cases, the Mere Gate was at first but a fisherman's station for the village of St. John's, which gathered about the old church at the south end of the existing town. But as the Northmouth closed up, and Sandwich Haven decayed, the Mere Gate naturally became the little local port for corn grown on the island and wool raised on the newly-reclaimed Minster Level. A wooden pier existed at Margate long before the reign of Henry VIII., when Leland found it "sore decayed," and the village was in repute for fishery and coasting trade. Throughout the Stuart period Margate was the ordinary place of departure and arrival for Flushing and the Low Countries. William of Orange frequently sailed hence, and Maryborough used it for almost all his expeditions. It was about the middle of the last century, however, that the real prosperity of Margate first began. Then it was that citizens of credit and renown in London first hit upon the glorious discovery of the seaside, and that watering-places tentatively and timidly raised their unobtrusive heads along the nearer beaches. The journey from London could be made far more easily by river than that to Brighton by coach; and so Margate, the nearest spot to town (by water) on the real sea with any accommodation for visitors, became in point of fact the earliest London seaside resort. It was, if not the first place, at least one of the first places in England to offer to its guests the perilous joy of bathing machines, which were inaugurated here about 1790.

With the introduction of steamers Margate's fortune was made. Floods of Cockneydom were let loose upon the nascent lodging-houses. Then came the London, Chatham and Dover, and South Eastern Railways, and with them an ever-increasing inundation of good-humoured cheap-trippers. The Hall-by-the-Sea and other modern improvements and attractions followed. Like the rest of Thanet, Margate has now become a mere suburb of London, and what it resembles at the present day a delicate regard for the feelings of the inhabitants forbids me to enlarge upon. I will merely add that the recognized modern name of Margate is an etymological blunder, due to the idea immortalized in the borough motto, "Porta maris, Portus salutis," that it means Door of the Sea. The true word is still universally preserved on the lips of the local fisher-folk, who always religiously call it either Meregate or Mergate.

Ramsgate, a much more attractive and enjoyable centre, rich in excursions to points of genuine interest, dates somewhat later. It first came into note about the beginning of the eighteenth century, when it did a modest trade with the Levant and the Black Sea, or, as contemporary English more prettily phrases it, 'with Russia and the east country.' In 1750 the first pier was built, as a national work, mainly to serve as a harbour of refuge for ships caught in gales off the Downs. The engineer was Smeaton, and he succeeded in creating an artificial harbour of great extent, which has lasted substantially up to the present time. This new port, rendered safer by the enlargement in 1788, made Ramsgate at once into an important seafaring town, the capital of the Kentish herring trade, alive with smacks in the busy season. The steamers did it less good at first than they did to Margate; but the completion of the two railways, and the building of the handsome extensions on the east and west cliffs, turned it at once into a frequented watering-place. It is the fashion nowadays rather to laugh at Ramsgate. Marine painters know better. Few harbours are livelier with red and brown sails; few coasts more enjoyable than the cliff walk looking across towards the Goodwins, the low shore by Sandwich, the higher ground about Deal and Dover, and the dim white line of Cape Blancnez in the distance.

Broadstairs, close by the lighthouse on the North Foreland (the Cantium Promontorium of Roman geography), is still newer as a place of public resort. But as a fishing village it dates back to the middle ages, when the little chapel of "Our Lady of Bradstow" stood in the gap of the cliffs, and was much addressed by anxious sailors rounding the dangerous point after the silting up of the Wantsum. Ships as they passed lowered their top-sails to do it reverence. Under Henry VIII. a small wooden pier was thrown out to protect the fishing boats; and about the same time, as part of the general scheme of coast defence inaugurated by the king, a gate and portcullis were erected to close the gap seaward, in case of invasion. The archway and portcullis groove remain to this day, with an inscription recording their repair in 1795 by Sir John Henniker. The railway has turned Broadstairs into a minor rival of Ramsgate and Margate and 'a favourite resort for gentry,' where 'those who require quietness, either from ill health or a retiring disposition,' says a local guide-book, may enjoy 'the united advantages of tranquillity and seclusion.' Hundreds of retiring souls indeed may be observed on the beach any day during the season, seeking tranquillity in a game of cards, repairing their health with the stimulus of donkey exercise, or soothing their souls in secret hour with music sweet as love, discoursed to them by gentlemen in loose pink suits and artificially imitated Æthiopian countenances.

Westgate is the very latest-born of these Thanet gates, a brand-new watering-place, where every house proclaims the futility of the popular belief that Queen Anne is dead, and where fashionable physicians send fashionable patients to cure imaginary diseases by a dose of fresh air. It has no history, for only a few years since it consisted entirely of a coastguard station and three or four cottages: but it is interesting as casting light on the nature of the revolution which has turned Thanet inside out and hind part before, making the open sea take the place of the Kentish mainland, and the railway to London that of the silted Wantsum.

At the present day Thanet as a whole consists of two parts: the live sea front, which is one long succession of suburban watering-places; and the agricultural interior, including the reclaimed estuary, which ranks among the best-farmed and most productive districts in all England, Yet till a very recent date the Thanet farmers still retained the use of the old Kentish plough, the coulter of which is reversed at the end of every furrow; and many other curious insular customs mark off the agriculture of the island even now from that which prevails over the rest of the country.

I don't know whether I'm wrong, but it often seems to me the very best way to gain an idea of the real history of England is thus to take a single district piecemeal, and trace out for one's self the main features of its gradual evolution. By so doing we get away from mere dynastic or political considerations, leave behind the bang of drums or the blare of trumpets, and reach down to the living facts of common human activity themselves, the realities of the workaday world of toilers and spinners. By narrowing our field of view, in fact, we gain a clearer picture on our smaller focus. We see how the big historical revolutions actually affected the life of the people; and we trace more readily the true nature of deep-reaching changes when we follow them out in detail over a particular area.

'Why, what did they want to build a city right up here for, anyway?' the pretty American asked, who had come with us to Fiesole, as we rested, panting, after our long steep climb, on the cathedral platform.

Now the question was a pertinent and in its way a truly philosophical one. Fiesole crests the ridge of a Tuscan hill, and in America they don't build cities on hill-tops. You may search through the length and breadth of the United States, from Maine to California, and I venture to bet a modest dollar you won't find a single town perched anywhere in a position at all resembling that of many a glowing Etrurian fastness, that 'Like an eagle's nest Hangs on the crest Of purple Apennine.' Towns in America stand all on the level: most of them are built by harbours of sea or inland lake; or by navigable rivers; or at the junction of railways; or at a point where cataracts (sadly debased) supply ample water-power for saw-mills and factories; or else in the immediate neighbourhood of coal, iron, oil wells, or gold and silver mines. In short, the position of American towns bears always an immediate and obvious reference to the wants and necessities of our modern industrial and commercial system. They are towns that have grown up in a state of profound peace, and that imply advanced means of communication, with a free interchange of agricultural and manufactured products.

Hence in America it is always quite easy to see at a glance the raison d'être of every town or village one comes across. New York, Boston, Philadelphia, Baltimore, New Orleans, Montreal, San Francisco, Charleston, are all great ports for the exportation of corn, pork, 'lumber,' cotton, or tobacco, and the importation of European manufactured goods. Chicago is the main collecting and distributing centre for the wide basin of the upper Great Lakes, as Cincinnati is for the Ohio Valley, and St. Louis for the Mississippi and Missouri confluents. Pittsburg bases itself upon its coal and its iron; Buffalo exists as the point of transfer where elevators raise the corn of Chicago from lake-going vessels into the long, low barges of the Erie Canal. In every case, in that newest of worlds, one can see for oneself at a glance exactly why so large a body of human beings has collected just at that precise spot, and at no other.

But when you have toiled up, hot and breathless, through olive and pine, from the Viale at Florence to the antique Cyclopean walls of Etruscan Fæsulæ, you wonder to yourself, like our American friend, as you pant on the terrace of the Romanesque cathedral, what on earth they could ever have wanted to build a town up there for, anyway.

If we look away from Tuscany to our own England, however, we shall find on many a deserted down or lonely tor ample evidence of the causes which led the people of this ancient Etruscan town to build their citadel at so great a height above the neighbouring valley. Fiesole, says Dante, in a well-known verse, was the mother of Florence. Even so in England, Old Sarum was indeed the mother of Salisbury, and Caer Badon or Sulis was the mother of Bath. And when there was first a Fæsulæ on the hill here there could be no Florence, as when first there was an Old Sarum on the Wiltshire downs there could be no Salisbury, and when first there was a Caer Badon on the heights of Avon there could be no Bath.

In very early times indeed, in the European land area, when men began first to gather together into towns or villages, two necessities determined their choice of a place to dwell in: first, food-supply (including water); and second, defence. Hence every early community stands, to start with, near its own cultivable territory, usually a broad river-valley, an alluvial plain, a 'carse' or lowland, for uplands as yet were incapable of tillage by the primitive agriculture of those early epochs. But it does not stand actually in the carse; it occupies as a rule the nearest convenient height or hill-top, most often the one that juts out farthest into the subjacent plain, by way of security against the attack of enemies. This is the beginning of almost every great historical European town; it is an arx or acropolis overhanging its own tilth or ager; and though in many cases the town came down at last into the valley, retaining still its old name, yet the remains of the old earthworks or walls on the hill-top above often bear witness to our own day to the original site of the antique settlement upon the high places.

One can mark, too, various stages in this gradual process of secular descent from the wind-swept hills into the valleys below, as freer communications and greater security made access to water, roads, and rivers of greater importance than mere defence or elevated position. At Bath, for example, it was the Pax Romana that brought down the town from the stockaded height of Caer Badon, and the Hill of Solisbury to the ford and the hot springs in the valley of the Avon. At Old Sarum, on the other hand, the hill-top town remained much longer: it lived from the Celtic first into the Roman and then into the West Saxon world; it had a cathedral of its own in Norman times; and even long after Bishop Roger Poore founded the New Sarum, which we now call Salisbury, at the point where the great west road passed the river below, the hill-top town continued to be inhabited, and, as everybody knows, when all its population had finally dwindled away, retained some vestige of its ancient importance by returning a member of its own for a single farmhouse to the unreformed Parliament till '32. As for Fiesole, though Florence has long since superseded it as the capital of the Arno Valley, the town itself still lives on to our own time in a dead-alive way, and, like Norman. Old Sarum, retains even now its beautiful old cathedral, its Palazzo Pretorio, and its acknowledged claims to ancient boroughship. In England, I know by personal experience only one such hill-top town of the antique sort still surviving, and that is Shaftsbury; but I am told that Launceston, with its strong castle overlooking the Tamar, is even a finer example. This relatively early disappearance of the hill-top fortress from our own midst is in part due, no doubt, to the early growth of the industrial spirit in England, and our long-continued freedom from domestic warfare. But all over Southern Europe, as everybody must have noticed, the hill-top town, perched, like Eza, on the very summit of a pointed pinnacle, still remains everywhere in evidence as a common object of the country in our own day.

I said above that Fiesole was the mother of Florence, and, in spite of formal objections to the contrary, I venture to defend that now somewhat obsolete and heretical opinion. For why does Fiesole stand just where it does? What made them build a city up there, anyway? Well, a town always exists just where it does exist for some good and amply sufficient reason. Even if, like Fiesole, it is mainly a survival (though at Fiesole there are, indeed, olives in plenty and other live trades to keep a town going), it yet exists there in virtue of facts which once upon a time were quite sufficient to bring the world to the spot, and it goes on existing, partly by mere conservative use and wont, no doubt, but partly also because there are houses, churches, mills, and roads all ready built there. Now, a town must always, from a very early period, have existed upon the exact site of Fiesole. And why? To answer that question you have only to look at the view from the platform. I do not mean to suggest that the ancient Etruscans came there to enjoy the prospect as we go nowadays to the hotels on the Rigi or to the summit of Mount Washington. The ancient Etruscan was a practical man, and his views about views were probably rudimentary. But gaze down for a moment from the cathedral platform upon the valley of the Arno, spread like a glowing picture at your feet, and see how immediately it resolves the doubt. Not, indeed, the valley of the Arno as it stands at present, thick set with tower and spire and palace. In order to arrive at the raison d'être of Fiesole you must blot out mentally Arnolfo's vast pile, and Brunelleschi's dome, and Giotto's campanile, and Savonarola's monastery, and the tall and slender tower of the Palazzo Vecchio, rising like a shaft sheer into the air far, far below, you must blot out, in short, all that makes the world now congregate at Florence, and all Florence itself into the bargain. Nowhere on earth do I know a more peopled plain than that plain of Arno in our own time, seen on a sunny autumn day, when the light glints clearly on each white villa and church and hamlet, from this specular mount of antique Fiesole. But to understand why Fiesole itself stands there at all you must neglect all this, neglect all the wealth of art that makes each inch of that valley classic ground, and look only, if you can for a brief moment, at the bare facts of primitive nature.

And what then do you see? Spread far below you, and basking in the sunshine, a comparatively flat and wide, open valley; olive and stone pine and mulberry on its slopes; pasture land and flowery vale in its midst. North and south, in two long ridges, the Apennines stretch their hard, blue outlines from Carrara to Siena against the afternoon sky, outlines of a sort that one never gets in northern lands, but which remind one so exactly of the painted background to a fifteenth-century Italian picture that nature seems here, to our topsy-turvy fancy, to be whimsically imitating an effect from art. But in between those two tossed and tumbled guardian ridges, the valley of the Arno, as it flows towards Pisa, with the minor basins of its tributary streams, expands for a while about Florence itself into a broad and comparatively level plain. In a mountain country so broken and heaved about as Peninsular Italy, every spare inch of cultivable plain like that has incalculable value. True, on the terraced slopes of the hillsides generation after generation of ingenious men have managed to build up, tier by tier, a wonderful expanse of artificial tilth. But while oil and wine can be produced upon the terraces, it is on the river valleys alone that the early inhabitants had to depend for their corn, their cheese, and their flesh-meat. Hence, in primitive Italy and in primitive England alike, every such open alluvial plain, fit for tilth or grazing, had overhanging it a stockaded hill-fort, which grew with time into a mediæval town or a walled city. It is just so that Caer Badon at Bath overhangs, with its prehistoric earthworks, the plain of Avon on which Beau Nash's city now spreads its streets, and it is just so that Old Sarum in turn overhangs, with its regular Roman fosses and gigantic glacis, the dale of the namesake river in Wilts, near its point of confluence with the stream of the Wily.

We find it hard, no doubt, to imagine nowadays that once upon a time England was almost as thickly covered with hill-top villages (though on minor heights) as Italy is in the present century. Yet such was undoubtedly the case in prehistoric times. I know no better instance of the way these stockaded villages were built than the magnificent group of antique earthworks in Dorset and Devon which rings round with a double row of fortresses the beautiful valley of the Axminster Axe. There, on one side, a long line of strongholds built by the Durotriges caps every jutting down and hill-top on the southern and eastern bank of the river, while facing them, on the opposite northern and western side, rises a similar series of Damnonian fortresses, crowning the corresponding Devonshire heights. Lambert's Castle, Musberry Castle, Hawksdown Castle, and so forth, the local nomenclature still calls them, but they are castles, or castra, only in the now obsolete Roman sense; prehistoric earthworks, with dyke and trench, once stockaded with wooden palings on top, and enclosing the huts and homes of the inhabitants. The river ran between the hostile territories; each village held its own strip of land below its fortress-height, and drove up its cattle, its women, and its children, in times of foray, to the safety of the kraal or hill-top encampment.

In such a condition of society, of course, every community was absolutely dependent upon its own territory for the means of subsistence. And wherever the means of subsistence existed, a village was sure to spring up in time upon the nearest hill-top. That is how the oldest Fiesole of all first came to be perched there. It was a hill-top refuge for the tillers and grazers of the fertile Arno vale at its feet.

But why did the people of the Arno Valley fix upon the particular site of Fiesole? Surely on the southern side of the river, about the Viale dei Colli, the hills approach much nearer to the plain. From San Miniato and the Bello Sguardo one looks down far more directly upon the domes and palaces and campaniles of Florence spread right at one's feet. Why didn't the primitive inhabitants of the valley fix rather on a spur of that nearer range, say the one where Galileo's tower stands, for the site of their village?

If you know Florence and have asked that question within yourself in all seriousness as you read, I see you haven't yet begun to throw yourself into the position of affairs in prehistoric Tuscany. You can't shuffle off your own century. For between the broad plain and the range of hills where the Viale dei Colli now winds serpentine on its beautiful way round the glens and ravines, the Arno runs, a broad torrent flood in times of freshet: the Arno, unbridged as yet (in the days I speak of) by the Ponte Vecchio, an impassable frontier between the wide territory of prehistoric Fiesole and the narrow fields of some minor village, long since forgotten, on the opposite bank. The great alluvial plain lies north of the river; the three streams whose silt contributes to form it flow into the main channel from Pistoja and Prato. To live across the river on the south bank would have been absolutely impossible for the owners of the plain. But Fiesole occupies a central spur of the northern heights, overlooking the valley to east and west, and must therefore have been always the natural place from which to command the plain of Arno. A little above and a little below Florence gorges once more hem the river in. So that the plain of Florence (as we call it nowadays), the plain of Fiesole, as it once was, formed at the beginning a little natural principality by itself, of which Fiesole was the obvious capital and stronghold.

For in order to understand Fiesole aright, we must always manage in our own minds to get rid entirely of that beautiful mushroom growth, Florence, and to think only of the most ancient epoch. While we are in Florence itself, to be sure, it seems to us always, by comparison with our modern English towns, that Florence is a place of immemorial antiquity. It was civilized when Britain was a den of thieves. While in feudal England Edward I. was summoning his barons to repress the rising of William Wallace, in Florence, already a great commercial town, Arnolfo di Cambio had received the sublime orders of the Signoria to construct for the Duomo 'the most sumptuous edifice that human invention could desire or human labour execute,' and had carried out those orders with consummate skill. While Edward III. was dreaming of his lawless filibustering expeditions into France, Ciotto was encrusting the face of his glorious belfry with that magnificent decoration of many-coloured marbles which makes northern churches look so cold and grey and barbaric by comparison. While Englishmen were burning Joan of Arc at Rouen, Fra Angelico was adorning the walls of San Marco with those rapt saints and those spotless Madonnas. Even the very back streets of Florence recall at every step its mediæval magnificence. But when from Florence itself one turns to Fiesole, the city by the Arno sinks at once by a sudden revulsion into a mere thing of yesterday by the side of the city on the Etruscan hill-top. Fiesole was a town of immemorial antiquity while Florence was still, what perhaps its poetical name imports, a field of flowers.

But why this particular height rather than any other of the dozen that jut out into the plain? Well, there we get at another fundamental point in hill-top town history. Fiesole had water. A spring at such a height is comparatively rare, but it is a necessary accompaniment, or rather a condition precedent, of all high-place villages. In the Borgo Unto you will still find this spring, a natural fountain, the Fonte Sotterra, in an underground passage, now approached (so greatly did the Fiesolans appreciate its importance) by a Gothic archway. The water supplies the whole neighbourhood; and that accounts for the position of the town on the low col just below the acropolis.

Who first chose the site it would be impossible to say; the earliest stockaded fort at Fiesole (enclosing the town and arx above) must go back to the very dawn of neolithic history, long before the Etruscans had ever issued forth from their Rhætian fastnesses to occupy the blue and silver-grey hills of modern Tuscany. Nor do we know who built the great Cyclopean walls, whose huge rough blocks still overhang the modern carriage road that leads past Boccaccio's Valley of the Ladies and

Fra Angelico's earliest convent from the town in the Valley. They are attributed to the Etruscans, of course, on much the same grounds as Stonehenge is attributed to the Druids, because in the minds of the people who made the attribution Etruscans and Druids were each in their own place the ne plus ultra of aboriginal antiquity. But at any rate, at some very early time, the people who held the valley of the Arno erected these vast megalithic walls round their city and citadel as a protection, probably, against the people who held the Ligurian sea-board. Throughout the early historical period at least we know that Fæsulæ was an Etruscan border-town against the Ligurian freebooters, and we can see that the arx or acropolis of Fæsulæ must have occupied the hill-top now occupied by the Franciscan monastery on the height above the town, while the houses must have spread, as they still do within shrunken limits, about the spring and over the col at its base.

Fæsulæ was not one of the great Etrurian cities, not one of the twelve cities of the Etruscan League. Volterra occupies the site of the large Tuscan town which lorded it over this part of the Lower Apennines. But Fæsulæ must still have been a considerable place, to judge by the magnitude and importance of its fortifications, and it must have gathered into itself the entire population of all the little Arno plain. As long as fortis Etruria crevit, Fæsulæ must always have held its own as a frontier post against the Ligurian foe. But when fortis Etruria began to decline, and Rome to become the summit of all things, the glory of Fæsulæ received a severe shock. Not indeed by conquest, that counts for little, but the Roman peace introduced into Italy a new order of things, fatal to the hill-tops. Sulla, who humbled Fæsulæ, did far worse than that: he planted a Roman colony in the valley at its foot, the colony of Florentia, at the point where the road crossed the Arno, the colony that was afterwards to become the most famous commercial and artistic town of the mediæval world as Florence.

The position of the new town marks the change that had come over the conditions of life in Upper Italy. Florence was a Fiesole descended to the plain. And it descended for just the selfsame reason that made Bishop Poore thirteen centuries later bring down Sarum from its lofty hill-top to the new white minster by the ford of Avon. Roads, communications, internal trade were henceforth to exist and to count for much; what was needed now was a post and trading town on the river to guard the passage from north to south against possible aggression. Fiesole had been but a mountain stronghold; Florence was marked from the very beginning by its mere position as a great commercial and manufacturing town.

Nevertheless, just as in mediæval England the upper town on the hill, the castled town of the barons, often existed for many years side by side with the lower town on the river, the high-road town of the merchant guilds, just as Old Sarum, for example, continued to exist side by side with Salisbury, so Fæsulæ continued to exist side by side with Florentia. As a military post, commanding the plain, it was needful to retain it; and so, though Sulla destroyed in part its population, he reinstated it before long as one of his own Roman colonies. And for a long time, during the ages of doubtful peace that succeeded the first glorious flush of the military empire, Fæsulæ must have kept up its importance unchanged. The remains of the Roman theatre on the slope behind the cathedral, great stone semicircles carved on a scale to seat a large audience, betoken a considerable Roman town. And from a very early period it seems to have possessed a Christian church, whose first bishop, according to a tradition as good as most, was a convert of St. Peter's, and was martyred, says his legend, in the Neronian persecution. The existing cathedral, its later representative, is still an early and very simple Tuscan basilica, with picturesque crypt and raised choir, of a very plain Romanesque type. It looks like a fitting church for the mother-town of Florence; it seems to recall in its own cold and austere fabric the more ancient claims of the sombre Etruscan hill-top city.

It was the middle ages, however, that finally brought down Fiesole in earnest to the plain. Pisa had been the earliest Tuscan town to attain importance and maritime supremacy after the dark days of barbarian incursion; but as soon as land-transit once more assumed general importance, Florence, seated on the great route from the north to Rome by Siena, and commanding the passage of the Arno and the gate of the Apennines, naturally began to surpass in time its distanced rival. As early as the Roman days a bridge is said to have spanned the Arno on the site of the existing Ponte Vecchio. The mediæval walls enclosed the southern tête du pont within their picturesque circuit, thus securing the passage of the river and giving Florence its little Janiculus, the Oltrarno, with its southern exit by the Porta Romana. The real 'makers of Florence' were the humble workmen who thus extended the firm hold of the growing republic to the southern bank. By so doing, they gave their city undoubted command of the imperial route from Germany Romeward, and brought in their train Dante and Giotto, Brunelleschi and Donatello, Fra Angelico and Savonarola, the Medici and the Pitti, Michael Angelo and Raffaele, and all the glories of the Renaissance epoch. For as at Athens, so in Florence, art and literature followed plainly in the wake of commerce. But the rise of Florence was the fall of Fiesole. Already in the eleventh century the undutiful daughter had conquered and annexed her venerable mother; and in proportion as the mercantile importance of the city in the plain waxed greater and greater, that of the city on the hill-top must slowly have waned to less and less. At the present day Fiesole has degenerated into a mere suburb of Florence, which, indeed, it had almost become when Lorenzo the Magnificent held his country court at the Villa Mozzi, or even earlier, when Boccaccio's lively narrators fled from the plague to the gardens of the Palmieri, though it still retains the dignity of its ancient cathedral, its municipal palace, its gigantic seminary, and its great overgrown Franciscan monastery, that replaces the citadel on the height above the town. Nay, more, with its local museum, its bishop's palace, and its quaint churches, it keeps up, to some extent, all the airs and graces of a real living town. But in reality these few big buildings, and the graceful campanile which makes so fair a show in all the neighbouring views, are the best of the little city. Fiesole looks biggest seen from afar. All that is vital in it is the ecclesiastical establishment, which still clings, with true ecclesiastical conservatism, to the hill-top city, and the trade of the straw plaiters, who make Leghorn straw goods and pester the visitor with their flimsy wares, taking no answer to all their importunities save one in solid coin of good King Umberto.

One last question. How does it come that in these southern climates the hill-top town has survived so much more generally to our own day than in Northern Europe? The obvious answer seems at first sight to be that in the warmer climates life can be carried on comfortably, and agriculture can yield good results, at a greater height than in a cold climate. Olives, vines, chestnuts, maize will grow far up on Italian hill sides, and that, no doubt, counts for something; but I do not believe it covers all the ground. Two other points seem to me at least equally important, especially when we remember that the hill-top town was once as common in the north as in the south, and that what we have really to account for in Italy is not its existence merely, but rather its late survival into newer epochs. One point is that in Southern Europe the state of perpetual internal warfare lasted much longer than in the feudal north. The other point is that each little patch of country in the south is still far more self-supporting, has had its economic conditions far less disturbed by modern rearrangements and commercial necessities, than in Northern Europe. In England every town and village stands upon some high road; the larger stand almost invariably upon some railway or some navigable river. In Italy it is still quite possible, where agricultural conditions are favourable, to have a comparatively flourishing town perched upon some out-of-the-way mountain height. Even a carriage road is scarcely a necessity; a mule path will do well enough for wine and oil and the other simple commodities of southern life. The hill-top town, in short, belongs to an earlier type of civilisation than ours; it survives, unaltered, on its own pinnacle wherever that type of civilisation is still possible.

And I sincerely hope our pretty American friend will pardon me for having thus publicly answered, at so great length, her natural question.

## A PERSISTENT NATIONALITY

Standing to-day before the dim outline of Orcagna's "Hell" in the Church of Santa Maria Novella, at Florence, and mentally comparing those mediæval demons and monsters and torturers on the frescoed wall in front of me with the more antique Etruscan devils and tormentors pictured centuries earlier on the ancient tombs of Etrurian princes, the thought, which had often occurred to me before, how essentially similar were the Tuscan intellect and Tuscan art in all ages, forced itself upon me once more at a flash with an irresistible burst of internal conviction. The identity of old and new seemed to stand confessed. Etruria throughout has been one and the same; and it is almost impossible for anyone to over-estimate the influence of the powerful, but gloomy, Etruscan character upon the whole tone, not only of popular Christianity, but of that modern civilisation which is its offspring and outcome.

I suppose it is hardly necessary, "in this age of enlightenment" (as people used to say in the last century), to insist any longer upon the obvious fact that conquest and absorption do not in any way mean extermination. Most people still vaguely fancy to themselves, to be sure, that, when Rome conquered and absorbed Etruria, the ancient Etruscan ceased at once to exist, was swallowed, as it were, and became forthwith, in some mysterious way, first a Roman, and then a modern Italian. And, in a certain sense, this is, no doubt, more or less true; but that sense is decidedly not the genealogical one. Manners change, but blood persists. The Tuscan people went on living and marrying under consul and emperor just as they had done under lar and lucumo; Latin and Gaul, Lombard and Goth, mingled with them in time, but did not efface them; and I do not doubt that the vast mass of the population of Tuscany at the present day is still of preponderatingly Etruscan blood, though qualified, of course (and perhaps improved), by many Italic, Celtic, and Teutonic elements.

Again, when we remember that Florence, Pisa, Siena, Perugia are all practically in Tuscany, and that Florence alone has really given to the world Dante and Boccaccio, Galileo and Savonarola, Cimabue and Giotto, Botticelli and Fra Angelico, Donatello and Ghiberti, Michael Angelo and Raffael, Leonardo da Vinci and Macchiavelli and Alfieri, and a host of other almost equally great names, it will be obvious to everyone that the problem of the origin of this Tuscan nationality must be one that profoundly interests the whole world. Nay, more, we must remember, too, that Etruria had other and earlier claims than these; that it spread up to the very walls of Rome; that the Etruscan element in Rome itself was immensely strong; that the Roman religion owed, confessedly, much to Tuscan ideas; that Latin Christianity, the Christianity of all the Western world, took its shape in semi-Tuscan Rome; that the Roman Empire was largely modelled by the Etruscan Mæcenas; that the Italian renaissance was largely influenced by the Florentine Medici; that Leo the Tenth was himself a member of that great house; and that the artists whom he summoned to the metropolis to erect St. Peter's and to beautify the Vatican were, almost all of them, Florentines by birth, training, or domicile. I think, when we have run over mentally these and ten thousand other like facts, we will readily admit to ourselves the magnitude of the world's debt to Tuscany, social, artistic, intellectual, religious, both in ancient, mediæval, and modern times.

And what, now, was this strong Tuscan nationality, which persists so thoroughly through all external historical changes, and which has contributed so large and so marvellous a part to the world's thought and the world's culture? It is a curious consideration for those who talk so glibly, about the enormous natural superiority of the Aryan race, that the ancient Etruscans were the one people of the antique European world, who, by common consent, did not belong to the Aryan family. They were strangers in the land, or, rather, perhaps they were its oldest possessors. Their language, their physique, their creed, their art, all point to a wholly different origin from the Aryans. I am not going, in a brief essay like this, to settle dogmatically, off-hand, the vexed question of the origin and affinities of the Etruscan type; more nonsense, I suppose, has been talked and written upon that occult subject by learned men than even learned men have ever poured forth upon any other sublunary topic; but one thing at least, I take it, is absolutely certain amid the conflicting theories of ingenious theorists about the Etruscan race, and that one thing is that the Rasennæ stand in Europe absolutely alone, the sole representatives of some ancient and elsewhere exterminated stock, surviving only in Tuscany itself, and in the Rhætian Alps of the Canton Grisons.

At the moment when the Etruscans first appear in history, however, they appear as a race capable of acquiring and assimilating culture with great ease, rapidity, and certainty. No sooner do they come into contact with the Greek world than they absorb and reproduce all that was best and truest in Greek civilization. 'Merely receptive, European Chinese,' says, in effect, Mommsen, the great Roman historian: to me, that judgment, though true in some small degree, seems harsh indeed on a wider view, when applied to a people who begot at last the 'Divina Commedia,' the campanile of Florence, the dome of St. Peter's, and the glories of the Uffizi and the Pitti Palace. It is quite true that the Etruscans themselves, like the Japanese in our own time, did at first accept most imitatively the Hellenic culture; but they gradually remoulded it by their own effort into something new, growing and changing from age to age, until at last, in the Italian renaissance, they burst out with a wonderful and novel message to all the rest of dormant Europe.

One of the most persistent key-notes of this underlying Etruscan character is the solemn, weird, and gloomy nature of so much of the true Etruscan workmanship. From the very beginning they are strong, but sullen. Solidity and power, rather than beauty and grace, are what they aim at; and in this, Michael Angelo was a true Tuscan. If we look at the massive old Etruscan buildings, the Cyclopean walls of Fæsulæ and Volterræ, with their gigantic unhewn blocks, or the gloomy tombs of Clusium, with their heavy portals, and then at the frowning façade of the Strozzi or the Pitti Palace, we shall see in these, their earliest and latest terms, the special marks of Tuscan architecture. 'Piled by the hands of giants for mighty kings of old,' says Macaulay, well, of the Cyclopean walls. 'It somewhat resembles a prison or castle, and is remarkable for its bold simplicity of style, the unadorned huge blocks of stone being hewn smooth at the joints only,' says a modern writer, of Brunelleschi's palatial masterpiece. Every visitor to Florence must have noticed on every side the marks of this sullen and rugged Etruscan character. Compare for a moment the dark bosses of the Palazzo Strozzi, the 'âpre énergie' of the Palazzo Vecchio, the 'beauté sombre et sévère' of the mediæval Bargello, with the open, airy brightness of the Doge's Palace, or the glorious Byzantine gold-and-blue of St. Mark's at Venice, and you get at once an admirable measure of this persistent trait in the Etruscan idiosyncrasy. Tuscan architecture is massive and morose where Venetian architecture is sunny and smiling.

Now, Tuscan religion has in all times been specially influenced by the peculiarly gloomy tinge of the Tuscan character. It has always been a religion of fear rather than of love; a religion that strove harder to terrorize than to attract; a religion full of devils, flames, tortures, and horrors; in short, a sort of horrible Chinese religion of dragons and monstrosities, and flames and goblins. In the painted tombs of ancient Etruria you may see the familiar devil with his three-pronged fork thrusting souls back into the seething flood of a heathen hell, as Orcagna's here thrust them back similarly into that of its more modern Christian successor. All Etruscan art is full throughout of such horrors. You find their traces abundantly in the antique Etruscan museum at Florence; you find them on the mediæval Campo Santo at Pisa; you find them with greater skill, but equal repulsiveness, in the work of the great Renaissance artists. The 'ghastly glories of saints' the Tuscan revels in. The most famous portion of the most famous Tuscan poem is the 'Inferno', the part that gloats with minute and truly Tuscan realism over the torments of the damned in every department of the mediæval hell. And, as if still further to mark the continuity of thought, here in Orcagna's frescoes at Santa Maria Novella you have every horror of the heathen religion incongruously mingled with every horror of the Christian, gorgons and harpies and chimæras dire are tormenting the wicked under the eyes of the Madonna; centaurs are shooting and prodding them before the God of Love from the torrid banks of fiery lakes; furies with snaky heads are directing their punishments; Minos and Æacus are superintending their tasks; and, in the centre of all, a huge Moloch demon is devouring them bodily in his fiery jaws, with hideous tusks as of a Japanese monster.

It would be a curious question to inquire how far these old and ingrained Etruscan ideas may have helped to modify and colour the gentler conceptions of primitive Christianity. Certainly, one must never for a moment forget that Rome was at bottom nearly one-half Etruscan in character; that during the imperial period it became, in fact, the capital of Etruria; that myriads of Etruscans flocked to Rome; and that many of them, like Sejanus, had much to do with moulding and building up the imperial system. I do not doubt, myself, that Etruscan notions large interwove themselves, from the very outset, with Roman Christianity; and whenever in the churches or galleries of Italy I see St. Lawrence frying on his gridiron, or St. Sebastian pierced through with many arrows, or the Innocents being massacred in unpleasant detail, or hell being represented with Dantesque minuteness and particularity of delineation, I say to myself, with an internal smile, 'Etruscan influence.'

How interesting it is, too, to observe the constant outcrop, under all forms and faiths, of this strange, underlying, non-Aryan type! The Etruscans are and always were remarkable for their intellect, their ingenuity, their artistic faculty; and even to this day, after so many vicissitudes, they stand out as a wholly superior people to the rough Genoese and the indolent Neapolitans. They have had many crosses of blood meanwhile, of course; and it seems probable that the crosses have done them good: for in ancient times it was Rome, the Etrurianised border city of the Latins, that rose to greatness, not Etruria itself; and at a later date, it was after the Germans had mingled their race with Italy that Florence almost took the place of Rome. Nay, it is known as a fact that under Otto the Great a large Teutonic colony settled in Florence, thus adding to the native Etrurian race (especially to the nobility) that other element which the Tuscan seems to need in order that he may be spurred to the realisation of his best characteristics. But allow as we may for foreign admixture, two points are abundantly clear to the impartial observer of Tuscan history: one, that this non-Aryan race has always been one of the finest and strongest in Italy; and the other, that from the very dawn of history its main characteristics, for good or for evil, have persisted most uninterruptedly till the present day.


## CASTERS AND CHESTERS

Everybody knows, of course, that up and down over the face of England a whole crop of places may be found with such terminations as Lancaster, Doncaster, Manchester, Leicester, Gloucester, or Exeter; and everybody also knows that these words are various corruptions or alterations of the Latin castra, or perhaps we ought rather to say of the singular form, castrum. So much we have all been told from our childhood upward; and for the most part we have been quite ready to acquiesce in the statement without any further troublesome inquiry on our own account. But in reality the explanation thus vouchsafed us does not help us much towards explaining the real origin and nature of these ancient names. It is true enough as far as it goes, but it does not go nearly far enough. It reminds one a little of Charles Kingsley's accomplished pupil-teacher, with his glib derivation of amphibious, 'from two Greek words, amphi, the land, and bios, the water.' A detailed history of the root 'Chester' in its various British usages may serve to show how far such a rough-and-ready solution as the pupil-teacher's falls short of complete accuracy and comprehensiveness.

In the first place, without troubling ourselves for the time being with the diverse forms of the word as now existing, a difficulty meets us at the very outset as to how it ever got into the English language at all. 'It was left behind by the Romans,' says the pupil teacher unhesitatingly. No doubt; but if so, the only language in which it could be left would be Welsh; for when the Romans quitted Britain there were probably as yet no English settlements on any part of the eastern coast. Now the Welsh form of the word, even as given us in the very ancient Latin Welsh tract ascribed to Nennius, is 'Caer' or 'Kair;' and there is every reason to believe that the Celtic cathir or the Latin castrum had been already worn down into this corrupt form at least as early as the days of the first English colonisation of Britain. Indeed I shall show ground hereafter for believing that that form survives even now in one or two parts of Teutonic England. But if this be so, it is quite clear that the earliest English conquerors could not have acquired the use of the word from the vanquished Welsh whom they spared as slaves or tributaries. The newcomers could not have learned to speak of a Ceaster or Chester from Welshmen who called it a Caer; nor could they have adopted the names of Leicester or Gloucester from Welshmen who knew those towns only as Kair Legion or Kair Gloui. It is clear that this easy off-hand theory shirks all the real difficulties of the question, and that we must look a little closer into the matter in order to understand the true history of these interesting philological fossils.

Already we have got one clear and distinct principle to begin with, which is too often overlooked by amateur philologists. The Latin language, as spoken by Romans in Britain during their occupation of the island, has left and can have left absolutely no directs marks upon our English tongue, for the simple reason that English (or Anglo-Saxon as we call it in its earlier stages) did not begin to be spoken in any part of Britain for twenty or thirty years after the Romans retired. Whatever Latin words have come down to us in unbroken succession from the Roman times, and they are but a few, must have come down from Welsh sources. The Britons may have learnt them from their Italian masters, and may then have imparted them, after the brief period of precarious independence, to their Teutonic masters; but direct intercourse between Roman and Englishman there was probably little or none.

Three ways out of this difficulty might possibly be suggested by any humble imitator of Mr. Gladstone. First, the early English pirates may have learnt the word castrum (they always used it as a singular) years before they ever came to Britain as settlers at all. For during the long decay of the empire, the corsairs of the flat banks and islets of Sleswick and Friesland made many a light-hearted plundering expedition upon the unlucky coasts of the maritime Roman provinces; and it was to repel their dreaded attacks that the Count of the Saxon Shore was appointed to the charge of the long exposed tract from the fenland of the Wash to the estuary of the Rother in Sussex. On one occasion they even sacked London itself, already the chief trading town of the whole island. During some such excursions, the pirates would be certain to pick up a few Latin words, especially such as related to new objects, unseen in the rude society of their own native heather-clad wastes; and amongst these we may be sure that the great Roman fortresses would rank first and highest in their barbaric eyes. Indeed, modern comparative philologists have shown beyond doubt that a few southern forms of speech had already penetrated to the primitive English marshland by the shores of the Baltic and the mouth of the Elbe before the great exodus of the fifth century; and we know that Roman or Byzantine coins, and other objects belonging to the Mediterranean civilisation, are found abundantly in barrows of the first Christian centuries in Sleswick, the primitive England of the colonists who conquered Britain. But if the word castrum did not get into early English by some such means, then we must fall back either upon our second alternative explanation, that the townspeople of the south-eastern plains in England had become thoroughly Latinised in speech during the Roman occupation; or upon our third, that they spoke a Celtic dialect more akin to Gaulish than the modern Welsh of Wales, which may be descended from the ruder and older tongue of the western aborigines. This last opinion would fit in very well with the views of Mr. Rhys, the Celtic professor at Oxford, who thinks that all south-eastern Britain was conquered and colonised by the Gauls before the Roman invasion. If so, it maybe only the western Welsh who said Caer; the eastern may have said castrum, as the Romans did. In either of the latter two cases, we must suppose that the early English learnt the word from the conquered Britons of the districts they overran. But I myself have very little doubt that they had borrowed it long before their settlement in our island at all.

However this may be, and I confess I have been a little puritanically minute upon the subject, the English settlers learned to use the word from the first moment they landed in Britain. In its earliest English dress it appears as Ceaster, pronounced like Keaster, for the soft sound of the initial in modern English is due to later Norman influences. The new comers, Anglo-Saxons, if you choose to call them so, applied the word to every Roman town or ruin they found in Britain. Indeed, all the Latin words of the first crop in English, those used during the heathen age, before Augustine and his monks introduced the Roman civilisation, belong to such material relics of the older provincial culture as the Sleswick pirates had never before known: way from via, wall from vallum, street from strata, and port from portus. In this first crop of foreign words Ceaster also must be reckoned, and it was originally employed in English as a common rather than as a proper name. Thus we read in the brief Chronicle of the West Saxon kings, under the year 577, 'Cuthwine and Ceawlin fought against the Welsh, and offslew three kings, Conmail and Condidan and Farinmail, and took three ceasters, Gleawan ceaster and Ciren ceaster and Bathan ceaster.' We might modernise a little, so as to show the real sense, by saying 'Glevum city and Corinium city and Bath city.' Here it is noticeable that in two of the cases, Gloucester and Cirencester, the descriptive termination has become at last part of the name; but in the third case, that of Bath, it has never succeeded in doing so. Ages after, in the reign of King Alfred, we still find the word used as a common noun; for the Chronicle mentions that a body of Danish freebooters 'fared to a waste ceaster in Wirral; it is hight Lega ceaster;' that is to say, Legionis castra, now Chester. The grand old English epic of Beowulf, which is perhaps older than the colonisation of Britain, speaks of townsfolk as 'the dwellers in ceasters.'

As a rule, each particular Roman town retained its full name, in a more or less clipped form, for official uses; but in the ordinary colloquial language of the neighbourhood they all seem to have been described as 'the Ceaster' simply, just as we ourselves habitually speak of 'town,' meaning the particular town near which we live, or, in a more general sense, London. Thus, in the north, Ceaster usually means York, the Roman capital of the province; as when the Chronicle tells us that 'John succeeded to the bishopric of Ceaster'; that 'Wilfrith was hallowed as bishop at Ceaster'; or that 'Æthelberht the archbishop died at Ceaster.' In the south it is employed to mean Winchester, the capital of the West Saxon kings and overlords of all Britain; as when the Chronicle says that 'King Edgar drove out the priests at Ceaster from the Old Minster and the New Minster, and set them with monks.' So, as late as the days of Charles II., 'to go to town' meant in Shropshire to go to Shrewsbury, and in Norfolk to go to Norwich. In only one instance has this colloquial usage survived down to our own days in a large town, and that is at Chester, where the short form has quite ousted the full name of Lega ceaster. But in the case of small towns or unimportant Roman stations, which would seldom need to be mentioned outside their own immediate neighbourhood, the simple form is quite common, as at Caistor in Norfolk, Castor in Hunts, and elsewhere. At times, too, we get an added English termination, as at Casterton, Chesterton, and Chesterholme; or a slight distinguishing mark, as at Great Chesters, Little Chester, Bridge Casterton, and Chester-le-Street. All these have now quite lost their old distinctive names, though they have acquired new ones to distinguish them from the Chester, or from one another. For example, Chester-le-Street was Conderco in Roman times, and Cunega ceaster in the early English period. Both names are derived from the little river Cone, which flows through the village.

Before we pass on to the consideration of those castra which, like Manchester and Lancaster, have preserved to the present day their original Roman or Celtic prefixes in more or less altered shapes, we must glance briefly at a general principle running through the modernised forms now in use. The reader, with his usual acuteness, will have noticed that the word Ceaster reappears under many separate disguises in the names of different modern towns. Sometimes it is caster, sometimes chester, sometimes cester, and sometimes even it gets worn down to a mere fugitive relic, as ceter or eter. But these different corruptions do not occur irregularly up and down the country, one here and one there; they follow a distinct law and are due to certain definite underlying facts of race or language. Each set of names lies in a regular stratum; and the different strata succeed one another like waves over the face of England, from north-east to south-westward. In the extreme north and east, where the English or Anglian blood is purest, or is mixed only with Danes and Northmen to any large extent, such forms as Lancaster, Doncaster, Caistor, and Casterton abound. In the mixed midlands and the Saxon south, the sound softens into Chesterfield, Chester, Winchester, and Dorchester. In the inner midlands and the Severn vale, where the proportion of Celtic blood becomes much stronger, the termination grows still softer in Leicester, Bicester, Cirencester, Gloucester, and Worcester, while at the same time a marked tendency towards elision occurs; for these words are really pronounced as if written Lester, Bister, Cisseter, Gloster, and Wooster. Finally, on the very borders of Wales, and of that Damnonian country which was once known to our fathers as West Wales, we get the very abbreviated forms Wroxeter, Uttoxeter, and Exeter, of which the second is colloquially still further shortened into Uxeter. Sometimes these tracts approach very closely to one another, as on the banks of the Nene, where the two halves of the Roman Durobrivæ have become castor on one side of the river, and Chesterton on the other; but the line can be marked distinctly on the map, with a slight outward bulge, with as great regularity as the geological strata. It will be most convenient here, therefore, to begin with the casters, which have undergone the least amount of rubbing down, and from them to pass on regularly to the successively weaker forms in chester, cester, ceter, and eter.

Nothing, indeed, can be more deceptive than the common fashion, of quoting a Roman name from the often blundering lists of the Itineraries, and then passing on at once to the modern English form, without any hint of the intermediate stages. To say that Glevum is now Gloucester is to tell only half the truth; until we know that the two were linked together by the gradual steps of Glevum castrum, Gleawan ceaster, Gleawe cester, Gloucester, and Gloster, we have not really explained the words at all. By beginning with the least corrupt forms we shall best be able to see the slow nature of the change, and we shall also find at the same time that a good deal of incidental light is shed upon the importance and extent of the English settlement.

Doncaster is an excellent example of the simplest form of modernisation. It appears in the Antonine Itinerary and in the Notitia Imperii as Danum. This, with the ordinary termination affixed, becomes at once Dona ceaster or Doncaster. The name is of course originally derived in either form from the river Don, which flows beside it; and the Northumbrian invaders must have learnt the names of both river and station from their Brigantian British serfs. It shows the fluctuating nature of the early local nomenclature, however, when we find that Bæda ('the Venerable Bede') describes the place in his Latinised vocabulary as Campodonum, that is to say, the Field of Don, or, more idiomatically, Donfield, a name exactly analogous to those of Chesterfield Macclesfield, Mansfield, Sheffield, and Huddersfield in the neighbouring region. The comparison of Doncaster and Chesterfield is thus most interesting: for here we have two Roman Stations, each of which must once have had two alternative names; but in the one case the old Roman name has ultimately prevailed, and in the other case the modern English one.

The second best example of a Caster, perhaps, is Lancaster. In all probability this is the station which appears in the Notitia Imperii as Longovico, an oblique case which it might be hazardous to put in the nominative, seeing that it seems rather to mean the town on the Lune or Loan than the Long Village. Here, as in many other cases, the formative element, vicus, is exchanged for Ceaster, and we get something like Lon-ceaster or finally Lancaster. Other remarkable Casters are Brancaster in

Norfolk, once Branadunum (where the British termination dun has been similarly dropped); Ancaster in Lincolnshire, whose Roman name is not certainly known; and Caistor, near Norwich, once Venta Icenorum, a case which may best be considered under the head of Winchester. On the other hand, Tadcaster gives us an instance where the Roman prefix has apparently been entirely altered, for it appears in the Antonine Itinerary (according to the best identification) as Calcaria, so that we might reasonably expect it to be modernised as Calcaster. Even here, however, we might well suspect an earlier alternative title, of which we shall get plenty when we come to examine the Chesters; and in fact, in Bæda, it still bears its old name in a slightly disguised form as Kaelca ceaster.

First among the softer forms, let us examine the interesting group to which Chester itself belongs. Its Roman name was, beyond doubt, Diva, the station on the Dee, as Doncaster is the station on the Don, and Lancaster the station on the Lune. Its proper modern form ought, therefore, to be Deechester. But it would seem that in certain places the neighbouring rustics knew the great Roman town of their district, not by its official title, but as the legion's Camp, Castra Legionis. At least three such cases undoubtedly occur, one at Deva or Chester; one at Ratæ or Leicester; and one at Isca Silurum or Caerleon-upon-Usk. In each case the modernisation has taken a very different form. Diva was captured by the heathen English king, Æthelfrith of Northumbria, in a battle rendered famous by Bæda, who calls the place 'The City of Legions.' The Latin compilation by some Welsh writer, ascribed to Nennius, calls it Cair Legion, which is also its name in the Irish annals. In the English Chronicle it appears as Lege ceaster, Læge ceaster, and Leg ceaster; but after the Norman Conquest it becomes Ceaster alone. On midland lips the sound soon grew into the familiar Chester. About the second case, that of Leicester, there is a slight difficulty, for it assumes in the Chronicle the form of Lægra ceaster, with an apparently intrusive letter; and the later Welsh writers seized upon the form to fit in with their own ancient legend of King Lear. Nennius calls it Cair Lerion; and that unblushing romancer, Geoffrey of Monmouth, makes it at once into Cair Leir, the city of Leir. More probably the name is a mixture of Legionis and Ratæ, Leg-rat ceaster, the camp of the Legion at Ratæ. This, again, grew into Legra ceaster, Leg ceaster, and Lei ceaster, while the word, though written Leicester, is now shortened by south midland voices to Lester. The third Legionis Castra remained always Welsh, and so hardened on Cymric lips into Kair Leon or Caerleon. Nennius applies the very similar name of Cair Legeion to Exeter, still in his time a Damnonian or West Welsh fortress.

Equally interesting have been the fortunes of the three towns of which Winchester is the type. In the old Welsh tongue, Gwent means a champaign country, or level alluvial plain. The Romans borrowed the word as Venta, and applied it to the three local centres of Venta Icenorum in Norfolk, Venta Belgarum in Hampshire, and Venta Silurum in Monmouth. When the first West Saxon pirates, under their real or mythical leader, Cerdic, swarmed up Southampton Water and occupied the Gwent of the Belgæ, they called their new conquest Wintan ceaster, though the still closer form Wæntan once occurs. Thence to Winte ceaster and Winchester is no far cry. Gwent of the Iceni had a different history. No doubt it also was known at first as Wintan ceaster; but, as at Winchester, the shorter form Ceaster would naturally be employed in local colloquial usage; and when the chief centre of East Anglian population was removed a few miles north to Norwich, the north wick, then a port on the navigable estuary of the Yare, the older station sank into insignificance, and was only locally remembered as Caistor. Lastly, Gwent of the Silurians has left its name alone to Caer-Went in Monmouthshire, where hardly any relics now remain of the Roman occupation.

Manchester belongs to exactly the same class as Winchester. Its Roman name was Mancunium, which would easily glide into Mancunceaster. In the English Chronicle it is only once mentioned, and then as Mameceaster, a form explained by the alternative Mamucium in the Itinerary, which would naturally become Mamue ceaster. Colchester of course represents Colonia, corrupted first into Coln ceaster, and so through Col ceaster into its present form. Porchester in Hants is Portus Magnus; Dorchester is Durnovaria, and then Dorn ceaster. Grantchester, Godmanchester, Chesterfield,

Woodchester, and many others help us to trace the line across the map of England, to the most western limit of all at Ilchester, anciently Ischalis, though the intermediate form of Givel ceaster is certainly an odd one.

Besides these Chesters of the regular order, there are several curious outlying instances in Durham and Northumberland, and along the Roman Wall, islanded, as it were, beyond the intermediate belt of Casters. Such are Lanchester in Durham, which maybe compared with the more familiar Lancaster; Great Chesters in Northumberland, Ebchester on the northern Watling Street, and a dozen more. How to account for these is rather a puzzle. Perhaps the Casters may be mainly due to Danish influence (which is the common explanation), and it is known that the Danes spread but sparingly to the north of the Tees. However, this rough solution of the problem proves too much: for how then can we have a still softer form in Danish Leicester itself? Probably we shall be nearer the truth if we say that these are late names; for Northumberland was a desert long after the great harrying by William the Conqueror; and by the time it was repeopled, Chester had become the recognised English form, so that it would naturally be employed by the new occupants of the districts about the Wall.

No name in Britain, however, is more interesting than that of Rochester, which admirably shows us how so many other Roman names have acquired a delusively English form, or have been mistaken for memorials of the English conquest. The Roman town was known as Durobrivæ, which does not in the least resemble Rochester; and what is more, Bæda distinctly tells us that Justus, the first bishop of the West Kentish see, was consecrated 'in the city of Dorubrevi, which the English call Hrofæs ceaster, from one of its former masters, by name Hrof.' If this were all we knew about it, we should be told that Bæda clearly described the town as being called Hrof's Chester, from an English conqueror Hrof, and that to contradict this clear statement of an early writer was presumptuous or absurd. Fortunately, however, we have the clearest possible proof that Hrof never existed, and that he was a pure creation of Bæda's own simple etymological guesswork. King Alfred clearly knew better, for he omitted this wild derivation from his English translation. The valuable fragment of a map of Roman Britain preserved for us in the mediæval transcript known as the Peutinger Tables, sets down Rochester as Rotibis. Hence it is pretty certain that it must have had two alternative names, of which the other was Durobrivæ. Rotibis would easily pass (on the regular analogies) into Rotifi ceaster, and that again into Hrofi ceaster and Rochester; just as Rhutupiæ or Ritupæ passed into Rituf burh, and so finally into Richborough. Moreover, in a charter of King Ethelberht of Kent, older a good deal than Bæda's time, we find the town described under the mixed form of Hrofi-brevi. After such a certain instance of philological blundering as this, I for one am not inclined to place great faith in such statements as that made by the English Chronicle about Chichester, which it attributes to the mythical South Saxon king Cissa. Whatever Cissanceaster may mean, it seems to me much more likely that it represents another case of double naming; for though the Roman town was commonly known as Regnum, that is clearly a mere administrative form, derived from the tribal name of the Regni. Considering that the same veracious Chronicle derives Portsmouth, the Roman Portus, from an imaginary Teutonic invader, Port, and commits itself to other wild statements of the same sort, I don't think we need greatly hesitate about rejecting its authority in these earlier and conjectural portions.

Silchester is another much disputed name. As a rule, the site has been identified with that of Calleva Atrebatum; but the proofs are scanty, and the identification must be regarded as a doubtful one. I have already ventured to suggest that the word may contain the root Silva, as the town is situated close upon the ancient borders of Pamber Forest. The absence of early forms, however, makes this somewhat of a random shot. Indeed, it is difficult to arrive at any definite conclusions in these cases, except by patiently following up the name from first to last, through all its variations, corruptions, and mis-spellings.

The Cesters are even more degraded (philologically speaking) than the Chesters, but are not less interesting and illustrative in their way. Their farthest northeasterly extension, I believe, is to be found at Leicester and Towcester. The former we have already considered: the latter appears in the Chronicle as Tofe ceaster, and derives its name from the little river Towe, on which it is situated. Anciently, no doubt, the river was called Tofe or Tofi, like the Tavy in Devonshire; for all these river-words recur over and over again, both in England and on the Continent. In this case, there seems no immediate connection with the Roman name, if the site be rightly identified with that of Lactodorum; but at any rate the river name is Celtic, so that Towcester cannot be claimed as a Teutonic settlement.

Cirencester, the meeting-place of all the great Roman roads, is the Latin Corinium, sometimes given as Durocornovium, which well illustrates the fluctuating state of Roman nomenclature in Britain. As this great strategical centre, the key of the west, had formerly been the capital of the Dobuni, whose name it sometimes bears, it might easily have come down to us as Durchester, or Dobchester, instead of under its existing guise. The city was captured by the West Saxons in 577, and is then called Ciren ceaster in the brief record of the conquerors. A few years later, the Chronicle gives it as Cirn ceaster; and since the river is called Chirn, this is the form it might fairly have been expected to retain, as in the case of Cerney close by. But the city was too far west not to have its name largely rubbed down in use; so it softened both its initials into Cirencester, while Cissan ceaster only got (through Cisse ceaster) as far as Chichester. At that point the spelling of the western town has stopped short, but the tongues of the natives have run on till nothing now remains but Cisseter. If we had only that written form on the one hand, and Durocornovium on the other, even the boldest etymologist would hardly venture to suggest that they had any connection with one another. Of course the common prefix Duro, is only the Welsh Dwr, water, and its occurrence in a name merely implies a ford or river. The alternative forms may be Anglicised as Churn, and Churnwater, just like Grasmere, and Grasmere Lake.

I wish I could avoid saying anything about Worcester, for it is an obscure and difficult subject; but I fear the attempt to shirk it would be useless in the long run. I know from sad experience that if I omit it every inhabitant of Worcestershire who reads this article will hunt me out somehow, and run me to earth at last, with a letter demanding a full and explicit explanation of this silent insult to his native county. So I must try to put the best possible face upon a troublesome matter. The earliest existing form of the name, after the English Conquest, seems to be that given in a Latin Charter of the eighth century as Weogorna civitas. (Here it is difficult to disentangle the English from its Latin dress.) A little later it appears in a vernacular shape (also in a charter) as Wigran ceaster. In the later part of the English Chronicle it becomes Wigera ceaster, and Wigra ceaster; but by the twelfth century it has grown into Wigor ceaster, from which the change to Wire ceaster and Worcester (fully pronounced) is not violent. This is all plain sailing enough. But what is the meaning of Wigorna ceaster or Wigran ceaster? And what Roman or English name does it represent? The old English settlers of the neighbourhood formed a little independent principality of Hwiccas (afterwards subdued by the Mercians), and some have accordingly suggested that the original word may have been Hwiccwara ceaster, the Chester of the Hwicca men, which would be analogous to Cant-wara burh (Canterbury), the Bury of the Kent men, or to Wiht-gara burh (Carisbrooke), the Bury of the Wight men. Others, again, connect it with the Braunogenium of the Ravenna geographer, and the Cair Guoranegon or Guiragon of Nennius, which latter is probably itself a corrupted version of the English name. Altogether, it must be allowed that Worcester presents a genuine difficulty, and that the facts about its early forms are themselves decidedly confused, if not contradictory. The only other notable Ceasters, are Alcester, once Alneceaster, in Worcestershire, the Roman Alauna; Gloucester or Glevum, already sufficiently explained; and Mancester in Staffordshire, supposed to occupy the site of Manduessedum.

Among the most corrupted forms of all, Exeter may rank first. Its Latin equivalent was Isca Damnoniorum, Usk of the Devonians; Isca being the Latinised form of that prevalent Celtic river name which crops up again in the Usk, Esk, Exe, and Axe, besides forming the first element of Uxbridge and Oxford; while the tribal qualification was added to distinguish it from its namesake, Isca Silurum, Usk of the Silurians, now Caerleon-upon-Usk. In the west country, to this day, ask always becomes ax, or rather remains so, for that provincial form was the King's English at the court of Alfred; and so Isca became on Devonian lips Exan ceaster, after the West Saxon conquest. Thence it passed rapidly through the stages of Exe ceaster and Exe cester till it finally settled down into Exeter. At the same time, the river itself became the Exe; and the Exan-mutha of the Chronicle dropped into Exmouth. We must never forget, however, that Exeter, was a Welsh town up to the reign of Athelstan, and that Cornish Welsh was still spoken in parts of Devonshire till the days of Queen Elizabeth.

Wroxeter is another immensely interesting fossil word. It lies just at the foot of the Wrekin, and the hill which takes that name in English must have been pronounced by the old Celtic inhabitants much like Uricon: for of course the awkward initial letter has only become silent in these later lazy centuries. The Romans turned it into Uriconium; but after their departure, it was captured and burnt to the ground by a party of raiding West Saxons, and its fall is graphically described in the wild old Welsh elegy of Llywarch the Aged. The ruins are still charred and blackened by the West Saxon fires. The English colonists of the neighbourhood called themselves the Wroken-sætas, or Settlers by the Wrekin, a word analogous to that of Wilsætas, or Settlers by the Wyly; Dorsætas, or Settlers among the Durotriges; and Sumorsætas, or Settlers among the Sumor-folk, which survive in the modern counties of Wilts, Dorset, and Somerset. Similar forms elsewhere are the Pecsætas of the Derbyshire Peak, the Elmedsætas in the Forest of Elmet, and the Cilternsætas in the Chiltern Hills. No doubt the Wroken-sætas called the ruined Roman fort by the analogous name of Wroken ceaster; and this would slowly become Wrok ceaster, Wrok-cester, and Wroxeter, by the ordinary abbreviating tendency of the Welsh borderlands. Wrexham doubtless preserves the same original root.

Having thus carried the Castra to the very confines of Wales, it would be unkind to a generous and amiable people not to carry them across the border and on to the Western sea. The Welsh corruption, whether of the Latin word or of a native equivalent cathir, assumes the guise of Caer. Thus the old Roman station of Segontium, near the Menai Straits, is now called Caer Seiont; but the neighbouring modern town which has gathered around Edward's new castle on the actual shore, the later metropolis of the land of Arfon, became known to Welshmen as Caer-yn-Arfon, now corrupted into Caernarvon or even into Carnarvon. Gray's familiar line about the murdered bards, 'On Arvon's dreary shore they lie'—keeps up in some dim fashion the memory of the true etymology. Caermarthen is in like manner the Roman Muridunum or Moridunum, the fort by the sea, though a duplicate Moridunum in South Devon has been simply translated into English as Seaton. Innumerable other Caers, mostly representing Roman sites, may be found scattered up and down over the face of Wales, such as Caersws, Caerleon, Caergwrle, Caerhun, and Caerwys, all of which still contain traces of Roman occupation. On the other hand, Cardigan, which looks delusively like a shortened Caer, has really nothing to do with this group of ancient names, being a mere corruption of Ceredigion.

But outside Wales itself, in the more Celtic parts of England proper, a good many relics of the old Welsh Caers still bespeak the incompleteness of the early Teutonic conquest. If we might trust the mendacious Nennius, indeed, all our Casters and Chesters were once good Cymric Caers; for he gives a doubtful list of the chief towns in Britain, where Gloucester appears as Cair Gloui, Colchester as Cair Colun, and York as Cair Ebrauc. These, if true, would be invaluable forms; but unfortunately there is every reason to believe that Nennius invented them himself, by a simple transposition of the

English names. Henry of Huntingdon is nearly as bad, if not worse; for when he calls Dorchester 'Kair Dauri,' and Chichester 'Kair Kei,' he was almost certainly evolving what he supposed to be appropriate old British names from the depths of his own consciousness. His guesswork was on a par with that of the schoolboys who introduce 'Stirlingia' or 'Liverpolia' into their Ovidian elegiacs. That abandoned story-teller, Geoffrey of Monmouth, goes a step further, and concocts a Caer Lud for London and a Caer Osc for Exeter, whenever the fancy seizes him. The only examples amongst these pretended old Welsh forms which seem to me to have any real historical value are an unknown Kair Eden, mentioned by Gildas, and a Cair Wise, mentioned by Simeon of Durham, undoubtedly the true native name of Exeter.

Still we have a few indubitable Caers in England itself surviving to our own day. Most of them are not far from the Welsh border, as in the case of the two Caer Caradocs, in Shropshire, crowned by ancient British fortifications. Others, however, lie further within the true English pale, though always in districts which long preserved the Welsh speech, at least among the lower classes of the population. The earthwork overhanging Bath bears to this day its ancient British title of Caer Badon. An old history written in the monastery of Malmesbury describes that town as Caer Bladon, and speaks of a Caer Dur in the immediate neighbourhood. There still remains a Caer Riden on the line of the Roman wall in the Lothians. Near Aspatria, in Cumberland, stands a mouldering Roman camp known even now as Caer Moto. In Carvoran, Northumberland, the first syllable has undergone a slight contraction, but may still be readily recognised. The Carr-dyke in Norfolk seems to me to be referable to a similar origin.

Most curious of all the English Caers, however, is Carlisle. The Antonine Itinerary gives the town as Luguvallium. Bæda, in his barbarised Latin fashion calls it Lugubalia. 'The Saxons,' says Murray's Guide, with charming naïveté, 'abbreviated the name into Luel, and afterwards called it Caer Luel.' This astounding hotchpotch forms an admirable example of the way in which local etymology is still generally treated in highly respectable publications. So far as we know, there never was at any time a single Saxon in Cumberland; and why the Saxons, or any other tribe of Englishmen, should have called a town by a purely Welsh name, it would be difficult to decide. If they had given it any name at all, that name would probably have been Lul ceaster, which might have been modernised into Lulcaster or Lulchester. The real facts are these. Cumberland, as its name imports, was long a land of the Cymry, a northern Welsh principality, dependent upon the great kingdom of Strathclyde, which held out for ages against the Northumbrian English invaders among the braes and fells of Ayrshire and the Lake District. These Cumbrian Welshmen called their chief town Caer Luel, or something of the sort; and there is some reason for believing that it was the capital of the historical Arthur, if any Arthur ever existed, though later ages transferred the legend of the British hero to Caerleon-upon-Usk, after men had begun to forget that the region between the Clyde and the Mersey had once been true Welsh soil. The English overran Cumberland very slowly; and when they did finally conquer it, they probably left the original inhabitants in possession of the country, and only imposed their own overlordship upon the conquered race. The story is too long a one to repeat in full here: it must suffice to say that, though the Northumbrian kings had made the 'Strathclyde Welsh' their tributaries, the district was never thoroughly subdued till the days of Edmund the West Saxon, who harried the land, and handed it over to the King of Scots. Thus it happens that Carlisle, alone among large English towns, still keeps unchanged its Cymric name, instead of having sunk into an Anglicised Chester. The present spelling is a mere etymological blunder, exactly similar to that which has turned the old English word igland into island, through the false analogy of isle, which of course comes from the old French isle, derived through some form akin to the Italian isola, from the original Latin insula. Kair Leil is the spelling in Geoffrey; Cardeol (by a clerical error for Carleol, I suspect) that in the English Chronicle, which only once mentions the town; and Carleol that of the ordinary mediæval historians. The surnames Carlyle and Carlile still preserve the better orthography.

To complete the subject, it will be well to say a few words about those towns which were once Ceasters, but which have never become Casters or Chesters. Numerous as are the places now so called, a number more may be reckoned in the illimitable chapter of the might-have-beens; and it is interesting to speculate on the forms which they would have taken, 'si qua fata aspera rupissent.' Among these still-born Chesters, Newcastle-upon-Tyne may fairly rank first. It stands on the Roman site, called, from its bridge across the Tyne, Pons Aelii, and known later on, from its position on the great wall, as Ad Murum. Under the early English, after their conversion to Christianity, the monks became the accepted inheritors of Roman ruins; and the small monastery which was established here procured it the English name of Muneca-ceaster, or, as we should now say, Monk-chester, though no doubt the local modernisation would have taken the form of Muncaster. William of Normandy utterly destroyed the town during his great harrying of Northumberland; and when his son, Robert Curthose, built a fortress on the site, the place came to be called Newcastle, a word whose very form shows its comparatively modern origin. Castra and Ceasters were now out of date, and castles had taken their place. Still, we stick even here to the old root: for of course castle is only the diminutive castellum, a scion of the same Roman stock, which, like so many other members of aristocratic families, 'came over with William the Conqueror.' The word castel is never used, I believe, in any English document before the Conquest; but in the very year of William's invasion, the Chronicle tells us, 'Willelm earl came from Normandy into Pevensey, and wrought a castel at Hastings port.' So, while in France itself the word has declined through chastel into château, we in England have kept it in comparative purity as castle.

York is another town which had a narrow escape of becoming Yorchester. Its Roman name was Eburacum, which the English queerly rendered as Eoforwic, by a very interesting piece of folks-etymology. Eofor is old English for a boar, and wic for a town; so our rude ancestors metamorphosed the Latinised Celtic name into this familiar and significant form, much as our own sailors turn the Bellerophon into the Billy Ruffun, and the Anse des Cousins into the Nancy Cozens. In the same way, I have known an illiterate Englishman speak of Aix-la-Chapelle as Hexley Chapel. To the name, thus distorted, our forefathers of course added the generic word for a Roman town, and so made the cumbrous title of Eoforwic-ceaster, which is the almost universal form in the earlier parts of the English Chronicle. This was too much of a mouthful even for the hardy Anglo-Saxon, so we soon find a disposition to shorten it into Ceaster on the one hand, or Eoforwic on the other. Should the final name be Chester or York?—that was the question. Usage declared in favour of the more distinctive title. The town became Eoforwic alone, and thence gradually declined through Evorwic, Euorwic, Eurewic, and Yorick into the modern York. It is curious to note that some of these intermediate forms very closely approach the original Eburac, which must have been the root of the Roman name. Was the change partly due to the preservation of the older sound on the lips of Celtic serfs? It is not impossible, for marks of British blood are strong in Yorkshire; and Nennius confirms the idea by calling the town Kair Ebrauc.

Among the other Ceasters which have never developed into full-blown Chesters, I may mention Bath, given as Akemannes ceaster and Bathan ceaster in our old documents, so that it might have become Achemanchester or Bathceter in the course of ordinary changes. Canterbury, again, the Roman Durovernum, dropped through Dorobernia into Dorwit ceaster, which would no doubt have turned into a third Dorchester, to puzzle our heads by its likeness to Dorne ceaster in Dorsetshire, and to Dorce ceaster near Oxford; while Chesterton in Huntingdonshire, which was once Dorme ceaster, narrowly escaped burdening a distracted world with a fourth. Happily, the colloquial form Cantwara burh, or Kentmen's bury, gained the day, and so every trace of Durovernum is now quite lost in Canterbury. North Shields was once Scythles-ceaster, but here the Chester has simply dropped out. Verulam, or St. Albans, is another curious case. Its Romano-British name was Verulamium, and Bæda calls it Verlama ceaster. But the early English in Sleswick believed in a race of mythical giants, the Wætlingas or Watlings, from whom they called the Milky Way 'Watling Street.'

When the rude pirates from those trackless marshes came over to Britain and first beheld the great Roman paved causeway which ran across the face of the country from London to Caernarvon, they seemed to have imagined that such a mighty work could not have been the handicraft of men; and just as the Arabs ascribe the rock-hewn houses of Petra to the architectural fancy of the Devil, so our old English ancestors ascribed the Roman road to the Titanic Watlings. Even in our own day, it is known along its whole course as Watling Street. Verulam stands right in its track, and long contained some of the greatest Roman remains in England; so the town, too, came to be considered as another example of the work of the Watlings. Bæda, in his Latinised Northumbrian, calls it Vætlinga ceaster, as an alternative title with Verlama ceaster; so that it might nowadays have been familiar to us all either as Watlingchester or Verlamchester. This is one of the numerous cases where a Roman and English name lived on during the dark period side by side. In some of Mr. Kemble's charters it appears as Walinga ceaster. But when Offa of Mercia founded his great abbey on the very spot where the Welsh martyr Alban had suffered during the persecution of Diocletian, Roman and English names were alike forgotten, and the place was remembered only after the British Christian as St. Albans.

There are other instances where the very memory of a Roman city seems now to have failed altogether. For example, Bæda mentions a certain town called Tiowulfinga ceaster, that is to say, the Chester of the Tiowulfings, or sons of Tiowulf. Here an English clan would seem to have taken up its abode in a ruined Roman station, and to have called the place by the clan-name, a rare or almost unparalleled case. But its precise site is now unknown. However, Bæda's description clearly points to some town in Nottinghamshire, situated on the Trent; for St. Paulinus of York baptized large numbers of converts in that river at Tiowulfinga ceaster; and the site may therefore be confidently identified with Southwell, where St. Mary's Minster has always traditionally claimed Paulinus as its founder. Bæda also mentions a place called Tunna ceaster, so named from an abbot Tunna, who exists merely for the sake of a legend, and is clearly as unhistorical as his piratical compeer Hrof, a wild guess of the eponymic sort with which we are all so familiar in Greek literature. Simeon of Durham speaks of an equally unknown Delvercester. Syddena ceaster or Sidna cester, the earliest see of the Lincolnshire diocese, has likewise dropped out of human memory; though Mr. Pearson suggests that it may be identical with Ancaster, a notion which appears to me extremely unlikely. Wude cester is no doubt Outchester, and other doubtful instances might easily be recognised by local antiquaries, though they may readily escape the general archæologist. In one case at least, that of Othonæ in Essex, town, site, and name have all disappeared together. Bæda calls it Ythan ceaster, and in his time it was the seat of a monastery founded by St. Cedd; but the whole place has long since been swept away by an inundation of the Blackwater. Anderida, which is called Andredes-ceaster in the Chronicle, becomes Pefenesea, or Pevensey, before the date of the Norman Conquest.

It must not be supposed that the list given here is by any means exhaustive of all the Casters and Chesters, past and present, throughout the whole length and breadth of Britain. On the contrary, many more might easily be added, such as Ribbel ceaster, now Ribchester; Berne ceaster, now Bicester; and Blædbyrig ceaster, now simply Bladbury. In Northumberland alone there are a large number of instances which I might have quoted, such as Rutchester, Halton Chesters, and Little Chesters on the Roman Wall, together with Hetchester, Holy Chesters, and Rochester elsewhere, the county containing no less than four places of the last name. Indeed, one can track the Roman roads across England by the Chesters which accompany their route. But enough instances have probably been adduced to exemplify fully the general principles at issue. I think it will be clear that the English conquerors did not usually change the names of Roman or Welsh towns, but simply mispronounced them about as much as we habitually mispronounce Llangollen or Llandudno. Sometimes they called the place by its Romanised title alone, with the addition of Ceaster; sometimes they employed the servile British form; sometimes they even invented an English alternative; but in no case can it be shown that they at once disused the original name, and introduced a totally new one of their own manufacture. In this, as in all other matters, the continuity between Romano-British and English times is far greater than it is generally represented to be. The English invasion was a cruel and a desolating one, no doubt; but it could not and it did not sweep away wholly the old order of things, or blot out all the past annals of Britain, so as to prepare a tabula rasa on which Mr. Green might begin his History of the English People with the landing of Hengest and Horsa in the Isle of Thanet. The English people of to-day is far more deeply rooted in the soil than that: our ancestors have lived here, not for a thousand years alone, but for ten thousand or a hundred thousand, in certain lines at least. And the very names of our towns, our rivers, and our hills, go back in many cases, not merely to the Roman corruptions, but to the aboriginal Celtic, and the still more aboriginal Euskarian tongue.

## Grant Allen – A Short Biography

Charles Grant Blairfindie Allen was born on February 24th, 1848 at Alwington, near Kingston, Canada West (now part of Ontario). He was the second son of the Rev. Joseph Antisell Allen, a Protestant minister from Dublin, Ireland and Catharine Ann Grant, the daughter of the fifth Baron of Longueuil.

Grant was educated at home until he was thirteen at which time the family moved, initially to the United States, then France and finally settling in the United Kingdom.

Whilst growing up the family background was obviously religious but Grant developed his own views on life and the world and turned to agnosticism and socialism.

He was educated at King Edward's School in Birmingham and Merton College in Oxford. After graduating, Grant studied in France and also taught at Brighton College. By 1870, still only in his mid-twenties, he became a professor at Queen's College, a black college in Jamaica.

Whilst in Jamaica Grant met and married his first wife Ellen Jerrard in 1873 and they produced a son five years later; Jerrard Grant Allen, who grew up to become a theatrical agent/manager.

In 1876 Grant and his family left Jamaica to return to England with both the talent and ambition to become a writer.

He quickly turned to writing essays, gaining a reputation for his work on science and literary works. An early article, 'Note-Deafness' a description of what is now called amusia, was published in 1878 in the learned journal Mind and was cited approvingly by Oliver Sacks very recently.

From essays in magazines and journals he now turned to books, initially on scientific subjects. These include Physiological Æsthetics 1877 and Flowers and Their Pedigrees 1886.

His first major influence was associationist psychology, as then expounded by Alexander Bain and Herbert Spencer, the latter is often considered the most important individual in the transition from associationist psychology to Darwinian functionalism. In Grant's many articles on flowers and perception in insects, Darwinian arguments now replaced the old Spencerian terms.

On a personal level, a long friendship that started when Grant met Herbert Spencer on his return from Jamaica, turned eventually to one of unease over its long course. Grant was to write a critical and revealing biographical article on Spencer that was published after Spencer was dead.

In the early 1880's Grant began to assist Sir W. W. Hunter in his Gazeteer of India. It is at this time that Grant now turned his full attention away from the factual and towards the world of imagination and fiction.

Between this shift to fiction in 1884 and his death fifteen years later Grant was to write about 30 novels.

Many were adventure novels which were very common in the late Victorian period as writers turned their literary talents to the voracious appetites of the weekly or monthly serial magazines.

Some however were to cause quite a stir. For instance in 1895 Grant took the subject of children born out of wedlock as his subject matter. The result was The Woman Who Did, that suggested, indeed pushed, for its time, certain quite startling views on marriage and related areas. In keeping with his then glowing reputation it became a bestseller despite it being seemingly at odds with society's unease at its provocative subject matter.

Interestingly Grant wrote novels under female pseudonyms. One of these was the short novel The Type-writer Girl, which he wrote under the name Olive Pratt Rayner.

Another work, The Evolution of the Idea of God 1897, propounding a theory of religion on heterodox lines, has the disadvantage of endeavoring to explain everything by one theory. This "ghost theory" was often seen as a derivative of Herbert Spencer's theory. However, at the time, it was well known and brief references to it can be found in a review by Marcel Mauss, Durkheim's nephew, in the articles of William James and in the works of Sigmund Freud. The young G. K. Chesterton wrote on what he considered the flawed premise of the idea, arguing that the idea of God preceded human mythologies, rather than developing from them. Chesterton said of Grant Allen's book on the evolution of the idea of God "it would be much more interesting if God wrote a book on the evolution of the idea of Grant Allen".

From this and other instances, it can be seen that his work was in debate and whether agreed with or not could always ensure a lively discussion.

Grant also helped to pioneer science fiction, with the 1895 novel The British Barbarians. This book, was published at about the same time as H. G. Wells was to publish The Time Machine. The plots are quite different but both describe time travel. A few years later his short story The Thames Valley Catastrophe (published 1901 in The Strand magazine) describes the destruction of London by a massive volcanic eruption. Whilst the premise now may seem outlandish, at the time genuine panic and concern set in as, like his contemporary, Jules Verne, much of great science fiction writing is rooted in a plausibility that is set out very convincingly.

In detective fiction too his works include female detectives, very much an innovation in the young genre and his gentleman rogue, Colonel Clay, is seen as a forerunner to other, perhaps more famous characters, by other later writers.

In 1881 he had settled at Dorking, where he took great delight in botanical walks in the woods and sandy heaths. He never enjoyed particularly good health and so almost every winter he would depart for milder climes, to winter in the south of Europe, usually at Antibes, though occasionally as far as Algiers and Egypt.

In 1892 he bought land almost on the summit of Hind Head, and built himself a charming cottage which he called the Croft. Here he found that it was possible to endure the vagaries of the English winter and in landscape more beautiful and wilder than at Dorking and that his long scientific training could better appreciate.

His growing re-discovery and interest in art in the later part of his life allowed him to blend together literature, art and history in a series of guide books on Paris, Florence, Venice, and the cities of Belgium.

On October 25th 1899 Grant Allen died at his home in Hindhead, Haslemere, Surrey, England. He died just before finishing Hilda Wade. The novel's final episode, which he dictated to his friend, doctor and neighbour Sir Arthur Conan Doyle from his bed appeared under the appropriate title, The Episode of the Dead Man Who Spoke in the Strand Magazine in 1900.

Grant Allen is rarely heard of today, although an occasional short story can be heard on the radio or reprinted among magazine enthusiasts but in his time he did much to entertain the masses and push several genres along a richer journey they are still proceeding on today.

Grant Allen – A Concise Bibliography

Physiological Æsthetics. 1877
The Colour-Sense: Its Origin and Development. 1879
Evolutionist at Large. 1881
Vignettes from Nature. 1881
The Colours of Flowers. 1882
Colin Clout's Calendar. 1883
Flowers and Their Pedigrees. 1883
Philistia. 1884
Strange Stories. Short Stories. 1884
Babylon. A novel in 3 volumes. 1885
For Mamie's Sake. 1886
In All Shades. 1886
The Beckoning Hand & Other Stories. 1887
This Mortal Coil: A Novel. 1888
Force and Energy. 1888
The Devil's Die. 1888
The White Man's Foot. 1888
Falling in Love. 1889
The Tents of Shem. 1889
Wednesday the Tenth. 1890
The Great Taboo. 1890
Dumaresq's Daughter. 1891
What's Bred in the Bone. 1891
The Duchess of Powysland. 1892
The Scallywag. 1893
Michael's Crag. 1893
The Lower Slopes. 1894
Post-Prandial Philosophy. 1894
The British Barbarians. 1895
At Market Value. 1895
The Story of the Plants. 1895

The Desire of the Eyes. 1895
The Woman Who Did. 1895
The Jaws of Death. 1896
A Bride from the Desert. 1896
Under Sealed Orders. 1896
Moorland Idylls. 1896
An African Millionaire. Colonel Clay's novel. 1897
The Evolution of the Idea of God. 1897
Paris. 1897
The Type-writer Girl. (as Olive Pratt Rayner) 1897
Tom, Unlimited. (as Martin Leach Warborough) 1897
Flashlights on Nature. 1898
The Incidental Bishop. 1898
Venice. 1898
The European Tour. 1899
A Splendid Sin. 1899
Miss Cayley's Adventures. 1899
Twelve Tales: With a Headpiece, a Tailpiece, and an Intermezzo. 1899
Hilda Wade (finished by Arthur Conan Doyle). 1900
Linnet. 1900
The Backslider. 1901
Sir Theodore's Guest & Other Stories. 1902
Evolution in Italian Art. 1908
The Hand of God. 1909
The Plants. 1909


Short Stories
The Empress of Andorra. 1878
My New Year Among the Mummies. 1878
Lucretia. 1879
My Circular Tour. 1880
A Ballade of Evolution. 1880
Ram Das of Cawnpore. 1880
The Chinese Play at the Haymarket. 1880
The Senior Proctor's Wooing. 1881
Pausodyne. 1881
Caribbean Twelve Per Cents. 1882
An Episode in High Life. 1882
Mr Chung. 1882
Isadine and I. 1883
The Backsider. 1883
The Reverend John Creedy. 1883
The Foundering of the Fortuna. 1883
The Third Time
The Gold Wulfric
My Uncle's Will. 1884
Carvalho. 1884
The Mysterious Occurence in Piccadilly. 1884
Dr Greatex's Engagement. 1884
Hugh Portledown's Return from Normandy. 1884

The Child of Phalanstery. 1884
The Curate of Churnside. 1884
John Cann's Treasure. 1884
Olga Davidoff's Husband. 1884
The Search Party's Find. 1885
The Two Carnegie's. 1885
Professor Milliter's Dilemma. 1885
In Strict Confidence. 1885
The Beckoning Hand. 1885
The Third Time. 1886
Harry's Inheritance. 1886
The Gold Wulfric. 1886
Mr Pierpoint's Repentance. 1886
Claude Tyack's Ordeal. 1887
Leonard's Recovery. 1887
A Social Difficulty. 1887
Dr Palliser's Patient. 1888
My Christmas Eve at Marzin. 1888
The Sultan's Sister. 1888
His First Crime. 1889
The Mayfield Mystery. 1889
Andre Canivet's Curse. 1890
Old Margaret. 1890
My One Gorilla. 1890
Dick Prothero's Luck. 1890
A Deadly Dilemma. 1891
Jerry Stokes. 1891
Selwyn Utterton's Nemesis. 1891
General Passavant's Will. 1891
The Briefless Barrister. 1891
Melissa's Tour. 1891
Karen – A Canadian Romance. 1891
The Prisoner of Assiout. 1891
The Abbe's Repentance. 1891
Masie Bowman's Fate. 1891
Naomi's Christmas Eves. 1891
That Friend of Sylvia's. 1892
The Conscientious Burglar. 1892
The Minor Poet. 1892
The Governor's Story. 1892
The Pot Boiler. 1892
The Great Ruby. 1892
Ewen Murray's Swim. 1892
Ivan Greet's Masterpiece. 1892
Pallinghurst Barrow. 1892
Langalula. 1893
The Assasin's Knife. 1893
The Artist and the Penny-a-Liner. 1893
A Casual Conversation. 1893
How To Succeed in Literature. 1893
Torrigiano. 1893

A Modern Sibyl: A Florentine Sketch. 1893
Nemesis Wins. 1894
Cecca's Lover. 1894
A Self Respecting Servant. 1894
Passiflora Sanguinea. 1894
An Excellent Match. 1894
Major Kinfaun's Marriage. 1894
Grateful Joe. 1894
An Idyll of the Ice. 1894
Criss Cross Love. 1894
Poor Little Soul. 1894
Amour de Voyage. 1894
The Dynamiter's Sweetheart. 1894
A Triumph of Civilisation. 1894
Dr Wardroper's Lie. 1894
The Miraclous Explorer. 1894
Leon and Leonie. 1895
A Comic Emotion. 1895
Joe's Rascality. 1895
Evelyn Moore's Poet. 1895
Frasine's First Communion. 1895
TheDead Man Speaks. 1895
A Study From the Nude. 1895
Cecca's Choice. 1895
The Desire of the Eyes. 1895
The Making of a Poet. 1895
The Man From Cumbrae. 1895
Fogo Skerries. 1895
The Great Californian Heiress. 1895
Cap'n Tom Woolley. 1895
The Girl at the Fair. 1895
Love's Old Dream. 1895
A Modern Pygmalion. 1895
A Bride From the Desert. 1895
The Practical Test. 1896
A Confidential Communication. 1896
The Great Temperance Preacher. 1896
A Day on the River. 1896
The Episode of the Mexican Seer. 1896
A Midsummer Episode. 1896
The Episode of the Diamond Links. 1896
Omar at Marlow. 1896
A Mere Matter of Standpoint. 1896
Fair Exchange. 1896
The Cowardly Dynamiter. 1896
The Episode of the Old Master. 1896
The Episode of the Tyrolean Castle. 1896
Janet's Nemesis. 1896
Entirely Accidential. 1896
The Episode of the Drawn Game. 1896
Wolverden Tower. 1896

The Episode of the German Professor. 1896
The Episode of the Arrest of the Colonel. 1896
The Episode of the Seldom Gold Mine. 1897
The Camisard's Bride. 1897
The Episode of the Japanned Dispatch Box. 1897
Llanfihangel Skerries. 1897
The Episode of the Game of Poker. 1897
The Episode of the Bertillon Method. 1897
A Lady of Florence. 1897
The Episode of the Old Bailey. 1897
A British Verdict. 1897
A Domestic Tragedy. 1897
A College Charm. 1897
A Freak of Memory. 1897
The Judge's Cross. 1897
The Thames Valley Catastrophe. 1897
The Great Oriental Seer. 1897
The Adventures of the Cantankerous Old Lady. 1898
The Adventure of the Supercilious Attache. 1898
The Pirate of Cliveden Reach. 1898
The Adventure of the Amateur Commission. 1898.
The Adventure of the Impromptu Mountaineer. 1898
Joe's Wife. 1898
The Adventure of the Urbane Old Gentleman. 1898
The Adventure of the Unobtrusive Oasis. 1898
The Adventure of the Pea Green Patrician. 1898
Isenberg's Regiment. 1898
The Adventure of the Magnificent Maharajah. 1898
A Woman's Hand: A Story. 1898
The Adventure of the Cross Eyed QC. 1898
The Christmas Eve Concert. 1898
The Adventure of the Oriental Attendant. 1899
Joseph's Dream. 1899
The Adventure of the Unprofessional Detective. 1899
Hobbling Mary. 1899
The Episode of the Patient Who Disappointed Her Doctor. 1899
The Episode of the Gentleman Who Had Failed For Everything. 1899
The Episode of the Wife Who Did Her Duty. 1899
The Episode of the Man Who Would Not Commit Suicide. 1899
A Regrettable Error. 1899
Peace-At-Any-Price Bill. 1899
The Episode of the Letter with a Basingstoke Post-Mark. 1899
The Episode of the Stone That Looked About It. 1899
His Ways Inscrutable. 1899
The Episode of the European With A Kaffir Heart. 1899
The Episode of the Lady Who Was Very Exclusive. 1899
The Episode of the Guide Who Knew the Country. 1899
Luigi and the Salvationist. 1899.
A Christmas Adventure. 1899.
The Episode of the Officer Who Understood Perfectly. 1900
Meriel Stanley, Poacher. 1900

The Episode of the Dead Man Who Spoke. 1900
A Question of Colour. 1900
Fra Benedett's Medal: A Story. 1900
The Temple of Fate: A Fable. 1900
The Way to Keronan. 1902
Lucy Lockett. 1902
Spencerian. 1904

## Articles

1878. Hellas and Civilization, Gentleman's Magazine, Vol. CCXLIII
1878. Nation-making: A Theory of National Characters, Gentleman's Magazine, Vol. CCXLIII
1878. The Origin of Fruits, in Popular Science Monthly Volume 13
1879. Why Do We Eat our Dinner? in Popular Science Monthly Volume 14
1879. A Problem in Human Evolution, in Popular Science Monthly Volume
1879. Pleased with a Feather, in Popular Science Monthly Volume 15
1880. Why Keep India? The Contemporary Review, Vol. XXXVIII
1880. The Growth of Sculpture, The Cornhill Magazine, Vol. XLII
1880. The English Chronicle, Gentleman's Magazine, Vol. CCXLV
1880. The Venerable Bede, Gentleman's Magazine, Vol. CCXLIX
1880. The Dog's Universe, Gentleman's Magazine, Vol. CCXLIX
1880. Evolution and Geological Time, Gentleman's Magazine, Vol. CCXLIX
1880. Geology and History, in Popular Science Monthly Volume 17
1880. Aesthetic Feeling in Birds, in Popular Science Monthly Volume 17
1880. Aesthetic Evolution in Man, in Popular Science Monthly Volume 18
1881. The Story of Wulfgeat, Gentleman's Magazine, Vol. CCLI
1882. An English Shire, Gentleman's Magazine, Vol. CCLII
1882. The Welsh in the West Country, Gentleman's Magazine, Vol. CCLIII
1882. The Colours of Flowers, The Cornhill Magazine, Vol. XLV
1882. An English Weed, The Cornhill Magazine, Vol. XLV
1882. Sir Charles Lyell, in Popular Science Monthly Volume 20
1882. Hyacinth-Bulbs, in Popular Science Monthly Volume 20
1882. Who was Primitive Man? in Popular Science Monthly Volume 22
1883. The Pedigree of Wheat, in Popular Science Monthly Volume 22
1883. From Buttercups to Monk's-Hood, in Popular Science Monthly Volume 23
1883. Honeysuckle, Gentleman's Magazine, Vol. CCLV
1884. The Garden Snail, Gentleman's Magazine, Vol. CCLVI
1884. Our Debt to Insects, Gentleman's Magazine, Vol. CCLVI
1884. Idiosyncrasy, in Popular Science Monthly Volume 24
1884. The Ancestry of Birds, in Popular Science Monthly Volume 24
1884. The Milk in the Cocoa-Nut, in Popular Science Monthly Volume 25
1884. Our Debt to Insects, in Popular Science Monthly Volume 25
1884. Hickory-Nuts and Butternuts, in Popular Science Monthly Volume 25
1884. Queer Flowers, in Popular Science Monthly Volume 26
1885. Food and Feeding, in Popular Science Monthly Volume 26
1885. Concerning Clover, in Popular Science Monthly Volume 28
1886. A Thinking Machine, Gentleman's Magazine, Vol. CCLX
1886. Fish Out of Water, in Popular Science Monthly Volume 28
1886. A Thinking Machine, in Popular Science Monthly Volume 28
1886. Thistles, in Popular Science Monthly Volume 30, November 1886
1887. A Mount Washington Sandwort, in Popular Science Monthly Volume 30

1887. Among the Thousand Islands, in Popular Science Monthly Volume 31

1887. The Progress of Science from 1836 to 1886, in Popular Science Monthly Volume 31

1887. American Cinque-Foils, in Popular Science Monthly Volume 32

1888. Gourds and Bottles, in Popular Science Monthly Volume 33

1888. A Living Mystery, in Popular Science Monthly Volume 33

1888. Evolving the Camel, in Popular Science Monthly Volume 34

1889. From Africa, Gentleman's Magazine, Vol. CCLXVII

1889. Genius and Talent, in Popular Science Monthly Volume 34

1889. Plain Words on the Woman Question, in Popular Science Monthly Volume 36

1890. The Girl of the Future, Universal Review, Vol. VII.

1891. Democracy and Diamonds, The Contemporary Review, Vol. LIX

1892. A Desert Fruit, in Popular Science Monthly Volume 41

1893. Ghost Worship and Tree Worship I, in Popular Science Monthly Volume 42

1893. Ghost Worship and Tree Worship II, in Popular Science Monthly Volume 42

1897. Spencer and Darwin, in Popular Science Monthly Volume 50

1898. The Romance of Race, in Popular Science Monthly Volume 53

1898. The Season of the Year, in Popular Science Monthly Volume 54


Poetry


Grant Allen wrote various poems published in many magazines etc. We have not listed them here but hope to record some of them in the future.

www.ingramcontent.com/pod-product-compliance
Lightning Source LLC
Chambersburg PA
CBHW071405170626
46811CB00003B/1267